A
MUR

A gripping murder mystery full of twists

LINDA MATHER

The Zodiac Mysteries Book 5

JOFFE
BOOKS

Joffe Books, London
www.joffebooks.com

First published in Great Britain in 2022

Cover art by Nick Castle

ISBN: 978-1-80405-501-4

CHAPTER ONE

The long grasses on the dunes had a way of rippling at this time of the morning that slightly deceived the eye. Meredith loved the metallic light as the dawn lifted over the horizon in winter, but then she loved it in all seasons. She was well insulated from the nipping wind in her wax coat and layers underneath. The leather of her boots creaked in rhythm with her walk and the gun lay weighted on her arm. Always slightly ahead, the dog weaved knowledgably through her secret paw-paths, Meredith's boots following more heavily on the slippery scree.

A duck flew up, startled by Cleo, and Meredith raised the gun. The light was deceptive. More shadowy, more grey through the gun scope. Steady arm and silent mind. One shot.

There was a satisfying fall from grace and other mallards took to the air but Meredith didn't shoot again. As she hefted the gun into the crook of her arm, the dog streaked towards the bird. She would only shoot what she and Peter would eat or give away. Later she would butcher the bird and anything she didn't assign to the pot would go to Cleo. The springer spaniel understood her part in this well and she was as focused on the enterprise as her mistress.

Meredith sensed that something was out of kilter when she found herself following a different direction from the dog. She reached the bird first. Then she checked the gun and called Cleo. Her voice sang across the air, seeming to sway the sedge. When she called again, the dog whimpered, half in alarm, half fear.

Meredith knew how to run with a firearm. All the same, it was a while since she'd done it and her breath was coming in gusts by the time she reached the lakeside.

Tail down, nose to the water's edge, Cleo's sensitive snout was nudging at a dead man's hairy white wrist.

* * *

That morning at around the same time, Jo Hughes was switching on the lights and heating at the Rivermill Bookshop and Café. Dawn had not yet stretched into the deep Gloucestershire valley to reach the shop's long, narrow windows. The Rivermill was the first unit in the mill building to open up so, over the last few months while she had been helping her friend Hanni to run the place, Jo had got used to the drill of unlocking and shoving open the main doors, then moving swiftly to switch off the alarms. It meant that, at this hour, their little corner of the old mill had the only lights showing.

Jo always kept her coat and gloves on for the first half an hour during the winter and made an instant coffee to keep herself warm while she checked the tills and the stock and turned on the proper coffee machine. While the machine heated the water, she tidied some baubles on the Christmas tree in the corner window and plugged in the coloured lights. She glanced up at the main road, a third of the way up the valley. The tree was as bright and prominent as they could make it, although it would take a sharp-eyed driver or a very alert passenger to notice it. At least the mill estate had erected an outdoor tree this year, which stood swaying in the light breeze in the courtyard outside. *You really can't miss that*, Jo thought.

She crossed the room to the café at the front of the shop. The books never needed any attention because Hanni left them immaculate. Inevitably, there was more preparation needed for the café, with cakes, milk and cream to retrieve from the fridge, coffee beans to refill and dishes to be dried and set out. When she'd done these jobs, she tweaked the furniture, moving tables and chairs and switching some of the cushions to hide the ones that were becoming thin and faded. Through the long front windows, passers-by would see a jumble of comfy armchairs with mismatched cushions, surrounded by books and posters about books. This was the image they were striving for, but Jo knew Hanni would prefer to have seen the whole space filled with bookshelves. The accounts told a different story, however, and it was the café that enabled Hanni to pay the rent.

By the time the coffee machine was ready to churn out its first cappuccino and the water was trickling noisily through the radiators, it was still half an hour until the bakery delivery. Jo sat down with her laptop and started work on her monthly blog. She was proud of the following she was building on her astrology website but keeping it up to date took a fair amount of maintenance, and these undisturbed early mornings were turning out to be a productive time to work on it. This month, she intended to focus on the movements of the powerful slow planets, seeing as they were threatening a bumpy end to the year and she wanted to give the best astrological advice to help people avoid the worst of their impact.

Before she had even got as far as Saturn, she was aware of a subtle change in the light. A shadow fell on the window. Had the lights on the outdoor Christmas tree gone out? Then she heard an engine running and realized that a vehicle had pulled up on the narrow estate road just outside. Jo checked the time, although it was still too early for the Sayers' delivery. Without standing, she stretched, craning her neck to better make out the shape of a small white van blocking the window.

A few other businesses on the estate would already be open. But if the van driver was delivering something for the garden centre around the corner, they would soon realize they had taken a wrong turn. Jo returned to her blog, but the van didn't move on. She checked the time again, frowning. It would be eight thirty before the other retailers in the building would arrive. The people from the jewellery workshop were invariably late starters and the carpenter, who held the other corner plot, was no early riser either.

After a couple of minutes, Jo sighed and got to her feet. *Maybe the poor driver is lost*, she thought. He seemed to be looking through their lighted window and, if he were heading to the garden centre, the van was facing the wrong way. She could still hear the engine but it was too dark to see much of the driver. She'd just go and see if they needed any help with directions.

As she opened the café door, the van moved swiftly away. She said the registration number out loud, knowing this would help her to remember it, and stayed on the worn doorstep, watching the van's progress.

In that direction, the narrow estate road only led towards the car park and picnic tables over the river. At seven forty-five on a November morning, she figured that a picnic was unlikely so she waited, arms folded, until the van had to perform a U-turn.

It barrelled past her, making for the main road. She glimpsed a solo driver, travelling too fast for the twisty route through the estate and saw them swerve onto the A road heading west.

She returned indoors, shivering. Before going back to her blog, she jotted down the van registration number on the nearest notepad, which lay on the bookshop counter. She couldn't really have said why she did this. If pressed, she would have put it down to having spent three years working as a private investigator but, now that she had founded her own astrology business here in Stroud, she didn't often think about that period of her life.

As she replaced Hanni's pen, she noticed that the notepad was lying beside the accounts book. Hanni must have been working on the finances after closing time the evening before. Jo set aside a palm-sized crystal that was resting on top of the hardback book and quickly leafed through the year's accounts. That was all it took to confirm what she had already guessed — Hanni's business was barely covering the rent for the site. This was not something the two friends had discussed in any detail but it explained why Hanni had seemed so worried and distracted lately. There was nothing Jo could do about it right now, however, so she replaced the crystal and tried to concentrate on the planets.

Twenty minutes later, when Aman from Sayers arrived with the pastries and sandwiches, Jo's first question was about the white van. He looked at her from under his long fringe, poised in taking a plastic tray out of the back. 'You expect me to remember a white van? Do you know how many white vans I see in a day?'

Jo reached in for the next tray, greeted by the luscious scent of almonds and icing sugar. 'This bloke was driving like an idiot.'

'Tell me something I couldn't guess.' Aman led the way into the shop and Jo followed, kicking the door shut behind her to keep out the cold air.

'I think you'd have noticed this guy because of the way he was driving. Man on his own, woolly hat . . .' Jo ran out of description at this point and licked the icing sugar off her finger instead.

'You are definitely having me on now.' He peered at her across the café. 'What are you on about? Have the early mornings got to you?'

Jo shrugged. 'No, it was just — he was acting oddly, that's all. No one ever comes down here at this hour. Apart from you.'

'Satnav error,' Aman said. 'Took him to the wrong estate, I bet. Cainscross Business Park is just up the road, that's where he'd be heading.' He picked up the two empty trays and Jo opened the door for him. 'Trust me, I'm a white van driver.' He grinned. 'And as for you, don't watch so many scary late-night movies.'

Jo told him in no uncertain terms what she thought of that advice and they parted with a laugh and a wave.

She wandered back in and returned to her blog. She had progressed as far as Neptune when Hanni arrived, her slight form swathed in multicoloured scarves, a fluffy hat and the sort of cape that Sherlock Holmes might have worn on the moor.

'Jo, I am a walking icicle,' she said. 'There was no heating on the bus today. Is Lola up and working?'

'She sure is.' Jo was proud to have bent the temperamental coffee machine to her will. 'A coconut skinny latte in short order.'

While Hanni unwound a skein of crocheted wool from her neck, Jo told her about the fleeting visit by the anonymous van driver.

'I know that a white van on the estate is hardly an unusual thing,' Jo said. 'But the driver did seem to be looking in at us and, well, it was just a bit odd.' She handed Hanni a large coffee.

'If you intuited something ominous then that makes it significant.' Hanni took a seat at one of the tables and cupped her mug between woollen gloves. 'We don't want to invite negative energies into our healing space.' She raised her almost lashless, almond-shaped eyes as if to heaven. In fact, she was referring to their consulting rooms above the café.

'Oh, well. It's gone now anyway.' Jo shrugged and, feeling a little guilty about her sneaky peak at the accounts, she added, 'Let's concentrate instead on how we can make this the most profitable Christmas ever for the Rivermill.'

Hanni gave a serene smile. 'You are already doing your bit towards that, Jo. I only wish I could pay you what you deserve for the hours you put in. Which reminds me, I have a crystal healing session this afternoon so if you wouldn't mind staying a bit later today, that would really help.'

Jo nodded her agreement. She and Hanni had been friends a long time and as a member of the Mind, Body and Spirit network, Hanni had helped her become established locally as an astrologer. Jo had pledged to help while Hanni's business partner, Chloe, was on maternity leave. So far it wasn't proving too difficult to fit in with her own business.

Hanni took her coffee over to the bookshop counter. 'I have placed some pyrite for manifestation on the accounts book and that should assist in raising our profits.'

Jo sighed, wishing she could share her friend's faith in the power of crystals, and returned to her laptop.

Despite their hopes, it was a quiet day at the Rivermill, not helped by the wild weather tossing the tops of the trees on the steep side of the valley and steady rain. If Hanni had not been meeting a crystal healing client in the afternoon, Jo would certainly have gone home. Left to herself as the skies blurred into darkness, she went round switching on all the lights again, made herself yet another coffee and sat down to finish her blog. She was in the middle of another rewrite of the paragraph on Jupiter when the door pinged.

'Hope you've got some cakes left,' said a familiar voice. 'Cherry bakewells are my favourite.'

She looked up to see the tall figure of her old boss, David Macy, shaking the rain off his umbrella. She didn't want to gratify him by asking how he had known she was here. Tracing people was his job after all.

She had not seen Macy since September, when she had sought him out for his PI skills and he had dutifully come to her assistance. Since then they had hardly been in touch. He had other skills too, she recalled, as she watched him unfold his long body onto the sofa while she listed the available cakes and waited while he havered between carrot cake and a fruit scone. 'This is the best — it's freshest,' she said eventually, cutting him a generous slice of the carrot and walnut cake. 'So, what are you doing in my part of the world?'

Macy ran his business from Birmingham and made no secret of the fact that he found the Cotswold valleys too sleepy for his liking. 'Just passing through.'

This made Jo smile. She carried their coffee and cake to the window table. 'Are you going to tell me what's going on?'

She could see there was something bothering him although it didn't seem to have affected his appetite.

'Honestly, can't I drop in to see an old friend without having to explain why?' He tried to feign outrage through a mouthful of cake. Jo also noted his slight hesitation over the word 'friend'. They were more than that to each other and they both knew it, which was one of the reasons she was certain this was not just a casual visit. But she waited patiently while he ate.

He looked around the bookshop, fork in hand. 'Good range of books,' he commented. 'Although I couldn't work here as I would eat the profits.'

'There aren't any,' Jo confided, surprising herself at how easy it was to tell him a difficult truth. 'That's one of the reasons I'm here, helping out virtually for free.'

He brought his dark eyes back to meet hers and nodded. 'How's your business going?'

'Good, thanks. I get time to work on it while I'm here and can hold consultations in the room above the shop. That's where Hanni is now. She offers crystal healing sessions.'

'Maybe that's what I need,' he said under his breath, but when she threw a questioning look at him, he didn't elaborate. 'I've come to bring you some business, actually, and to ask a favour. I need you to cast a horoscope for a case we're working on. The woman's name is Flora Howell and she was born on the ninth of November 1995 in Maidenhead, Berkshire at 4.15 p.m.'

Jo nodded approvingly at the level of detail. 'OK, she's Scorpio and she's just had her twenty-fourth birthday. Just a baby, still in her twenties.' Lately, Jo had been feeling the subtle pressure of having turned thirty-three in September. 'Twenty-four is significant in astrological terms but I'll tell you more when I draw up the chart. How do you know her? What does she do?'

'She works for a training company called Upwards, which is based in Bournemouth and specializes in helping underprivileged kids get jobs.' He paused. 'And to answer your first question, we have Flora on surveillance.'

'Whatever for?' Jo said, amused. 'She sounds positively saintly.'

Macy flattened out his lips in frustration. 'That's the problem. Upwards have lost an important contract and the new owner of the company thinks it's her fault.'

'Why not just sack her? That would be a lot more straightforward.'

'No evidence, for one thing. But now that's part of my problem too. We can't find anything on her — neither can her boss, incidentally — but the owner is convinced she's the one who sold them out.'

'And the owner is the person paying you?' Jo said and had the satisfaction of seeing from his expression that she had guessed right.

'Yes, my contract is with a guy called Louis Carswell, who runs an events business in Bournemouth and has just bought the training company Flora works for. Reading between the lines, he is worried he's been sold a pup and is looking closely at the whole business, including Flora.'

'New brooms sweep clean or however it goes,' Jo said.

Macy nodded. 'I know Carswell because he worked for me about five years ago, but he's always had his finger in lots of pies. Since then he's moved south, where he seems to have found much bigger and richer pies. A month or so ago, he got in touch with this latest job. Right at this moment he's not too happy with us because we're not bringing him the results he expected.' Macy looked up at her with a wry smile. 'He loved the idea of a horoscope for Flora though. Like a psychological profile, that sort of thing.'

'Steady on,' Jo said. 'I wouldn't go that far. But I can make you a formal-looking report for this Carswell guy, if that's what you want.' She thought for a second. 'So, what is it you're looking for? What do you want to know about Flora?'

'I suppose to throw some light on her character. She seems fairly bland to us so far. Can you tell if she has tendencies to deception, lying — criminality even? That sort of thing? You can charge me top whack,' he added.

'I can tell you straight away that Scorpios are very comfortable with secrets and they invariably have emotional depths. I've never met a bland one.' Jo sipped the last of the froth from her coffee cup. 'What about this man Carswell? He also sounds interesting.'

'That's one word for him. Honestly? I don't trust him an inch but he's our client now so I have to manage him. But he is not a man who takes disappointment well.'

Macy rested his elegant hands on the table. He thanked Jo and told her how good it was to see her, but Jo wasn't fooled for a moment. She had known him too long and sensed there was more coming.

'What about the favour?' she prompted. 'You said you had some business for me and a favour to ask.'

'Ye-es.' He held her gaze while he searched for the right words. 'This is a bit weird,' he began.

Jo waved a hand at the display of crystals and related literature behind her. 'Go on, you're in the right place.'

'How do you fancy attending a business seminar in Bournemouth? Upwards are holding a seminar for local businesses on "Future Skills". It's mainly a promotion event, if you ask me. Their MD, Carolyn Ash, has an eye for publicity. When I told Carswell about you, he suggested you might like to attend. Astrology is all about the future, isn't it?' He gesticulated vaguely in the air. 'You never know, you might get some business out of it. That's what it's about after all. It's a networking event after work with drinks and nibbles, you know the sort of thing.'

His tone was so uncharacteristically positive that Jo found she was searching for the catch. 'Just a business drinks evening?'

'Yes.' He caught her eye and grinned. 'OK, it would also be great if you could spend as much time as possible with Flora. I want to understand her relationship with Carolyn Ash. Flora is Carolyn's business manager, a recent promotion and they seem to be very chummy.'

The jingle of the doorbell made them both look up and Hanni entered the shop. Jo called her over and introduced them. Hanni, a head shorter than Jo and still wearing her brightly coloured Peruvian hat over her fine urchin-cut hair, smiled at Macy and offered him her delicate hand. She looked pleased when he told her how much he liked the place and asked for a card so he could order some books.

'We get good rates from our suppliers,' she said. 'We can even beat the internet sometimes. And of course, fabulous cakes too.'

'I can attest to that,' Macy smiled, as he stood. Jo went with him to the shop door and he looked at her questioningly while they hesitated in the doorway. 'Will you be able to do it? It's the day after tomorrow.'

'Oh, so not very much notice then.'

It was still raining heavily and he stepped out to put up the umbrella. 'I'll book you into the swanky hotel overnight so you can have a few cocktails and I'll even give you a lift down there if you want. I'm constantly ferrying back and forth between the office and Bournemouth, it seems. What do you say?'

Behind him, the light was flickering in rain-slanted waves between the arc lights on the estate, the pale rectangles of the shop windows and the swaying Christmas tree, so she couldn't make out his expression. She was certain there was still a lot he wasn't telling her. *Nothing new there*, she thought. And yet, this was different. There was something troubling him about these people.

'OK,' she agreed from her vantage point on the doorstep. 'I'll do it. But only on condition that you tell me what is really bothering you.'

'That'll take longer.' Macy looked at the sky. 'Tell me there's a pub in this little town that does a decent meal and I'll fill you in you over dinner later.'

'I finally get to meet Macy,' Hanni commented when Jo came back indoors. 'He's an old soul, isn't he? Handsome man, though.'

'He was here on business,' Jo said. She was still turning over the unexpected visit in her mind.

'Oh, I see.' Hanni said no more but looked at the rain-streaked windows. 'We're not going to get any more customers tonight. Let's close up.'

* * *

In Dorset, Meredith was finally gutting the duck with Cleo waiting patiently, nose raised, in her basket. The whole routine for the day had been thrown out by their gruesome find that morning. Instead of letting the duck hang while she continued with the house renovations as planned, it had lain in the boot of the car most of the day while she was being interviewed at the police station. The taste would be compromised as a result, but she was not going to let the kill go to waste. Cleo wasn't likely to object and there would still be a casserole in the oven by the time Peter came home.

Having seen active service herself, not much shocked Meredith. Or Peter, come to that, who was still a serving officer in the army. The police had been complimentary about the level of detail she had been able to provide about the crime scene: the exact time of day, the angle of the body and its proximity to a floating sculpture. This gave her a modicum of satisfaction, and she was glad she had retained her military calm and resilience.

'Still got it, Cleo,' she remarked to the dog, who banged her tail in anticipation. All the same, she opened the red wine a little earlier than usual. While the dog wolfed down her well-earned dinner, Meredith sat at the kitchen table with her glass, trying not to dwell on the way the man's stomach had been split from his sternum to his navel.

CHAPTER TWO

Jo chose a pub in one of the surrounding villages, where the food was reliable and they would be guaranteed a quiet table on a Monday night. Macy said he had phone calls to make and was happy to meet her there, so she gave herself enough time to go home and get ready. She chose her clothes and make-up carefully but not *too* carefully. *It's only Macy after all,* she thought as she gave herself the final once-over in the wardrobe mirror. She had known him for years and they were long past anything between them. They both had other people now. She had lovely Teddy, who was currently running a golf tournament in Spain. And Macy had Rowanna — or she thought he did. That was one of the many important details she was determined to find out.

Driving to the pub, she called Teddy and they talked about their very different days. He had been outdoors in the chilly sunshine, 'herding people about', as he put it. 'I'm no good at sorting out people's problems for them. Unless it's a golf problem, which it hardly ever is. I could use your organizing skills,' he told her. 'Listen, why don't you come over at the end of the tournament? Everyone will be gone by then, thank God. It finishes next week but we can still use the apartment for a few days.'

He had mentioned this before and there was no doubt the offer was tempting. But so far she hadn't committed herself, partly because of her promise to help Hanni. She dodged the invitation again and said she would call him later. She felt a little guilty for not mentioning that she was on her way to meet her old flame but as it was purely a business arrangement with Macy, she decided it was forgivable.

Macy was standing at the bar and turned his head when she came in. 'What can I get you?' He was smiling but his face showed signs of strain.

'Beer, thanks.' She resisted the temptation to kiss him on the cheek.

As she had hoped, the bar was empty apart from a couple with a Labrador by the fire. After they'd ordered, she chose a settle in the corner furthest away from them and Macy brought the beers over.

'Come on then, tell me what I am getting into,' she said.

'You won't be getting into anything,' Macy was quick to reassure her. She waited for more, as he took a long drink of his beer. 'It really is just finding out a bit more about Flora's relationships at work because her job is the part of her life where we could do with more access.'

'Why me? I thought you had a team on this?'

'Not a very big team.' He sighed. 'I haven't got that many people who are prepared to spend their weeks in Bournemouth. I probably need to recruit locally, but that's not been easy either. And for this business event, I want to make sure it is someone who is completely new to the team at Upwards. And someone who is convincing.' He sat back against the hard wooden bench and took another thirsty drink.

'What do you mean "the team at Upwards"? I thought it was just Flora you were interested in.' At this rate, she was going to be fetching a second round shortly. She glanced at the bar and recognized the barman. She and Teddy regularly came here to eat, and she was a little distracted by the hope that the barman would not mention tonight's visit to Teddy.

Macy placed his half-empty glass on the mat. 'All right. I said that because I don't know who to trust among this lot. I'm not convinced that Flora Howell has done anything wrong, so now I am just as suspicious about the people she works with. Including Louis Carswell.'

'He's the guy employing you, isn't he?' The other couple had stopped talking and suddenly Jo was aware that the pub was essentially a small, enclosed room. Maybe she would have been better off choosing somewhere a bit livelier. Only in conversations with Macy did she ever have to think about such things, she realized. She lowered her voice. 'Why would he think that it was her fault Upwards lost their contract? That is what he suspects her of, isn't it?' She recalled the thin details Macy had given her in the bookshop.

Macy nodded. 'It was for a big government contract. He thinks Flora gave information to a rival company. Apparently only Flora had access to the contract documentation, including the pricing.' As Macy was speaking, a group of younger, noisier customers arrived and took over the bar area. Jo was grateful for the additional background noise and Macy also seemed to relax a bit more as he tucked into his steak.

'Looks bad for Flora,' Jo acknowledged as she surveyed her duck with noodles in anticipation. She'd eaten this dish before and had found herself looking forward to it while driving over. 'Presumably, knowing what Upwards was going to quote enabled this other company to undercut them?'

'Exactly,' Macy said. 'But Upwards still has a very good reputation for training apprentices and getting young people into work. Louis Carswell bought it from Carolyn Ash and she is well respected locally. She built it up from scratch. She wants to devote more time to campaigning on behalf of deprived kids these days, but she is still managing the business for Louis.'

Jo had been observing Macy closely. They had been friends and lovers, and had worked together for many years, but she had rarely seen him troubled by his work. Usually he had a laconic, cynical style, which allowed him to stay detached. 'So what's bothering you?' she asked. 'Is it this Louis Carswell? Or is it Flora herself?'

Macy's eyes flicked up to meet hers and he gave the merest of nods. 'It's both. Carswell has done very well for himself since moving to Bournemouth. When I first knew him, he'd just moved from South Africa and needed a job. Now he owns Planet Events, an ever-expanding exhibitions company.' Macy put down his fork as if eating was a distraction and looked at her intently. 'About a month ago, Carswell called me and I went down to see him. He had just bought Upwards and he asked me to find out what we can about Flora Howell because of this contracts business. Now we get to the crux of the problem.' He sighed. 'We have been monitoring Flora for six weeks and found absolutely zero.' He paused to take a few mouthfuls and then corrected himself with irony. 'Well, that's not true. We've established that Flora is a twenty-four-year-old single woman who lives in a one-bedroomed flat in Boscombe, a little seaside suburb of Bournemouth. She cycles to work every day and enjoys reading and knitting.'

'You haven't answered my question,' Jo pointed out.

He groaned. 'It's late and I've been driving all day, cut me some slack.'

They exchanged looks.

'OK, I said I'd be upfront with you,' he went on. 'My worry is she's just a quiet, harmless young woman and nothing we've found tells me anything different.'

'Ah well, her natal chart will tell us if she's really harmless,' Jo said with a knowing look. 'What are you actually doing to keep her under surveillance?'

'It's only limited surveillance — we can't access her once in work or at home. We've been focused on finding out about her contacts, her social network. That's the brief. We've been taking two- or three-day shifts at a time: me, Alan and Jess.'

'Alan?' Jo and Alan had often worked together when they had both been PI operatives for Macy and Wilson but they had very little else in common. Alan had used to drive her mad with his bigotry and unfunny sense of humour, but he had got her out of a few tricky situations too. 'Isn't he supposed to be retired?'

'He's not a regular for me anymore but, thank the Lord, this job is right up his street. He takes his bike down on the train so he can "maintain visuals on the target" on Flora's commute to work.' Macy shot her an amused glance over his beer. 'I've found my car is just as effective, and I don't get wet if it rains.'

'It doesn't seem like Alan has changed much. But if you haven't found anything on Flora, why not just make your report and Carswell will have to deal with it?' As soon as she had asked the question, she realized with a first hint of foreboding that it was probably not that simple. Macy didn't respond, but his sombre silence reinforced her sense of unease.

Had they not both been driving, they would definitely have had more beers and maybe shared more confidences but, as it was, they switched to coffee with their puddings and the conversation moved on to practicalities. Jo turned down the offer of a lift, preferring to get to Bournemouth under her own steam, which meant she could open up at the bookshop for Hanni beforehand. They agreed to meet at the hotel in Bournemouth late afternoon on Wednesday.

'It's just a local business event with some so-called experts to talk about future skills,' he said before they parted. 'And I won't be far away throughout the evening, so you've no need to worry. It's not like these people are dangerous or anything.'

Jo frowned. 'I didn't think they were,' she said.

She was still doubtful after they had said a chaste good-night in the car park. Sitting at the steering wheel, she didn't even try to sort out the mix of feelings that Macy's unexpected arrival had caused. It was only as she was forced to wait while a van pushed its way out of the car park in front of her that she remembered the unexplained white van outside the Rivermill that morning. Aman had been right to scoff at her concerns on that score. Now that Macy was back in her life, there were real worries on the horizon.

CHAPTER THREE

The street lights and signs from restaurants and bars lit Jo's entry into Bournemouth. She surveyed the shopfronts to see if there was anything about the seaside town that she found familiar. Her last visit had been on a family holiday when she was about eight, which would have made her sister, Marie, eleven, and they had perfected the art of how to wind each other up as only sisters can. She mainly remembered the arguments, a chilly apartment and some gorgeous mint chocolate chip ice cream. She wondered if she could track down a version of that ice cream before she left.

A glimpse of the Christmas lights on the pier gave her a sudden surge of childlike excitement at being unexpectedly away from home on a strange mission. She smiled inwardly and turned her thoughts to the more mundane matter of locating the Metropole Hotel. This didn't prove too difficult as the grand white Georgian building held a commanding position on the seafront. The hotel appeared to be the sort of well-established, self-confident place that had probably looked much the same for decades and Jo wondered idly if her parents had strolled past its grand façade with their two squabbling daughters in tow twenty-five years ago.

By her third lap of the tiny Metropole car park, she reckoned she had memorized every car, was on nodding terms with the woman locking her bike into the cycle racks and was starting to feel tense. Having arrived early, she now had only five minutes before she was due to meet Macy in the hotel lobby. She spotted a space near the entrance, blocked by a large black BMW.

'If you move back a bit, I can get into that space,' Jo said to the driver through her window. At least, she assumed the guy in the Gucci sportswear, leaning against the side of the car, was the driver.

He surveyed her with startlingly handsome eyes from under a haircut that was both extravagantly curled and part shaved. 'I'm waiting for someone,' he muttered, spread his legs wider and dropped his eyes to his phone screen.

Jo, not easily deterred, started to explain that she was late for a meeting when she was interrupted. The cyclist had been observing their exchange from the doorway, where she had swapped a purple waterproof for a smarter, more businesslike silk jacket. She leaned over, tapped the driver politely on the arm and murmured something.

Whatever she said was effective. The driver returned with sullen slowness into the driving seat. The woman scurried into the hotel while he inched the large black car backwards, leaving Jo just enough space to park.

She threw him a grin as she strolled past. 'Thanks, mate, and thanks for moving.'

He stared at her, a brown elbow sticking out of the driver's window.

'This is where the Futures event is being held, right?' she asked.

'Yeah, that's right. My boss's girlfriend is running it.' He smirked at the word 'girlfriend' as if to indicate that they were too old for this epithet. Now she was over thirty, could she still refer to Teddy as her 'boyfriend'?

'Carolyn Ash?'

'That's right. You going to it?'

'I certainly am,' she said cheerfully. 'I'm Jo Hughes and I'm an astrologer. And you?'

'No, not likely, I'm busy here.' He indicated the car with a tap of his finger on the paintwork. 'I'm Andre Souto. And it's a name worth remembering if you want to impress Carolyn Ash.'

'Then I will remember it,' she said. 'I'm just curious, by the way, who was the cyclist?'

He raised his eyebrows, one of which had a notch cut out of it, drawing attention to his striking dark eyes. 'Some woman that works for Carolyn. Name's Flora.'

So that was Flora, Jo thought, fighting an urge to dash after the young woman like Alice following the white rabbit. 'Well it was nice to meet you Andre Souto. I should get in there — in fact, I'm meant to be meeting my colleague now.' She knew, as she breezed past him, that she sounded far more confident than she felt and trusted she could keep this up for the rest of the evening.

After she'd checked in, Jo scanned the hotel lobby, with its impressive set of 1920s revolving doors on the seafront side and pillars with fluted stained glass, Tiffany-style. The place thrummed with chatter and faint piano music drifting from a bar on one side of the wide atrium. Jo climbed a few steps up the grand staircase to gain a better view and found herself looking down on Macy's tall, narrow-hipped figure exiting the bar with a woman whose bright red topknot barely came up to his shoulder. She was laughing and they paused beside the huge corporate Christmas tree to share a quick handclasp before parting. Jo had an impression of the woman's easy stride, leather jacket and boots as Macy watched her leave through the revolving door.

Jo's instant reaction of indignation, even outrage and, she had to admit it, a flash of jealousy was completely irrational. There was nothing between her and Macy nowadays, and they had only shaken hands. She had accepted that he and his employee Rowanna were probably an item. But this tiny, leather-jacketed, red-headed woman definitely wasn't

Rowanna. The question she asked herself was, why did she care?

Macy had noticed her and was loping up the staircase before she could entirely clear her head of all such illogical thoughts. 'You got here OK,' he said. 'Good timing. Carswell is due to meet us at five thirty. Is there anything you need to know beforehand?'

The one question she wanted to ask felt impossible, so she kept to the task in hand and instead blithely informed him that she'd already met Flora.

'I know.' He led the way back down into the bustling lobby. Catching her puzzled look, he grinned sheepishly. 'Don't forget, she is under surveillance.'

'You mean you were watching me?' Jo demanded, stung. She would have said more but Macy put a hand on her arm, pointing discreetly towards the revolving doors.

'This is Carswell,' he said. 'Oh, and Carolyn is with him.'

Jo turned her head to see a conspicuous couple entering through the revolving doors. They were both in their forties, Jo guessed. Carolyn was animated, using her hands to make her point and Carswell nodded, head down, listening. Carolyn's short, well-styled haircut and trouser suit of peacock silk seemed designed to catch the eye.

'She doesn't know about the surveillance on Flora by the way,' Macy said in a low voice. 'I don't suppose she would sanction it.'

'Marvellous,' Jo muttered. 'If I've got this right, you are investigating a key member of her staff but she's not been told because she wouldn't allow it.' She saw from his expression that she'd hit the nail on the head.

Neither of them had time to say more because Louis Carswell was bearing down on them. The man had height and some bulk but moved lightly. His suit and tie were immaculate, his dark hair styled into careful waves. His white teeth showed in a wide smile.

'Macy, you're here ahead of me.' He flicked ostentatiously at a showy watch. 'Although I don't know why I expected any different. You've never let me down, after all.' Although he bestowed a genial smile and bland brown eyes on them, he didn't appear to register Jo until Macy introduced her. Then she felt the full attention of Carswell's undeniable presence.

'So, this is Jo.' Carswell took a step back and opened his arms so that Jo feared she may be drawn into an unwanted hug. Instead he remained poised on the balls of this feet, emanating a faint, expensive scent of cedar. 'At last. I can't say we've heard a lot about you. I am sure you know what he's like.' Carswell shot a glance at Macy that was as sharp as a physical dig in the ribs. 'He's as silent as the tomb. That's why we know we can trust Macy and Wilson,' he added. 'Welcome to our merry band, Jo Hughes, and I hope you enjoy the evening we've got planned. I'm looking forward to reading the profile you're preparing on our subject. It's a whole new way of looking at the problem.' He grinned at Macy. 'And it shows Carolyn isn't the only one who can be innovative.'

'I'm confident astrology will bring you new insights,' Jo said. She meant it.

'Good, good,' Carswell went on smoothly. 'Leaving aside the astrology and any other job he's got you doing—' this was accompanied by another pointed sideways look — 'I hope you will also engage with the work of Upwards, which is making a massive difference in upskilling young adults. And not just locally. I can promise you that by the end of the evening, you will be impressed by what young people are capable of given the right chances to earn a wage, and you may even find yourself supporting the campaigning work, which Carolyn is leading on.'

'I'm looking forward to it,' Jo said when she managed to get a word in.

'I'm really disappointed I can't be there to see how astrology holds up against the competition.' His smile grew wider and his eyes glinted.

'Competition?' Jo repeated, unable to resist a darting glance at Macy. His face told her nothing.

'Oooh, didn't he tell you?' Carswell said, drawing out the first word teasingly. 'You're up against academics from the proper, factual, evidence-based sciences like climatology and physics. It's going to be a hoot to see how they react when you start to tell them all about the dawning of the Age of Aquarius.'

'You're showing your age, I'm afraid. That's the title of a very old song.' Jo said with a smile.

Carswell chuckled. 'Is that so? Well, I want to hear all about this evening anyway. And I mean *all*.' He delivered another telling look to Macy and then beamed at Jo again. 'Good luck. The seminar is in the Lord Bute room at six thirty. Can't wait to see your report.'

'Jo won't be delivering the report,' Macy replied. 'She's only here for this evening, but you and I are meeting at your office tomorrow, you'll recall. Jo, don't you need to go and find your hotel room before the meeting?'

She was grateful for the chance to escape, and left, vowing to take the surprise details up with Macy as soon as she could. The opportunity came when he phoned her twenty minutes later.

'You didn't tell me I was going head-to-head with a bunch of academics,' Jo said from her bed in the cramped, over-furnished room looking onto the car park. 'You know that scientists love pouring cold water on astrology.'

'It won't be anything you can't handle,' he said. 'Now tell me what you thought of Carswell.'

'He likes to rattle people, doesn't he? Likes to shake things up.' She eyed her little black cocktail dress, which was hanging on the back of the wardrobe. 'Remind me, how much are you paying me for this again?'

'You won't have to see much of Carswell,' Macy said, ignoring this question. 'Remember, it's Flora Howell we're interested in.'

'I've looked up her boss too by the way. Carolyn Ash is a Leo. They don't exactly shun the limelight and, on first impression, she seems typical of the star sign. She certainly makes an entrance.' Realizing they had limited time, she changed the subject. 'OK, tell me specifically what you need to know. Seeing as I'm here, I might as well get on with it.'

'Everything you can find out about Flora's work set-up, really,' Macy replied. 'What we haven't been able to establish is how much influence she has within the training company. We need to verify if she really was the only one with access to the contract documents. Also, what Flora's relationships are like with the rest of the Upwards team.'

'Not much then. Just some forensic business process analysis and occupational psychology.' Before Macy could comment on her sarcastic tone, she went on. 'What about Carolyn Ash? What's her relationship like with Carswell? They looked pretty close at first sight.'

'Close in a business way, but I'm certain there's nothing more to it. Louis keeps his private life very much to himself, insofar as he even has one. He's all business. Their relationship is actually more strained now Carolyn effectively works for him. Listen, I will only be a phone call or text away,' he said. 'I'm staying in town overnight, somewhere distinctly less swish, I can tell you. I'm picking up surveillance on Flora when she leaves the hotel after the event and again in the morning. Once she's in work tomorrow, we can meet up and you can give me the lowdown. Let's say ten o' clock.' He gave the name of a coffee lounge on the seafront and Jo made a mental note.

She continued to stare at her dress while her mind was busy going over the plan. 'Can you get me into the room while the Upwards people are setting up?' she said. 'I might find out more about life behind the scenes then.'

'No problem. You're a guest of Planet Events, so I'll sort that. Just go down to the meeting room when you're ready. What else do you need?'

'Nothing. Unless you've got any designer bling.' The image of Carswell and Carolyn Ash making an entrance in the hotel lobby was still fresh in her mind. 'I somehow think my matching earrings and necklace from Accessorize are not going to cut it with this crowd.'

'You'll look gorgeous,' Macy said.

Jo felt her jaw drop slightly. She couldn't remember receiving such a compliment from him before. Maybe this was the moment to ask him about the woman he was with in the bar? And yet she didn't.

'You know, you are being remarkably positive and helpful,' she said instead. 'You really are worried about something, aren't you?'

But Macy didn't hear her — or feigned not to — and reminded her about the arrangement to meet in the morning. 'After that, you're free to go back to hippy town.'

She rolled her eyes, knowing what Macy thought of Stroud, her adopted town. She did what she could with her dress and make-up. The hotel hairdryer was not up to the job of taming her thick, wavy hair but, as she left the room, she reminded herself that she was not there to impress anyone. In fact, she would learn more from simply blending in. The silky black dress and heels plus a rather smart evening bag she had found at the back of her wardrobe would suffice.

As she approached the Lord Bute room on the ground floor, she was marshalling her arguments against any potential challenges from the scientists. She realized that she had allowed Carswell to needle her, which made her dislike him even more, and she couldn't for the life of her fathom what had possessed Macy to take this job. And now, so was she. *But only for one evening,* she reminded herself.

CHAPTER FOUR

According to the noticeboard with its gold lettering, Jo was an hour early, which was exactly what she had intended. Nevertheless, she turned the handle on the door with surprisingly sweaty fingers. *This is ridiculous*, she thought. *It's just an evening with people I'll never meet again.*

A short, stocky man in a rugby shirt and jeans bounded up to her, grinning aggressively. 'Really sorry, but you're way too early. We're not quite ready yet.' Behind him, a bright blue-and-green laminated banner reached from one end of the long, wood-panelled room to the other, bearing the message, *Future Planet, Future Skills*. 'Can I get them to order you a coffee in the bar? I'm Vinny Harrison, PR man for Upwards by the way.' He thrust square-shaped, spread fingers in her direction.

Jo introduced herself and explained she was just looking for a quiet corner.

'Oh, you're the lady Louis mentioned. Welcome, Jo, any guest of Planet is a friend of ours. Fraser!' He called over his shoulder to two young people who were struggling to erect a roll-up poster. 'This is the guest from Planet Events. Where is the material Louis left for her?'

Fraser, a waif of a youth with a wide smile, produced a glossy folder from among the name cards piled up on a side table and handed it to her. 'Louis said you would need this. You can sit anywhere.' He indicated the boardroom table.

'Well, there's meant to be a seating plan somewhere,' Vinny said. While he rummaged through the paperwork, Jo surveyed the room. She spotted her helpful cyclist immediately. Flora was carefully placing a line of small herbs in pots down the centre of the long table. Her dark head was lowered but Jo recognized the vivid green silk jacket, which jarred with her floral dress.

'Flora! Where is our seating plan?' Vinny asked from across the room.

She looked up with round, startled eyes. 'That's not me, I wasn't doing the seating plan. Isn't it with Liang?'

'Look, I'll just sit here.' Jo took the closest seat. She spread out the brochure about Planet Events and pretended to study it in depth while observing Flora Howell. Her impression was of a slight, round-shouldered woman with large eyes, an array of freckles across her nose and a bamboozled expression. Her dark brown curly hair was tied on either side of her head in bunches, a style Jo had last worn at about the same period as the family holiday in Bournemouth. How could this mild-mannered woman have ever become the focus of surveillance?

Although she had not asked for one, Vinny appeared at her side with a coffee, eager to tell her about the company. He enthused about the awards they had won for training young people. 'And we have two of our own apprentices here.' There was no doubting the pride in his voice. 'Fraser works for Planet Events and Bex is our own Upwards apprentice.' He beckoned to the young woman who had been setting up the poster with Fraser.

'What do you think?' Bex demanded, hands on hips. 'I want it to hit people between the eyes so they know this is all about our future.' She stood back to admire her work.

'Bex has the joy of working for me mainly, don't you?' Vinny said. 'I'm in charge of PR at Upwards including marketing and communications—'

'And the rest,' Bex chimed in. 'Go on, give her the list.' The young woman clearly didn't lack confidence and from the way she regarded Vinny, she had his measure.

'OK, let's see.' He tipped his head back. 'I also do recruitment and I'm the schools coordinator. Oh yes, health and safety and further education lead. Basically, give me a broom and I'll sweep up.' He ran his hand through thick brown hair, which was already tousled. 'But hey, that's life in a small company that's trying to change the world.'

Fortunately for Jo, his phone rang and he excused himself. It seemed to her that the youngest people in the room, Bex and Fraser were doing most of the work. Vinny's management style consisted of telling them they were marvellous and racing off to take phone calls. 'Carolyn says' and 'Carolyn wants' peppered their conversation. The boss's word was clearly law.

Another member of the Upwards team entered the room, carrying the sought-after seating plan, which she promptly handed to Flora. The newcomer presented herself to Jo with a direct smile and handshake as Liang Han, Training Manager. As Flora wandered off to place the name cards around the table, Liang turned to Jo with interest. 'I've never met an astrologer before, I'm dying to hear about it.'

Jo was surprised that anyone knew much about her but Liang had clearly done some research and could even quote from Jo's website.

'That's Carolyn's training.' Liang confessed when Jo complimented her. 'She likes us to be prepared.' It wasn't long, however, before Liang was enthusing to Jo about her own role, explaining how she had been 'poached' by Carolyn from her previous job with an estate agency. 'I was actually on one of Upwards's courses but Carolyn spotted that I would be good at training people,' she confided, 'so she offered me this job, which is amazing. And there will always be work here. That's what this event is all about, so we can put together a training programme for the future.'

While Jo was listening politely, Flora announced to no one in particular that she was going to fetch Carolyn and drifted out past Vinny, who was still on the phone. Jo watched her leave with a feeling that she had lost the first round of this strange game.

'I'm sure Carolyn doesn't need to be fetched,' Liang remarked with a sharp sigh. 'Look, our next guests are arriving and we could do with people to hand out programmes.'

With this talk of seating plans and programmes, Jo felt another twinge of apprehension. This was not the networking 'drinks and nibbles' social event Macy had described. And, as Liang told Jo about the guests, her heart sank. The two men being greeted by Fraser were Bart Klaassen, a climatologist from the university, Emily Anderson, a research fellow in health sciences, and Baljit Bawa. 'He's our expert on technological change,' Liang said. 'I'd better go and say hello.'

'Just tell me you haven't got an astrophysicist coming.' When Liang looked puzzled, Jo added, 'Scientists tend to disagree with astrologers on most things.'

'Oh, don't worry on that score. On the Upwards team, we are looking forward to the astrology bit the most. There are no other experts — except our speaker, who is a futurologist.'

Jo didn't like to admit that she wasn't sure what a futurologist was and wondered exactly what Liang had in mind for 'the astrology bit'. To amuse herself, she made a mental list of what Macy owed her for getting her into this.

'Don't worry, it won't be dry and boring,' Liang said, misreading Jo's expression. 'The most important session is straight after the break anyway.' She waved towards Bex and Fraser. 'Our apprentices have made a little movie to showcase our campaign work. We're trying to get firms to offer more apprenticeships. You wait, it will be trending again tomorrow. It's already all over TikTok.'

Jo decided to approach the little enclave of academics to introduce herself. They regarded her with polite reserve, except for Baljit Bawa, the technological expert, who went out of his way to be sociable. Jo chatted to him while keeping one eye on the door for Flora's return.

'Tell me, are you planning something light-hearted, like a sort of spoof?' The Dutch accent cut across Jo's conversation and came from a man with wire-rimmed glasses and a runner's build, who had introduced himself as Bart Klaassen from Bournemouth University. 'We could do with a jokey bit or it might all be too dire, don't you think?' He looked at his fellow academics.

Baljit looked embarrassed but Emily Anderson chuckled alongside him. 'Like a sort of panto, you mean, which would be appropriate, given the time of year.' She half-suppressed a smirk. 'I wonder if there is a clairvoyant coming too?'

'I suppose in one way or another we are all being asked to foretell future events.' Jo might have said more but was interrupted by a warm clear voice, which carried across the room.

'I see you've met Jo Hughes.' Carolyn Ash walked towards the group. 'I'm so jealous you got to her before me.' She included the wider room with a sweeping gaze and a challenging smile. 'Jo is an astrologer, running a business with a global reach from the Cotswolds. You know, I'm always fascinated by businesses whose success depends on understanding the future. That's what this whole event is about.'

Jo thought she caught a sceptical sneer from the Dutchman but before she could speak, Carolyn took her arm. 'Sorry, I must steal her before we start.'

She beamed a farewell and propelled Jo across the room. 'We've all been so excited to meet you, Jo. I mean it,' Carolyn added with a comprehensive look that dismissed the previous scene. 'I've really been impressed with how astrology has captured the imagination of our team. They've been talking about their star signs ever since we knew you were coming. That's its power, isn't it? It's instantly relatable.'

'Yes, most people are interested — sometimes despite themselves.' Jo smiled. 'Thanks for your support. They're a tough crowd.'

Carolyn waved this away. 'Rubbish, you could handle them. Now, Louis has been telling me all about you, and I'm specifically interested in how astrology can help make the future appealing to young people. Bart was right about that, at least. Sometimes it can seem bleak.'

Jo found herself being steered through the hubbub with Carolyn bobbing at her shoulder. 'There is someone you absolutely must meet, and it will give me the chance to tell you a bit about Upwards. We want our training programme to be future-proofed and that's why we need to understand the trends. I'm hoping that astrology will provoke some creative thinking. Maybe with a lighter, dare I say more spiritual, touch? It can't all be about serious science, can it?'

'I don't know about spiritual exactly, but the planets can give a sense of the energies that will be needed in the future,' Jo said. She had done her homework so she decided she may as well demonstrate it. 'Such as the way we will need to transform our relationship with the earth. That will need sensitivity and collaboration, for instance.'

'Perfect. That's just the sort of thing that people need to hear.' They had come to a halt beside Jo's place at the table. 'Young people want to understand what skills they need to learn, not just data and analysis.' Her lively eyes swooped around the room. 'Now, I've designated Flora to look after you this evening, so she can tell you anything else you need to know. Where is she? Flora knows my diary and I want to put in a date that suits you.'

'A date for what?'

The other woman turned an impish smile on her. 'For a reading, of course. Or what do you call it in astrology? I go to have my cards read sometimes and the chap calls that a reading. Is that the right terminology?'

'Yes, or you might say a consultation.' It was hard not to be warmed by the woman's enthusiasm, especially when she was offering future business. Carolyn's bubbliness had an intelligence about it, which was now directed at Jo.

'Good,' she said. 'We like to get things right.'

'What would you like a consultation about?' Jo asked. 'Most people like to know about their natal chart, which outlines your personality and future trends. Or I could focus on a business venture. I bet you know the date you started Upwards, don't you?'

'Oh, I was thinking of a birth chart all about me, me, me,' Carolyn said with a laugh. 'Actually though, maybe we could have a company chart for Upwards's birthday which is in a couple of weeks.' She shot Jo an admiring look. 'You know, that's not a bad idea. Will you come into the office and see us?'

At the front of the room, Vinny was gesticulating in Carolyn's direction and pointing at his watch to indicate they should start.

'Absolutely,' Jo assured her. 'I'm sitting next to Flora. I'll mention it to her and get a date in.'

Carolyn hurried off to take her place at the head of the table as the latecomers took their seats. Flora slipped into the room and bobbed down next to Jo, apparently not realizing that her place had been changed, just as her boss began to speak.

Poised and confident at the head of the table, Carolyn had no problem holding the attention of the room as she talked about 'equipping young people as the workforce of the future'. She welcomed not just the experts but the views of local businesspeople as well. Here she caught the eye of a couple of people around the boardroom table, including the florist who had provided the potted herbs, who twinkled back at her. With a nod towards Jo, she added, 'We are bring-ing together experts from a wide range of fields in the spirit of collaboration.'

Jo relaxed a little as Carolyn warmed to her subject. 'We need you to give us your views on what the next five to ten years will be like and what skills the country will need,' Carolyn went on. 'This is important because I believe that work is the saviour of our young people, offering not just wages — although they really matter when you don't have very much, believe me,' she said with feeling. 'But also a structure, training and the ability to learn while being paid. I know this first-hand. I was in care as a teenager and even, for a while, in juvenile detention. For those who don't know,' she said in a dry aside, 'I was caught shoplifting hair slides and shampoo and was absent from school so much, I excluded myself. Social workers, teachers and probation officers despaired of me. It wasn't until I got a job behind the tills at a DIY shop at the age of sixteen that I started to work out how to save myself from a life of thieving and probably drugs or other abuse. I earned money by working all the hours I could, and I learned everything they could teach me.'

Jo related some of Carolyn's story to her own life. Although she'd been part of a secure family and done well enough at school to get to university, she had never found any subject that really motivated her until she started to work for herself. Whether that was astrology or the strange jobs that Macy had put her way, they were the times she felt truly satisfied. At the end of the short speech, she caught sight of Flora's face, which was glowing as she clapped along with everyone else.

'Carolyn must be inspiring to work for,' Jo whispered. 'Is she the reason you started to work for Upwards?'

Flora shot her a look. 'No, I just needed a job,' she answered and fell silent as Carolyn called upon the 'experts in the room' to talk about their subjects. Even the inference of being an expert made Jo feel nervous and she was relieved when a wispy white-haired man got to his feet and launched into a prepared presentation. Alexander Booth, the man who styled himself a futurologist, described a picture of the future using infographics, which Jo found fascinating, although she didn't agree with all of it. After his speech, Carolyn simply asked for the others' views, which was a relief to Jo as, contrary to what Louis Carswell had said, she didn't have to defend astrology against the scientists present. She managed to make her contribution and even enjoyed the discussion. In fact, when Vinny announced a break, she felt a pang of guilt as she had precious little to report to Macy so far.

She leaned forward and smiled at Flora. 'Is this what you were expecting?' she asked.

Flora looked puzzled. 'Yes, it makes you think further ahead than just next week, I suppose. Though I didn't know what to expect, really.' She glanced at her watch. 'Sorry, I need to go and sort something out . . .' The rest of her words were lost as she pushed out of her chair and weaved her way through the clusters of people towards the back of the room.

Jo was not going to let her quarry out of her sight for the second time that evening and managed to catch up with her at a bottleneck near the door. She followed Flora's dark curly head along the corridor, threading her way through a sociable crowd streaming in the opposite direction. Flora seemed to be heading towards the ladies and Jo sighed in frustration. *All this effort for a pee.*

But Flora hurried past the queue, slipping her phone out of her dress pocket. Jo quickened her pace. The slight woman trotted knowledgeably through a series of short corridors, leading to the car park at the back of the hotel, while reading messages on her phone.

As she stepped outside, Jo saw her bring her phone to her ear. Cold gusts sent salty rain swirling around the car park, batting at Flora's dress. Jo shivered, hanging back in shadow near the automatic doors. Too far away to hear what Flora was saying, she watched her sneak between the parked cars and the side of the building in an effort to keep out of the rain. Flora ended the short call and studied the phone screen again, her shoulders hunched and face hidden. She found a number and started another call.

Jo reached into her bag for her car keys and scurried towards a car near to Flora, brandishing the keys in front of her as if it was hers. She didn't have much of a plan as her own blue Seat was parked at the opposite end of the car park but, as she got closer, Flora said, 'Shit!'

'You OK?' Jo paused, car keys in hand.

Flora jumped and stepped back against the wall of the hotel. 'Phone's died,' she said, after a beat.

'Oh no,' Jo groaned. 'Is it urgent? You can borrow mine.' She dug her phone out of her bag and held it across the rainy space between them. 'If you know the number, that is,' she went on. 'I hardly know anyone's phone number off by heart.'

Flora stood, her phone in her hand, her thin dress increasingly spattered by the rain and her moon-shaped face stricken. 'I know the number.'

'Here you go.' Jo guessed that Flora might be reluctant to make a call in front of her. 'I've unlocked it and you can give it back to me indoors. I'm just going to get some tablets from my car. Terrible headache.' She prodded her temple with her free hand. 'It's just come on.'

'OK, thanks.' Flora took the phone uncertainly. She turned away and pressed the keypad. This was fortunate, as Jo had to make a pantomime of going to a car that wasn't hers and ducking out of view as if she was rooting around inside it. She struggled to hear what Flora was saying. She seemed to be leaving a straightforward message asking someone to call her. The rain continued to fall relentlessly while, from her strange vantage point, she watched Flora finish the brief call and, without looking around, return quickly indoors, her head down.

Jo dashed across the car park and through the sliding doors, congratulating herself that she finally had some information for Macy. Including a phone number, she assumed, once she retrieved her phone. She hurried to make herself look more presentable for the second half of the evening and, in the ladies, she met up with Flora, who was doing exactly the same thing.

'Oh — er — thank you.' Flora was blotting her dress with paper towels. She produced Jo's phone from her pocket.

'Any luck?' Jo asked, studying her own bedraggled reflection in the mirror.

'Unfortunately no. My friend's phone seems permanently switched off and I haven't heard from him for a few days. It's really not like him. He's always around. I've even tried his home number, but that just rings out.'

Jo was bent over sponging mud off her shoe, though she was listening hard. 'Is there anyone else you could call who might know where he is?'

This suggestion received an emphatic shake of the head while Flora reapplied some pink lipstick. Surveying the long damp streaks on her silk dress with a sigh, Jo tried again. 'Or, if you're worried, could you go to his house?'

'If Carolyn will let me get away at a decent hour, I could go over there tonight.' She bit her lips, effectively chewing off the lipstick she had just applied. 'He's just always around. I can't understand it,' she said to her reflection.

A couple of women emerged from the cubicles at the same time, banging doors and talking loudly, which put an end to their conversation. However, on the way back to their seats, Jo mentioned Carolyn's request for a natal chart reading. Flora rather grudgingly offered some dates in the following week. She couldn't be persuaded that Carolyn would find an online or phone session just as effective. 'No, she always likes to meet in person if at all possible.'

Jo ended up agreeing to come back to Bournemouth on Wednesday. *Oh well, maybe I can cadge a lift with Macy,* she mused while Bex and Fraser introduced their 'short movie about how Upwards helped us and people like us'.

She soon forgot about her schedule for next week as she was drawn into the video, which was more professional and smarter than she'd expected, with a good-quality music track and infused with the sort of rapport and energy she had already seen in the way Bex and Fraser got along. This was followed by more discussion, led by Carolyn, and by now Jo was feeling confident enough to contribute more about future skills such as empathy and partnership. She noticed that both Bex and Fraser responded enthusiastically to her comments and felt that, after all, she had acquitted herself satisfactorily.

As soon as people started to move away from the table, Jo turned to Flora. 'Are you going to find your friend now?' she pressed before the woman could drift off again. 'Sorry, I don't know his name.'

'I'm going to charge up my phone and I'll try again later. Then if he still doesn't answer, I'll go and see him tomorrow to check he's OK.'

'Is it far?'

'No he only lives in Pokesdown, but it means I'll have to try and get out of duties here. Carolyn's holding a press conference tomorrow morning. That's why she's paying for us all to stay at the hotel. So we can help set up. It's a big campaign launch and I don't think she will be too happy . . .' Her words faded away.

Jo guessed this would be news to Macy as he had been expecting Flora to travel home after the event. 'Can't you just go now? I mean, if you're worried,' she added. 'It would put your mind at rest. It's clearly a while since you heard from him.'

'Sunday. And yes, I'm going to try—'

Vinny Harrison arrived at her shoulder. 'I need some help moving these banners because the press conference is in a different room. And Carolyn says you will be needed in the Snug Bar later.'

Flora's expression was impassive although Jo was sure she discerned a small sigh of frustration. 'I'll go and see what she wants first,' she said.

'A woman of few words,' Jo remarked.

'And fewer actions,' Vinny responded. He strode away with a long-suffering sigh.

Jo smiled to herself and went to seek out Liang. 'Can I ask an odd question? Do you know where the Snug Bar is?'

'Oh, have you been invited? You are honoured.' Liang looked impressed. 'It's your introduction to the inner sanctum.' She pointed vaguely towards the back of the hotel. 'The bar's in the basement. I can't come with you though. We've got to stay here and get ready for the press conference tomorrow.'

Jo decided not to mention that she hadn't been invited. 'Who's in the inner sanctum?'

'Oh, it's Justin Fielding's crowd mainly,' Liang said. 'That's Carolyn's partner. I hope you haven't got an early start. Their parties go on into the small hours. Sorry, I've got to go and help Vinny.' She didn't sound too disappointed to be missing the after-show party. Jo wasn't all that keen on attending herself but she felt she should try.

Of course, getting into the Snug Bar could pose a problem, she acknowledged, but she liked a challenge.

CHAPTER FIVE

Jo recognized the man at the foot of the basement steps from the notch in his eyebrow. 'Oh hello, Andre,' she said. She had the satisfaction of catching the look of surprise not just from Andre himself but from the older man standing behind him, just inside the quilted door.

This must be Andre's boss, she guessed. In his fifties, with silver, cropped hair and a wiry build, he was wearing his shirt-sleeves rolled up and a fancy black-and-silver waistcoat. He was in good shape and there was a twitch of his shoulders and chest that seemed to hint he was looking for a fight, as opposed to Andre, who looked like he would rather go to sleep.

'Justin Fielding. How do you do?' The man gave a small bow in response to her silent appraisal and Jo felt slightly abashed. She hadn't realized she was being so obvious. Behind her, she could hear low, female voices as Carolyn and Flora were descending the staircase, heads together. 'Come in, come in.' He waved at all three of them, a genial sparkle in his narrow eyes. 'Drinks are doing the rounds and even some food, if you can call it that. It's just little bites of unrecognizable snacks.'

'Canapés,' Carolyn murmured, moving past him into the bar. Many of the businesspeople from the earlier meeting had already crowded into the tiny space plus a few others, mainly men, whom Jo didn't recognize. Andre resumed his position near the door although his superior, dark eyes slid to Jo's occasionally. Booth, the futurologist, was holding court in the corner, having brought some copies of his book with him, but no other academics were there, Jo was relieved to notice. A cluster formed around Carolyn to congratulate her on the evening, but Flora went straight to the bar, clutching her phone, and handed it to the barman.

Justin Fielding placed a glass of champagne in Jo's hand.

'Are we celebrating something?' she asked.

'Do you need an excuse?' His accent was local, south coast. 'But, seeing as you ask,' he went on, 'Westbourne Studios has just won a contract with an advertising agency. Besides the Future Skills event upstairs.' He jerked his head.

'Congratulations. So you've won a contract, and Upwards have lost one.'

He sucked in a breath through pursed lips to show she was on dangerous territory. 'What do you know about lost contracts?' He led the way to two leather tub chairs, taking the one opposite her.

'Oh, just gossip and hearsay.' Jo took a sip of champagne. Her opening remark seemed to have hit a nerve.

'Via Louis Carswell by any chance?' Justin Fielding shot her a direct look and Jo knew her expression gave her away. 'That man trusts everyone and no one.' He shook his head briefly, and then switched topics, glinting a smile across at her. 'But tell me about you. You obviously know something about the future or you wouldn't be here.'

'I run my own astrology business in Gloucestershire.' A reference to astrology was always a good distraction, so she paused for the inevitable reaction.

'Star signs and such like? Well, my birthday is the thirteenth of August, which is only a week before Carolyn's, so we're both Leos.' He crossed one perfect set of quads over the other and sent her a teasing look. 'So, go on, tell me some home truths.'

Jo allowed her glass to be filled up while she considered her response. 'Two fixed signs, both addicted to being right and pretty stubborn, so it's going to be hard to know who's boss.'

'I wouldn't like to say right now.' His eyes creased at the corners as he appeared to give the question some serious thought.

He was an odd energetic mixture of openness and aggression. Quite a bit of Sagittarius and Aries in his chart, Jo decided, as he expanded on his answer.

'Back in the day, it was definitely me. I've known Carolyn since we were kids together a few streets away from here. She idolized me and when she first went into business, she used to ask me about every little thing.' He spoke as if stating a matter of fact. 'She likes to go on about working in the DIY shop but she'd never have achieved all this if she'd carried on working for someone else. It was me who bought her a cleaning business and that got her started. Nowadays, I'm not so sure.' He glanced across the room to where Carolyn was chatting to the futurologist and took a considered sip of champagne.

He stretched out his arms, flexing his hands. 'I haven't flown far from the nest. I like it here. I don't really see why anyone would want to live anywhere else.' His eyes roamed around the plush little bar. 'Carolyn's restless though. She's got her eyes on a career in Westminster. Have the planets any advice about that?'

Jo wondered if he was always as expansive as this or whether it had anything to do with the champagne, which circulated generously past them again. 'Leos and their ambition? Well, I wouldn't like to stand in their way.'

'She wants to be an MP, for heaven's sake.' Justin scratched his cheek thoughtfully as he watched Carolyn move on to mingle among the other guests, clearly in her element.

'Leos love an audience,' Jo commented. 'But that would apply to you too, wouldn't it?'

Justin Fielding laughed and signalled for more champagne, which promptly arrived. 'We can't have you sober as a judge,' he said. 'Or you might remember too much in the morning.'

Jo glanced up. Flora was standing near Carolyn, who was now sitting chatting to a prosperous-looking elderly couple, although not without the occasional glance in Justin's direction. Flora had one hand on the back of Carolyn's chair and the other clutching a large gin glass.

'How about Flora?' she pressed. 'Do you know her at all? I was chatting to her earlier and she seems to have a lot on her mind.'

'Carolyn's little helper? A lot on her mind?' Justin didn't attempt to disguise his scepticism. 'She's away with the fairies most of the time. Or if she isn't, it's a damn good act. Of course, Carolyn's devoted to her,' he added, as if trying to redress a balance. 'In fact, they are devoted to each other and that's what matters.'

As he was speaking, Carolyn made her way over, play-acting a hand to her brow. 'I don't know about you, but I'm nearly ready to hit the sack. Are you and Jo talking astrology?' She placed a proprietorial hand on Justin's broad shoulder. Contrary to her words, she looked as fresh as a daisy with her still perfect make-up and lively expression.

'Jo has you and me taped, I can tell you,' Justin answered. 'She says she doesn't know who's the boss.'

A complex look went from each to the other, so swift Jo didn't know what to make of it: jokey, loaded, questioning. But then Carolyn picked up the conversational baton willingly and described how Jo was going to cast her horoscope and a chart for Upwards. Listening and joining in politely, Jo was struck by the thought that, while this seemed like promising business for her, none of it was going to matter to Macy. The person he really needed to know about was Flora Howell, who was glugging down a large gin and tonic at the bar. Just as she was contemplating how to make a graceful exit, Carolyn threw out a question.

'So, Jo, apparently you're Flora's guest tonight. That's nice, she's never invited anyone to the Snug Bar before. How do you two know each other?'

'Oh, I just helped her out with something,' Jo said. 'And she was very helpful at explaining the work of Upwards.' She could see from their faces that this was stretching the truth too far but something had made her want to support Flora. She quickly added, 'Actually, I found the event tonight inspiring, especially Bex and Fraser's video.'

'It's brilliant, isn't it?' Carolyn pointed a fingernail at Justin's cropped head. 'This is the mastermind behind that creative venture.'

'No, not guilty,' he said. 'I just gave them some studio space and some technicians. The energy and the ideas are all theirs — and the other students involved. It was lucky it all came together though, wasn't it, darling? After we had to wait for you to approve the final version.' He rolled his eyes at Jo. 'Too busy partying.'

'It was work, and I was double-booked,' she said. 'It was an extremely busy time.' She looked at Jo with bright, expectant eyes. 'The Upwards team loved your contribution tonight. And Bex came up with an amazing idea. We want to run this event again on the company's birthday. But this time we'll video it and invite an audience of young local workers who can ask questions. Then we can use clips as promotion over the year. Will you come along? You can invoice us at your usual rates, of course.'

Jo thanked her and heard herself agreeing to take part while her instincts registered some inner qualms. They agreed to discuss it further on Wednesday and Jo took this as the opportune moment to leave. She headed for the bar first as if she was paying a tab. As expected, there was no bill to settle, but it enabled her to move closer to Flora, who was now standing there alone, gazing behind the bar with a remote expression.

'Are you OK?' Jo asked.

'Yes,' Flora responded with a brittle smile. 'I've got to stay here because Carolyn wants to do some planning for studio time with Justin while he's here. But she's said I can miss the press conference tomorrow if I have to. I may not have to,' she rambled on, her words slurring slightly, 'because if I can get hold of Shane, then the problem goes away. That's why I'm charging up my phone but the barman says it's not ready, but that's OK, I'll be a while yet.'

She followed Flora's gaze to Carolyn and Justin, who were still seated on the bucket chairs, knees close and exchanging the occasional glance or word. 'Funny time of day for a planning meeting,' Jo said.

'That's typical of Justin, he never does anything you expect.' She squared her shoulders and put down her drink. 'Right, I'm going to work now, so you'll have to excuse me. Thanks again for the loan of the phone.'

'Oh, I'm not going to turn in yet,' Jo said. 'I'll wait here for you. I know you must still be worried about your friend — Shane, is it? When did you last see him?'

'No, please don't wait.' Flora avoided the questions. 'This meeting could take a while.'

'OK, but if you need a friendly ear and if I'm not holding onto this very chic bar, I can be found in room 116.' After that, Jo had little choice but to stay at a distance while Flora went over to join Carolyn and Justin. Jo watched discreetly as they asked Flora to draw up a chair. Once they were deep in conversation, she slipped out of the bar and sought a quiet space from which call Macy. Although it was past eleven, he picked up straight away. 'How's it going?'

'The evening's been fascinating, but I haven't found out much about Flora,' Jo said. She followed the midnight-blue corridors towards reception. 'Carolyn is with her boyfriend, Justin Fielding, in the Snug Bar and Flora is in a huddle with them. I thought you'd want to know she's got a room here tonight so there's no point in your waiting for her to leave. Apparently, they've got some sort of press announcement here tomorrow and half the company seem to be staying for that.'

'I know. Louis just told me. But thanks,' he added. 'I'm with him in the lounge bar. The one near the tree.'

Although he had said he wouldn't be far away, the knowledge that Macy was in the hotel sent Jo's mind on a very different track, which had nothing to do with Flora Howell or the work of Upwards. Maybe it was because he had mentioned where exactly he was, but she was struck by a sudden, very familiar and appealing sense of him being close by.

'So, you're not far away?' Her footsteps had led her to the lobby and she looked past the party guests towards the tree. 'Is Carswell still there?'

'Yes, unfortunately. Your call gave me a good reason to step out for a minute.'

'You're under the tree?'

'Well not actually under the tree.' She could hear him laughing. He sounded very sober, which she realized she wasn't. 'Although I can be.'

She spotted him moving towards the silver-and-blue tree, but stayed where she was, half-hidden behind a pillar. 'What do you know about Justin Fielding?' she asked. 'He and Carolyn seem to be a couple but Justin doesn't have anything to do with Upwards.'

'Not much. Flora had to visit Westbourne Studios about a week ago so we looked the place up and Justin Fielding owns it. They do promo videos and some music videos, that sort of thing. It's not a massive concern. Why are you interested in him?'

'I don't know, I've only just met him. By the way, I'm over to your left.' She smiled as he looked directly her. 'What does it feel like to be under surveillance?' Before he could answer, she added, 'Another thing about Flora. You didn't mention a boyfriend. Does she have a boyfriend?'

'No boyfriend.' Macy tipped his head on one side. 'Don't you think I would have said?'

'Well, there's a man she's concerned about. Shane. He's not picking up his calls. Flora is so worried that she's going to go to his house in Pokesdown tomorrow morning, even if it means missing the press conference.' She explained about the conversation she'd had with Flora in the car park.

Macy received this information in silence, which she took as a huge compliment as she knew she had managed to surprise him. Not an easy thing with a man like Macy.

'I suppose you are going to have to go back to see Louis,' Jo said.

Somehow he managed to meet her eyes over the lobby, which was still thronging with people and Christmas music. She could tell he was serious.

'I suppose I am,' he sighed. 'But you should call it a night. You've done a good job and I will pick up the trail on Flora tomorrow morning.'

'I'll find out what I can about this Shane guy,' she said. 'OK, goodnight. See you at the coffee place.'

She turned, somewhat clumsily, and found herself colliding with the hard chest of Justin Fielding, who was standing directly behind her. *How long has he been there?* she wondered.

'What are you doing here?' She tried to laugh off her confusion but he wasn't smiling.

'I don't think you're in a position to ask that, are you?' He stepped back quickly, holding his hands out in an exaggerated way to show there was no bodily contact intended.

'No, I guess not,' Jo conceded. Retreat was her best option. 'I was on my way to my room, thanks for the champagne. Please say goodnight to Carolyn for me.'

She made a hasty exit up the sweeping staircase and managed to locate her room. Sleep, however, seemed remote as she replayed conversations and questions in her head. *What exactly had Justin been doing there? He must have followed her,* she thought, *but why?* She wondered what, if anything, he would tell Carolyn and whether she had stupidly compromised Macy's surveillance operation.

Eventually, propped against the pillows, she viewed her recent calls. Flora had made two short calls to a mobile number at 20.09 p.m. and 20.16 p.m. and, between that, a longer call to a landline number. Jo hesitated for a minute or two and then, with a little 'what-the-hell' shrug, she dialled the first one. There was no answer on either of the numbers, which at least meant that she didn't have to come up with a reason for calling a complete stranger in the middle of the night. At least she had something concrete to report to Macy in the morning and not all of it was bad news.

* * *

Jo was dredged out of a deep sleep by an insistent knocking at her door. The room seemed almost pitch black and for a moment or two, she couldn't remember where she was in the world, much less where to find the light switch. The rapping came again, persistent and louder. She grasped for a switch and the cold room filled with ghoulish sage green light. The clock read one twenty-three. She dragged on a sweatshirt over her nightdress and went to the door, conscious of her own raised heartbeat.

The tiny, bevelled glass in the peephole revealed Flora with a disproportionately large head, chewing a fingernail and looking back down the corridor.

'Flora. You OK?' Jo's voice sounded as groggy as she felt.

'Oh, thank God you're awake. Can I come in?'

'Well I wasn't really. What's wrong?'

'Nothing.' Flora's voice was naturally high-pitched but it seemed to have risen by an octave. 'Nothing's wrong. I just need someone to talk to, that's all. Have you got anything to drink? They've closed the bar and everyone's gone to bed.'

'Only water. Or tea,' Jo said. If she hadn't been working for Macy, she would have told Flora to go to bed. *He owes me big time*, she thought, as she held the door open.

Flora walked in and threw herself onto the other bed. 'Fabulous. You have a spare bed. Do you mind if I stay here?' She started to remove her sandals. 'No one will ever think to look for me here.'

'What do you mean?' Jo pushed her hair out of her eyes and went to fetch two tumblers from the bathroom. She poured out two glasses of mineral water and handed one to Flora. 'What about your friend? I thought you were worried about him?' Jo's words were spoken with feeling but the other woman didn't appear to notice and simply struggled onto her elbows, promptly slopping water on the front of her dress. 'Oops, silly me. I knew I could rely on you to help me somehow.'

Jo sat down on her own bed and regarded the drunken Flora trying to sip her water while semi-supine. 'You'd be better off sitting up. And who's looking for you?'

Flora groaned. 'Carolyn, of course. She always is. She thinks this job is twenty-four seven.' She looked at her glass. 'I don't think there's any gin in this.'

'Why is Carolyn looking for you at one thirty in the morning?' Jo got back into bed, trying very hard to feel as supportive towards Flora as she had felt earlier in the evening. But it was hard not to conclude that the woman was an idiot and neither had she yet made much effort to find her friend, which weighed heavily against her in Jo's view.

'It's not just Carolyn, but the others. They're worse in some ways,' Flora babbled into her glass. She looked up askance. 'You know I was trying to charge my phone up at the bar? Well, the barman told me Justin Fielding told him not to do it. That's why it was taking hours.' She stumbled over her words as her voice rose in indignation. 'In fact, Justin held my phone over the ice bucket.'

'Hmm, why did he do that?' Jo asked tiredly, struggling to picture Justin bothering to taunt Flora. He'd acted like he hardly knew her. Maybe drunken games had got out of hand? 'And who are these others?'

'The pressure is intense lately and I'm making too many mistakes,' Flora continued. 'I've even thought about going back to live in London but — but I can't afford it.' She raised herself off the bed, carrying her glass. 'I think I'll have some more of this gin. Don't worry, I'll help myself.' Jo watched, arms folded while the other woman poured out more water. 'Carolyn had a hissy fit,' she said, 'because you monopolized Justin all evening.'

'I didn't monopolize him. The boot was on the other foot, I can assure you,' Jo began, but then subsided. *It might be more enlightening to let Flora ramble on.*

And ramble on she did. If, in the course of her drunken ruminations, Flora let fall a crucial nugget of information, it was lost on Jo, as she fell asleep after about twenty minutes.

The unmistakable ringtone of her own mobile awoke her and this time she was alert instantly. An unknown number was scrolling across the screen.

'Don't answer it!' Flora cried. 'Please don't answer it.'

The ringing stopped and Jo looked over at Flora in the queasy green light. Her face was smeared with make-up. She had got into bed fully clothed and had left the room light on.

'Why not?' Jo asked. 'Who do you think it is?'

'I don't know and you don't either, do you?' Flora looked younger, still drunk, but now large-eyed and terrified.

The ringing started up again. Same number. The two women looked at it.

Jo pressed 'accept' and Flora hissed 'No!'

A man's voice, measured and comfortable, said, 'Is that Jo Hughes?'

'Yes, who's this?'

Flora watched, holding the bedclothes to her chin like a child.

'It's Louis Carswell. Sorry to call so late.'

'It's two twenty-five,' Jo said. She began to pull on some more clothes one-handed. She remembered that Macy had been with Carswell and was struck by the half-formed, irrational conviction that something bad had happened to him. Whatever Carswell had to say to her, in any case, she didn't want to hear it with Flora in the room.

'Don't go,' Flora mumbled.

'I won't be a minute,' she mouthed. She grabbed her key and let herself quietly out of the door. Disconcertingly, the warm voice was laughing in her ear. 'Oh my dear,' he said. 'Do you have company? I'm so sorry to disturb your fun.'

There were so many retorts Jo could have made to this. She just wished she was awake enough to deliver them with aplomb. Instead, she snapped. 'What is it you want?'

But Carswell wasn't ready to drop this found treasure. 'How thoughtless of me, I should have forewarned you. Maybe a small text next time? And you can rely on my discretion with David. Some spidey-sense tells me that Mr Macy would not be overjoyed to hear such information.'

Jo had not realized it was possible to go from sound asleep to boiling angry in less than five minutes. 'You've no idea what you're talking about,' she shot back and, from the short silence that followed, she knew she had nettled him. Clearly Carswell did not like to be told he was ill-informed.

'I can see you and I are going to have a strong working partnership,' the mellow voice responded. 'But how we rub along could hardly matter less at the moment. Let me explain my reason for ringing.'

Jo said nothing. She found herself on the mezzanine floor overlooking the lobby, which by now had emptied out. A sole receptionist was stationed at the large desk and the music had been switched off.

'Justin Fielding has turned up, hasn't he? He and you were in cahoots all night in the Snug Bar,' Carswell said. 'I want you to tell me what exactly he is doing here.'

'His presence hasn't got anything to do with Flora Howell,' she said with more certainty than she felt.

Carswell's voice became impatient. 'Don't trot out what you think will make me go away.'

'My reason for being here is to find out additional information about Flora, about what influence she has in the company for instance,' Jo said. 'Justin Fielding has nothing to do with Upwards. He wasn't even at the event—'

'I don't know what rules David Macy plays to,' Carswell cut in. 'But these are house rules now and you don't get to choose what you do and don't do. That's my prerogative. So please find out what you can about Fielding and include it in your report to me tomorrow.'

'I'm reporting to Macy—'

'Of course you are,' Carswell interrupted again. 'And he has asked me to give you a call. How else do you think I got your number?'

Jo was not defeated but she recognized she had limited options. She simply rang off, still simmering. She thought about calling Macy to have the satisfaction of telling him what she thought of him for giving her number to Carswell and, still more irrationally, to check he was OK. But now it was after three and the prospect of sleep won the argument.

To her surprise and guilty relief, Flora was no longer occupying the spare bed when she got back to her hotel room. The only trace of her presence was the empty water glass on the bedside table and a smell of booze. Jo spent a chilly half-hour traipsing up and down hotel corridors looking for her. Eventually she had to concede it was a lost cause and went back to bed. Her feeling before drifting off to sleep was one of vague regret and missed chances.

CHAPTER SIX

The Works Lounge was a shade too noisy for Jo, who, at ten the following morning, was regretting the glasses of fizz. Every sound in the café seemed to reverberate off hard edges. The place was less like a lounge and more like a designer's idea of a factory floor with low metal girders, fixed benches and enamel beakers. She tried to block out the hiss of the coffee machine and the shouting of the baristas, who repeated every customer's name at volume. Whether or not it was part of her hangover, she still couldn't shake her misgivings about the night before. It was as if some of Flora's anxiety had rubbed off on her, leaving her with an uncomfortable sense that there was something crucial she should have done.

The coffee wasn't too bad at least. Better than the pallid liquid they had served at the Metropole. Breakfast had been a solitary affair, thankfully. There had been no further sign of Flora since her unexplained visit in the middle of the night. Neither was Carolyn in evidence, nor any of the Upwards team. Later, after checking out, Jo had tracked them down to a larger conference room and, peering through the open doorway, had seen Carolyn and Vinny, heads together over a phone screen. The room was laid out, cinema-style, for the press conference at ten thirty with the Upwards banners in place, transported from the Lord Bute room. Flora was, once again, conspicuous by her absence but Liang had spotted Jo hovering in the doorway and came up, holding a sheet of A3 paper.

'Hello, Jo. Are you coming to the press conference?'

'I can't. I've got to meet someone at ten o'clock. What's it about?'

Liang had turned the printed poster around so Jo could see it.

'We're offering free training places for managers if businesses will take on new apprentices,' Liang had informed her while smoothing the poster into place. 'It's a clever idea because we get paid by the government to train apprentices.'

'Provided you get the contracts,' Jo had said.

The other woman had looked injured. 'Well, yes, we did lose a big government one recently, but it's not the only contract. Anyway,' Liang added, 'you've got to see the bigger picture, Jo. It's all part of our campaign to help young people get into work. We already do lots of training free for people who don't even have jobs. So it doesn't matter who gets the business.'

Jo couldn't help but smile in the face of such serious enthusiasm. 'OK, I accept that. I can also see Carolyn is a good talent scout.'

Carolyn had been testing out a microphone but at the mention of her name she'd waved to Jo. 'This was all her idea,' Liang had said. 'And we can offer more free places now, due to Planet's money.'

'Louis Carswell's company?' There had been no sign of him but Jo still felt irritable when she thought of his late-night phone call.

'That's right, and they're letting us take the credit,' Liang had informed her. 'I really feel this is how companies can change society and make a practical difference.'

With Liang's idealistic words still in her head, Jo had tackled the blustery walk along the seafront to The Works

Lounge, reflecting that Upwards had made a good decision when they had poached the young woman from the estate agency. She was certainly quick on the uptake and invariably positive — the exact opposite of how Jo herself was feeling. Before she had left the Metropole, she'd asked Liang if she knew where Flora was, but there she had drawn a blank.

'I hadn't noticed she wasn't here.' Liang had stared around her with characteristic honesty. Jo had concluded that Flora must have agreed with Carolyn to miss the press conference in order to go and see her friend, and she trusted that Macy had picked her up on surveillance when leaving the hotel.

Now, in the harsh light of the coffee shop spotlights, Jo didn't feel quite so pleased with her trawl of information for Macy. There were quite a few notable gaps. One obvious one was that she knew very little about this mysterious missing friend, who Flora had been so desperate to contact. She had been sure it was a possible boyfriend. But now she questioned herself. Could she be certain how Flora had described him? Jo put her fingers to her temples as if to urge on her sluggish thought processes. There was also the slight issue about where Flora was at this actual moment. And the fact that last time Jo had seen Flora, the woman had been drunk, inexplicably scared and sitting up in bed, fully clothed. In Jo's own hotel room. She chewed her lip over that one.

On the other hand, she reasoned, surely all Macy had to do was to trace one of the two phone numbers Flora had been calling, now safely stored in Jo's phone, and it would lead him directly to her. How difficult could that be? Jo had already looked up the landline and knew it was a local number, which confirmed what Flora had told her. *Macy will probably want to get straight over there*, Jo thought as she drained her coffee cup. Which would mean she would be free to wend her way home and back to her normal life. Mission accomplished.

Still that apprehensive feeling gnawed at her gut. It was unusual for Macy to be late. She shifted uncomfortably on the hard bench, wishing he had chosen a calmer place to meet and remembering that she was still moderately annoyed with him for giving her number to Louis Carswell. And there was the identity of the woman with the red topknot, who had been with him in the lobby yesterday. She hadn't asked about that yet.

To kill some time, she returned to the counter and bought more coffees but he had still not arrived when she returned to her bench with the two mugs. By ten twenty-five, she had reached that irresolute state between impatience and anxiety. When she phoned him, he answered to say he was on his way and instantly rang off, which did not nothing to improve her mood.

However, as soon as she saw him walk into the coffee shop, his expression closed, long body tense and shoulders hunched, she knew there was something wrong. Her own feelings, including her hangover, went into suspense. For once, Macy came straight to the point as soon as he was seated opposite her.

'Flora has been in an accident. I followed her from the hotel at eight thirty-five and just before nine she was knocked off her bike on a steep hill coming into the town centre. It was a hit-and-run. I saw it all. The driver ran the lights. I even got a picture of the white van that hit her.' His words came out quietly but his face betrayed his shock. 'She just lay there on her back on the road, not moving. She couldn't answer me and the paramedics couldn't get her to regain consciousness either. She looked so vulnerable, Jo, and so young.' He placed his long fingers on the coffee cup but didn't drink. 'I followed the ambulance to the hospital.' He lapsed into silence.

'How bad is it?' Jo asked. Her throat had seized unexpectedly as a memory of Flora came back to her, of her wide eyes and wary face, her dress spattered with rain as she stood in the car park, uncertain whether to accept a stranger's phone. She felt a stab of guilt about her ungenerous impatience with the woman.

'She's in intensive care. They've sent for her brother, Theo. He's only twenty-two but he's her next of kin. Her mother's dead and her father's living abroad.'

'They must have other relatives?'

55

'I expect Theo will contact them if so but we haven't been able to trace anyone. The team went down that road when we first took the case.' He finally lifted the cold coffee to his lips. 'The thing is, I was a witness but I had to stay out of the way of the police because I suspected Carswell wouldn't want them to know about the surveillance. I couldn't tell the police half the truth — that's always a risky business. And I was right, he doesn't.'

'You've spoken to him?'

'Yep. I'm meeting him in an hour at his office. He didn't want to discuss it on the phone but I'm going to have to tell him I need to share this evidence with the police.'

'Won't it look a bit odd that you didn't come forward straight away?' Jo asked.

Macy didn't answer this. He was looking past her down the line of bench tables in the coffee shop but wasn't focusing on them. 'I saw it all in the rear-view mirror,' he said. 'I parked in a bus stop to let her catch up and I saw a van run the lights at the crossroads. He just ploughed straight into her. Then it kept moving, driving up the hill, away from the town centre. Another cyclist just behind her was caught too but he was OK, he just had a few scratches. He picked his bike up and he would have cycled off but I told him to wait. He was still in shock. It was a woman passer-by, who rang for the ambulance.' He stared at her, his face drawn and anxious. 'I tried to talk to Flora, Jo, but she was unconscious. And when the ambulance arrived, I offered to give her details but the paramedic told me to save it for the hospital. That's why I followed them there.'

'And the police, did they see you?'

'They arrived as the paramedics were assessing her so I was able to stay in the background then.' He came to a halt again.

'You said you got a photo?' Jo prompted.

Macy took out his phone and showed her the last three photographs. Two were very blurred but the third showed a white van taking a corner and a bicycle bent and upended in the middle of the road. No number plate was visible on the van. 'I know the registration though, so you see why I have to tell the police,' he said. 'This could be where Louis Carswell and I part company.' He sighed, staring at the table. 'Lying there on the tarmac, Flora looked completely blameless. I'm sure she has been dragged into something that has put her in danger. And I didn't spot it. We didn't see this threat coming at her.'

Impulsively, Jo touched his hand. 'You weren't told she was in any danger.' She paused for a second. 'Were you?'

'No, nothing like that. Carswell told me that she was the one who had been sharing secrets with other companies. Maybe for money, maybe just indiscretion or pure incompetence, but they were convinced Flora lost Upwards that big contract.' Jo stayed quiet and hoped it didn't show on her face that she thought incompetence most likely, from what she'd seen of Flora. Macy looked as anguished as she'd ever seen him so she didn't think it wise to share this view. 'Nothing I've seen about Flora makes me believe she is anything other than vulnerable and entirely innocent,' he went on. 'And I've got to be able to tell the police what I witnessed.'

A silence fell as they tacitly accepted that Carswell would not take well to dissent. 'He called me last night,' she said at last. 'He was demanding that I tell him all about Justin Fielding, but I'd only just met the man. What would I know?'

'Carswell phoned you? When was this?'

Jo took a breath. 'I'd better tell you what else I found out last night. It's not much. And I suppose it all seems a bit irrelevant now.'

'It could be more relevant than ever.' He looked across at her sharply. 'It wasn't an accident, Jo. I'm certain someone was trying to kill her.'

Jo's guts shifted unpleasantly and she swallowed. 'Well, Flora was in some distress but I wouldn't say she acted like someone whose life was in danger. She was anxious because she couldn't get hold of this friend of hers. I told you about that. But afterwards she turned up in my room, drunk and saying Carolyn was looking for her.'

'And was she?'

'I don't think so. Flora wasn't making a lot of sense. She seemed to have forgotten all about her missing friend and it took her till this morning to go and look for him.'

'Yes, but at least she went then. And you said she virtually had to beg her boss for permission,' Macy pointed out, apparently determined to defend the woman.

'I fell asleep while Flora was still rabbiting on,' Jo admitted. 'Then Carswell called me at two twenty-five. He wanted me to find out everything I could about Justin Fielding and put it in your report. But I'd only spoken to the guy for a few minutes, and he didn't exactly share his life story. When I got back, Flora had gone. I did look for her but I assumed she'd gone back to her own room.'

'This man that Flora was going to meet. Did she say how long he'd been missing?'

'No, but I know he lives in Pokesdown and these must be his numbers.' Jo held out her phone. 'Flora said she'd not been able to reach him since Sunday. I've tried and his mobile seems to be switched off and the landline just rings out.'

Macy put the numbers into his own phone. 'Go on,' he said.

'Well, that's about it. Surely you can trace those numbers to a person or an address and then you'll know where Flora was heading. And if we find him then that should tell us something more about Flora.'

'Maybe. But this man is not at home, we can be fairly certain about that. Even Flora couldn't contact him and we don't know the first thing about him. Do you know if she told Carolyn why she wanted the morning off? Or where she was going?'

Jo shook her head, feeling uncomfortable. 'No, sorry I haven't found out more—'

But Macy was frowning, following his own train of thought. 'Do you think Flora was genuinely scared?'

Jo nodded slowly.

'Do you have any idea what she was frightened of?'

She felt even worse. 'No.'

He gave the merest glance at his watch, which Jo didn't miss. There didn't seem to be much else she could add that would be worth making him late for his meeting with Carswell, except to confess that Justin Fielding had been standing behind her during their late phone call in the hotel lobby. 'I don't know why or what he heard,' she finished.

Macy said nothing but his expression made it clear that this news had done nothing to improve his day. Eventually he got to his feet, his tone brisk. 'OK, I'll get the team in the office onto those numbers. Alan is already on his way down by train and should be here by two. I've told him to go straight to the hospital. Until Carswell calls us off the case, we are still being paid to keep Flora under surveillance. One of us should be there now. I know the poor girl is clearly not going anywhere, but we should be monitoring visitors and staying informed as much as we can about how she is doing—'

'I can go to the hospital,' Jo said on an impulse. 'I don't need to be home till late. As long as I'm there to open up at the Rivermill tomorrow, it will be fine.'

Macy regarded her with unreadable brown eyes.

'Alan can meet me there when he arrives and he can take over,' she went on. 'And later you can tell me how your meeting with Carswell goes.'

Macy gathered up his phone, ready to leave. 'All right. That's decided then. Meet me and Alan in Soul Bar at six o'clock. It's in the town centre, you'll find it easily enough.'

CHAPTER SEVEN

On the drive to the hospital, Jo received a very brief phone call from Alan. His clipped tones came through her car speakers and it was clear he was on the train so the conversation was minimal. But then, conversation with Alan was always minimal. He said he would text her when he got to the hospital.

'It's hardly worth your going, I'll be there in an hour,' he said with a brusqueness she remembered well. When she said she was already on her way, he harrumphed and said, 'Well, don't make any contact with me. When you get my text, just leave and I will find my own way.'

Alan's charm and diplomacy did not seem to have improved in three and a half years, she noted. She wondered how exactly you were meant to carry out surveillance on someone in intensive care. She wouldn't mind betting that Alan would know the answer to this question but she didn't have the chance to ask him before he rang off. It turned out that the first test was to locate the ICU, which took her fifteen minutes of following a route led by signs, corridors and directions from enquiry desks. At the ICU desk finally, she asked for news of Flora and received a frosty grilling from a balding receptionist in a blue uniform.

'Are you family? Have you phoned in?'

'No, I'm a friend.'

'If you're not family, I'm afraid there's nothing we can tell you.'

Jo had not queued in traffic all the way across the town and spent ten minutes parking to be put off so easily, although she could tell this was going to be a struggle. 'Please can you just give me an update on her condition. I don't need to actually see her.'

'No one can visit her. This is ICU,' the man told her with exaggerated patience.

'I just want to know how she's doing,' Jo persisted. 'Or can you at least confirm she is here. Flora Howell. Is she on a list somewhere?'

'You should have phoned. This is not for drop-ins.' The man behind the desk halted, his attention turning to a thin, dark man who had appeared at Jo's shoulder.

'Are you asking about Flora?' The lean figure behind her had dark eyes, which were wide and shadowed, and his grey shirt was creased. 'I'm her brother, Theo,' he said. 'Are you a friend of hers?'

'Er — well, yes.' Jo had no idea how well Theo knew Flora's friends, but there was something about the open, stricken face opposite her which made it hard to stick to her story. 'A — a sort of friend through work. I was passing the hospital so I thought I would ask after her.'

'Oh. You're from Upwards? They seem a nice crowd. Flora is happy there.' Theo gave a small smile and wandered back to his seat, where he had left his backpack.

Jo followed. 'How is she?'

'I'm afraid it's not good news.' He sat down heavily and stared down at the palms of his hands. 'She has really serious injuries to her spinal column and neck and has to be kept stable. They can't operate yet until they are clearer about the extent of the injury.'

'I'm sorry,' Jo said. 'Is there anything I can do?' She glanced around the sparsely-populated waiting room, unsure if she was seeking an escape or inspiration. When Theo thanked her politely, her conscience got the better of her and she admitted she was not a colleague of Flora's. 'I only met her yesterday at an event run by Upwards,' she confessed. 'But I lent her my phone because she was trying to reach a friend of hers. Then I heard about her accident.'

Theo looked back at her with an expression that accepted and understood everything and nothing at the same time. 'Actually, there is something,' he said, with a sudden injection of energy. 'You could tell Upwards how she's doing for me. I've rung them once and I spoke to a chap called Vinny. I said I'd call back but I'm not good at talking on the phone — not official things, I mean, especially when there's nothing good to say.'

Jo agreed to pass on the news although she didn't exactly know how she was going to achieve this. He seemed reluctant to let her leave and launched into telling her that he was in his first year of his postgraduate medical degree and he was living in halls in London. 'I had another test paper all lined up to do this afternoon, but I'm not leaving here until I get to know what's going on with Flora. There's supposed to be a consultant coming into see her later. Maybe I should have brought the laptop.'

Jo recognized this flipping between anxiety and normality. She had seen it before. 'I think you're still suffering from shock yourself,' she said. 'Have you eaten anything? I passed a café on the way through, will you let me buy you a cup of tea and a bun or something? Or is there someone else you can call? A family member?'

Theo wasn't moving. He said he had eaten breakfast and phoned 'an auntie', but Jo wasn't sure she believed him. She saw a couple of vending machines in the corner. 'Look, let me get you a bottle of water or a machine tea at least.'

Theo nodded his head slightly at the notion of water so Jo went to see what she could buy. When she returned with a chunky bottle of water and a chocolate bar, Theo accepted them wordlessly, broke off the top of the bottle and drank some as if on autopilot. 'I don't know why Flora wasn't at work,' he said. 'She likes that job and her boss thinks the world of her. She told Flora that she was the only person who knew what the fuck was going on. Those were her exact words.' Theo gave a pale grin. 'Flora was shocked but I thought it was hilarious.'

'Can I ask you something about your sister?' she asked, breaking open the chocolate bar, which Theo had ignored, and sharing it out in his favour. 'Was Flora in any trouble?'

Theo's chin shot up, half-indignant and half-amused, 'That's not very likely,' he said. 'You are clearly right when you say you don't know my sister. She's the most rule-conscious, law-abiding citizen. She even cries when she gets a speeding ticket and she waits at crossings even when there's no traffic.'

'What about a boyfriend?' Jo pursued. 'She borrowed my phone because she was trying to track down a friend of hers who had gone missing. I think she was on her way to see him this morning. A guy called Shane?'

'No way.' He shook his head. 'She'd have told me. She doesn't want to get close to anyone. Flora's not uninterested in guys, but she's shy. And very wary, because of our parents.' Theo broke off another square of chocolate. 'Not a boyfriend. A friend, maybe.'

'Oh, OK, it could be just a friend. But she didn't mention anyone?' When Theo shook his head again, she helped herself to some more chocolate while she thought this over. Guiltily, she handed him the rest of the bar. 'You'd better finish this. What do you mean about your parents?'

Theo groaned as if this was a too-familiar story. 'It was our dad really. Mum died when I was fifteen and Flora seventeen, so it's not Mum's fault. Dad waited till Flora was eighteen — just — and went off to live in Greece with some woman. Well, let's say a woman he had known for some time. We've got other relatives out there but we know we're not welcome. He's basically ignored us since he left. That's why I had to call Aunt Miriam today when I heard about Flora.

She's on Mum's side of the family but she's miles away in Cheshire. She's going to come down, which is good of her.' Theo paused as two doctors went by. He followed them with his eyes and then regained his thread. 'Anyway, when Dad left, it all fell on Flora, you know, to look after me and so on. We had the house. He left us that. But she couldn't go to uni — she had to get a job because there was only the two of us. As a result of all that, she's always said she'll be a singleton and plans to remain that way.'

'That doesn't mean not having boyfriends though,' Jo said. In her pocket, her phone vibrated, taking it out she glanced at it. Alan had arrived at the hospital.

'She'd have told me,' Theo repeated. 'We speak most days and I come down once a week. Well, almost.' He looked away guiltily. 'Except when I'm doing exams.'

Maybe she would have told him, maybe not, Jo thought. She didn't have any brothers but there was plenty that Marie didn't know about her. She knew she should make her exit before Alan arrived and took some heart from the fact that Theo looked more animated and was sipping more water.

'Where are you going to sleep? You can't stay here all night,' she said.

'I'll stay until the consultant comes to see her again, which is later this afternoon. Then I'll go to Flora's. I've got a key to her flat and I can do some work there.'

Jo nodded. 'You can only do what you can,' she said, which sounded lame even to her ears, but Theo thanked and assured her that Aunt Miriam would arrive tomorrow.

Jo leaned against a wall outside the hospital and checked her phone. Alan's text simply said, *I'm in the hospital by the coffee bar and can take over from here. See you later at Soul Bar.*

To fulfil her promise to Theo, she called the number on the Upwards website in the hope that she could leave a brief message to a receptionist. The number was ringing out when Jo saw the unmistakable suited and heeled figure of Carolyn Ash step elegantly out of a taxi at the hospital entrance, carrying a large bouquet of flowers. Jo ended her call and walked swiftly across the shrubby garden but before she could reach Carolyn, the older woman had come to a halt. The yellow taxi stopped and the driver leaned out. 'Is everything OK? This is the hospital you asked for,' he shouted.

She watched as Carolyn waved him on but still she didn't move. Jo wondered if she was waiting for someone. The woman's slim, dark silhouette seemed to hesitate. She tweaked the flowers and then lifted her head and straightened her shoulders. Jo understood suddenly. She had stood on thresholds herself and felt equally uncertain. She picked up her pace and caught up with Carolyn as she entered the hospital.

The woman looked pale and anxious. 'Jo, you're here! Have you heard? Flora has been in an accident.'

Jo said she had stopped on the way home to see a friend who worked at the hospital. Listening to Carolyn explain what she knew about the accident, which wasn't much, she reflected in surprise at how easily these little inventions came to her. The subterfuges of a PI were back in her life whether she wanted them or not.

'The police rang me directly,' Carolyn said. The heavy make-up on her face, gave her a gaunt and vulnerable look. 'She had my number as her emergency contact — and Jo, I really don't know what to expect. I'm not very good with hospitals.'

'No, neither am I,' Jo said. 'But they probably won't let you see her.'

'Well, I will see what I can do,' Carolyn said, bracing herself behind the bouquet. There didn't seem to be anything to add so Jo had to let her go. There was no doubt that she would meet Theo, who would have to cope as best he could, and she would possibly also encounter Alan. Jo tapped out a quick text message to let her colleague know and received a speedy reply. *OK, got it.*

It was only four days since Macy had turned up at the Rivermill and introduced her to this strange crowd in Bournemouth, most of whom she didn't much like, and now she was inventing cover stories and following people about. She didn't know whether to be impressed with herself or appalled. Either way, thanks to her rash promise to meet Macy later, she was not yet free to go home. Instead, she decided to find the pier and a mint chocolate chip ice cream to see if either of these things made her feel any better.

CHAPTER EIGHT

When Jo arrived at the Soul Bar she was shown to a distant alcove in the whitewashed basement, where Alan was sitting puzzling over the menu like it was an exam paper. He hadn't changed. He had the same side-parting in sparse, sandy hair, and his clothes and square glasses still made him look like his mum had dressed him for school. Tonight he was wearing a grey crew-necked jumper, which looked slightly too small, over a white shirt. He approached the world as he always had, with a perpetual frown, but he got to his feet when he saw Jo and stuck his hand out. 'Long time no see.'

She smiled back and took it. 'Good to see you too.'

'Macy says you're still doing the horoscopes. We may need a heavenly intervention after the day we've had.'

'You do realize I can't actually manipulate the planets?' Jo said. She took off her down coat and scarf and sat down. 'But thanks, yes, the astrology business is doing really well.'

'I know. I follow you on Twitter.'

When she cast him a curious look, he added, 'Not as me, obviously.' He glanced across at the entrance. Macy had just arrived and was chatting to the woman who had greeted her. 'God knows why he chose this place,' Alan said in disgust. 'It's Lebanese food, so there's nothing normal on the menu.

I don't know what's wrong with Burger King. That's where I always go.'

Jo could tell from the enticing aromas that the food was going to be good. 'I thought you had retired, but I understand you're spending a fair bit of time with Macy.'

'*Early* retirement,' he corrected her. 'Yes, I've been down here two or three times a week since the middle of October. I've been doing most of the shifts.' He dropped his voice. 'No quibble about expenses, either. It's brilliant work, Jo. You should come and join us again if we get the contract extended.' He sighed. 'Although it might all go tits up after today.'

'I heard,' Jo said. 'So, tell me what's been happening up to now?'

'You know we've been tracking Flora Howell, who is suspected of selling on confidential commercial information. I've come across this sort of thing before. Very likely the woman is an aggrieved employee who saw the opportunity to get her own back on the company. We're doing external surveillance at the moment but we've built up a comprehensive picture over the last six weeks. We were just about to make our first stage report when the woman gets knocked down in a hit-and-run.' He jabbed a forefinger in Macy's direction. 'He got pictures of the van but we've been told not to share them with the police.'

'I don't suppose he's happy about that. Apart from anything else, he doesn't like being told what to do.'

'No, and that's not the only problem.'

'I didn't think it was,' Jo said. 'The poor girl's in intensive care.'

'Well, yes there is that.' Alan shot a glance at Macy, who was on his way over. 'The other issue is that he's got too attached. Flora Howell is our target, and you know it's always best to keep emotions out of it.'

Before Jo could respond, Macy arrived at the table at the same time as the wine and Alan turned abruptly to the menu. 'Hello. I was telling Jo that we can't go to the police with your photos of the van,' he said.

'On the contrary, I intend to make a full report to Bournemouth Police,' Macy said. 'I've spoken to Carswell and told him I'm going to the station tomorrow.'

Alan chuckled darkly. 'Go on then, tell us how it went. I bet you needed to put a book down the back of your trousers for that meeting.'

Macy took a seat opposite Jo. 'First, let's order some food. Jo needs to get home sometime tonight.' Selecting what to eat was some version of torture for Alan and while he quizzed the waiter about ingredients, Macy poured Jo a glass of wine. 'Same old team.' He raised his glass to her and she found herself smiling back, while her doubts continued to revolve in her mind.

'Any news on Flora?' she asked.

Macy turned to Alan. 'You're the one who's been at the hospital most of the day. Any progress?'

Alan's frown lines deepened and his jaw sagged. 'Nothing good, I'm afraid. No surgical operation planned yet, but they know it will be needed and a spinal op is always dodgy. The nurse I spoke to was not optimistic but that was off the record. They're not saying that to the family. Her brother is still there and their aunt had just arrived when I left. I got her name,' he added, anticipating Macy's question. 'I phoned the office and they're checking her out.'

'Aunt Miriam from Cheshire,' Jo murmured. 'Maybe Theo can get a break now. He was intending to go back to Flora's flat. Did you see Carolyn?'

'I could hardly have missed her. She was like a walking florist.' Alan snorted. 'What a dimwit, bringing flowers to an ICU.'

'She didn't know Flora was so seriously injured,' Jo said. 'And, to be fair, most bosses wouldn't have shown up at all.'

Their food arrived, which put a halt to any further argument on this score. Alan's consisted of a pint of lager as he stated that he didn't like the wine, nor much of the food, but Jo tucked in readily to her pomegranate, lamb and rocket salad. Macy poured himself another glass of wine and picked at his rice dish. He sighed. 'I suppose I'd better tell you the latest position with Carswell.'

Alan looked up in alarm. 'Tell me you haven't walked out on the contract?'

'I was never not going to the police,' Macy said with a shrug. 'Our licence to operate is more important than any client. Plus, a woman has been seriously injured. Flora could have been killed and I believe it was deliberate. The police need all the help they can get.'

'How did Carswell take that?' Jo asked.

'He calmed down after he realized there was no other option.'

'For fuck's sake, Macy, Carswell is the best paying client we've had for years.' Alan glared at his boss across the table. He clearly felt he could speak his mind, taking advantage of the fact that their relationship was probably as old as the Macy and Wilson agency itself. Possibly older, Jo reflected, watching with interest.

'Well, that's what's happening anyway.' Macy said with a bored look around the room, as if seeking out diners who were having more interesting conversations. 'We're completing the final report on Monday as planned and then that's it, there's no more Carswell and no more case.'

'What about Flora?' Jo said. 'And Theo. What do you think will happen to them?'

Macy gave another cold shrug. 'I don't know. They have Aunt Miriam, I suppose.'

The table fell silent. Jo and Alan both knew Macy in this mood and there was no point in arguing.

Macy scowled at them. 'For Christ's sake, both of you, cheer up. We haven't completed the final report yet and Jo, you still need to provide the birth chart. Carswell will pay good money for both. There is still work to be done. Plenty of it, in fact.'

'The chart's almost done,' Jo said offhandedly. 'I can email it to you tomorrow.'

Macy gave an impatient sigh. 'OK, look, if I am suddenly a shit for abandoning Flora, then I'm fine with that. But it's rich coming from you, Alan, seeing as you've been telling me for weeks that she's just a target. And you've got some extra business out of it too, Jo, thanks to Carolyn. I'd like you to remember that I'm the only one who actually cares about Flora.'

Jo was on the point of retorting that she was only in Bournemouth because he had asked for her help. But then she thought of Theo waiting for news of his sister and of Flora herself, drunk, clueless, distressed, and she fell silent, less certain what she thought. Meanwhile, Alan made one of his mercurial shifts of mood. 'Of course there is work to be done,' he stated, breezy and businesslike. 'And I will be at the office tomorrow afternoon for the final report meeting. Especially as I've done most of the work.'

Jo remembered he was an Aquarian with Gemini rising, so he could always be relied on to be rational, which provided a good antidote when Macy became brooding and crabby. While they ate, she turned to Alan and asked what he had found out from his surveillance on Flora so far.

He was more than willing to oblige. 'It's been a piece of piss, to be honest, because she doesn't do very much. Every Tuesday she goes to knitting class and she goes to the gym in Boscombe two or three times a week. It's pretty easy to keep an eye on her there because they let non-members into the café and you've got a fairly good view of all the comings and goings. Flora goes to classes — yoga or some other thing that needs a mat. Her brother came down from London to visit her one weekend and they went to see a film together. It was one of the Marvel movies. Flora doesn't see much of anyone outside work hours.'

'There's the motorbike man,' Macy said. 'I'm wondering now if Jo may have found us his phone number.'

'Jess calls him Flora's stalker,' Alan said. 'He's a courier who delivers to the Upwards office. Sometimes he talks to

Flora outside the office but that's it, they don't see each other anywhere else.'

'As a work romance goes, it's the slowest burn ever,' Macy commented. Jo met his eyes for a moment and quickly looked back at her salad.

'It's never a romance,' Alan chipped in. 'All they do is talk and not for long. It is winter, you know.'

Jo laughed appreciatively and Macy ordered him another lager and refilled his own glass. Jo put a hand over hers, thinking of the drive ahead.

'What about this horoscope on Flora?' Alan asked. 'You must be able to tell us something. I've been weeks on this case and all I can say is she cycles to work every weekday, works for her boss as a sort of bag carrier and has next to no social life.'

'She's very private, so it's not surprising that you're not finding out much. I think she has a rich internal life—'

'What does that mean?' Alan demanded. 'It's always the quiet ones, is that it?'

'There's a lot going on for her, which even those closest to her wouldn't know about,' Jo said. 'Flora has to contend with some deep emotions. She feels things strongly. Some are positive, like loyalty, but there's a lot of anger there too, probably very well suppressed. But I need to finish the chart before I say any more.'

Macy signalled for the bill. 'Look, Jo, if you can make it tomorrow afternoon, could you come into the office? We have to pull this final report together for Carswell on Monday and I'd like to get everyone in on it.'

She agreed to this. She was curious herself to see how all the pieces of the puzzle came together. Alan grinned at her over his pint. 'Good to have you back, Jo.'

When they left the restaurant, Macy walked her to her car. Alan had already said goodnight and faded away towards their hotel, she assumed. 'Being upfront with the police is the best way to help Flora you know,' he said. She wondered if he was convincing himself as much as her. 'Ultimately, they will be able to find out what happened to Flora.'

'You might have some difficult questions to answer though. About why you took so long to come forward and what you were doing there.'

'I'm up to those,' he said. They had reached Jo's car. 'Thanks for agreeing to come into the office tomorrow. If I'm not there, you'll know they've arrested me.'

She laughed and, before she got into the driving seat, reached up and kissed him. It wasn't a peck on the cheek either but a fully passionate kiss. Within a minute or so, sense of some sort or another prevailed and she said goodnight and drove off.

One question cycled around her mind as she headed towards the M27. *What exactly am I getting into here?*

CHAPTER NINE

By the morning, Jo was satisfied with the write-up of Flora's natal chart, which she emailed to Macy at ten o'clock. Later, at the Rivermill, she worked on a summary so that she could present it at his meeting in the afternoon. She had been slightly alarmed to discover she had a ten-minute slot on the agenda entitled 'Personal profile based on astrology'. At least they had stopped short of calling it a psychological profile. She was pretty sure that the agenda was Rowanna's influence. Back in the day when she used to work for Macy, a case review — if they had ever bothered to call it that — would have consisted of her, Alan and Macy sitting over bottles of beer at Brown's in Coventry, much like their night in Soul Bar.

She practised her presentation out loud in the car as she drove through the rabbit warren of a business park where Macy and Wilson's office was located. In ten minutes, she had to do justice to Flora's complex personality without making either Macy or Alan out to be wrong. Because, according to her birth chart, Flora Howell was not the straightforward, harmless young woman Macy seemed to want her to be. Nor was she likely to be the malicious saboteur that Alan would probably have liked to paint her. Although Jo had to admit that, according to the chart now neatly printed and contained in a smart plastic wallet on the passenger seat, Alan was closer to the mark.

The discreet plaque by the sliding glass door stated merely, *Macy and Wilson Unit 12.* Jo had discovered long ago that Wilson was no longer an active partner in the private investigation agency, if indeed he — or she — ever had been. There was a vague connection with Macy's ex-wife, Jo had once discovered but she had never got to the bottom of this. Macy was as circumspect about his personal life as the agency was about its business. Blinds at the windows ensured nothing was revealed about what went on inside the office, though they clearly allowed good visibility because Rowanna appeared promptly in the doorway.

The two women had only met a handful of times but Rowanna was much as Jo remembered: competent, blonde and oddly superior. Today she had trained her hair to curl at the ends and was wearing a long jacket over an autumnal brown woollen dress, which looked expensive. Jo, in her red down coat and boots, wondered if her look was 'corporate' enough for the occasion.

'We're all squashed in David's office, I'm afraid,' said Rowanna. 'He's the only one who actually has an office. I told him we should have hired a conference room at the Topham Hotel. Maybe we will have to expand into new premises in the fullness of time.' She led Jo through the square reception area. Jo glimpsed, in the larger open-plan office to her left, two clusters of desks with people on the phones. Straight ahead, visible through glass walls and door, were some familiar faces gathered around Macy's desk. 'Who knows, we may be able to contemplate that if we can extend this contract,' Rowanna went on. 'Would you like a coffee?'

'Love one,' Jo said. She noted that both Rowanna and Alan seemed to hold out hope of keeping the contract with Carswell, which was very different from what Macy had said last night. She had already exchanged looks with him and noted he was suited and booted today and looked tense. They had rearranged his office to get five seats around his desk and a flip chart at one end of the room. Rowanna's influence again, Jo didn't doubt. The date and agenda were written up in green marker pen and Rowanna took the seat at the top of the table nearest to it, having despatched a man to fetch Jo's coffee. Macy was in his usual seat in the middle of the long side of the desk with Alan squashed in beside him. Rather surprisingly, Alan winked at Jo as she took her own seat beside Jess, a carefully made-up Goth with sleek black hair and an impressive set of piercings.

No sooner had she sat down, Macy started the meeting. His gaze travelling from one to the other around the desk, he reminded them of the need to compile a report, 'bringing together everything we know about Flora Howell, for Rowanna to send to Louis Carswell by close of play on Monday'.

'Si is taking notes,' Rowanna added and the tousle-haired man at the opposite end of the table who had brought Jo's coffee gave a sheepish nod and ducked behind his laptop.

'There's a lot to cover,' Macy said, 'and Rowanna is going to start us off by giving some background about Upwards, the training company that Flora works for.'

Jo exchanged the hint of an eye-roll with Alan as Rowanna stood up and turned the page on the flip chart to reveal a hand-drawn organizational chart showing the hierarchy at Upwards. She started by describing the campaigning role of the business, which had increased since Louis Carswell had bought the company in September.

'Louis Carswell boasts about having influence with people in government and there's some connection with a minister called Paul James. I've seen some pictures of them at social events,' she said. 'He has pledged to get more high-profile support for Carolyn's campaigns. Flora is her business manager so maybe she wants to follow in Carolyn's wake as she rises to the top in her new career of influencer and fundraiser.'

'Flora seems more like a dogsbody to me,' Alan put in. 'And a pretty useless one at that.'

'A change of career explains why Carolyn Ash wanted to sell the business,' Macy said. 'And Louis Carswell seems keen to help her run it now he's involved.'

So keen that he puts her staff under surveillance without telling her, Jo thought. 'Maybe Carolyn is good at campaigning because she's genuine. When she told her life story, the audience were captivated — including Flora, even though she must have heard it a million times,' Jo said. 'I think Carolyn drives the company quite hard but she's inspirational, and they all admire her.'

Rowanna frowned and looked at her watch. 'Well, this is all just speculation, so if there are no questions, shall we move quickly on to Flora's weekend and evening activities? Alan and Jess, I believe you are going to update us.'

Alan took the lead and Jess gave the smallest of nods for him to carry on. His report of Flora's limited social activities was not as lively as the one he'd given last night at Soul Bar and Jo didn't learn much that was new. She was becoming aware of an odd, sweetish, stale smell which seemed to emanate from Alan's corner and the origin of this became clear when he lifted a carrier bag onto the table. 'There's more,' he said, 'because I've been doing a spot of garbology.'

Jo, as naturally fastidious as any Virgo, recoiled slightly as he lifted out a stack of stained and curled-up papers from the bag. The scent of ancient coffee grounds mingled in the stuffy room with old garlic and cabbage. 'Each week on my shift I've taken Flora's recycling box from outside her block of flats and gone through it in the evenings. Don't worry, I've cleaned it all up and I've chucked away the actual rubbish,' Alan reassured them.

Jo caught Macy hiding a smile behind his hand and had to avoid his eyes or the urge to giggle would have overtaken her.

'I hope your hotel doesn't hit us with a cleaning bill,' Rowanna said.

Alan ignored this. 'I've sorted the rubbish into categories, but now we need to divvy up the next stage to see what all this stuff tells us.' He pointed to a small pile held by a blue elastic band. 'Those are all her non-shredded receipts since the sixth of January.' The next pile turned out to be a stack of torn and battered magazines and a few old newspapers. 'Not much of interest that I can find,' Alan said, 'but you never know.'

'I'll take those,' Jess said, speaking up for the first time. She drew the disreputable bundle of papers towards her.

Alan withdrew another packet from the reeking carrier bag. 'These are all bills and other paperwork to do with the flat. I've got a whole pile of shredded stuff at home and I'm working through that, but I'm hoping you lot will tell me what I'm looking for.'

Macy gingerly picked up the bundle of bills. 'We haven't got much time. You'll have to email anything of interest by tomorrow lunchtime.'

'I'll go through the receipts,' Rowanna said. 'Put them in a plastic bag for me.'

With the carrier bag now empty, only two items remained on the desk. 'They don't fit any categories,' Alan said. Si had started to flick through a series of printed PowerPoint slides, leaving a thick, dog-eared official-looking report in old-fashioned comb binding with a hard plastic cover, now marked with brown stains. Jo pulled it towards her, feeling she ought to volunteer to take on something. The title page read, *Quality Assurance Review on Upwards Training Company.*

'The thing to focus on is what do these things tell us about Flora that we don't already know,' Macy said. 'What, if anything, was she up to? Was she in any trouble? What was she hiding?'

Jo recognized her cue and recounted her story of meeting Flora in the car park when the woman was trying to contact her missing friend. Now knowing that Flora was critically ill made the woman seem even more vulnerable, Jo felt, but she was careful to be brief and stick to the facts.

'Yes, we are trying to trace the numbers she was dialling,' Rowanna said with a pointed glance at the agenda. 'I'm aware of time, so can we move on to the astrology item please.'

Jo was more than happy to switch to her own subject and handed out her pristine folders around the now cluttered desk. Under Rowanna's beady eye, she was careful not to exceed her ten minutes. She summarized Flora's personality as quietly driven and family-oriented with emotional depths, not one to wear her heart on her sleeve so probably very comfortable with secrets. 'Flora almost certainly has ambitions herself but, unlike Carolyn, you wouldn't know it,' Jo said. 'She's a very private person and she's also stymied by her own lack of confidence and life experiences.'

'Well she's not exactly a high achiever at work,' Alan said.

'She did get promoted a few months ago,' Macy pointed out.

'Maybe her dreams are nothing to do with work,' Jess said, but when they turned to look at her, she gave a dismissive shrug of her shoulders.

'You may be right,' Jo said. 'The chart doesn't give much indication of career ambitions. But whatever they are, this is the year for Flora to achieve them as it is her Jupiter return. Every twelve years, Jupiter returns to its original place in our birth chart and, as Flora has just turned twenty-four, this could potentially give her the energy to live out some of these big dreams. But I don't know if she has the . . . the—' Jo searched for the right word — 'the gumption to achieve them.'

'Are we asking the right questions?' Macy mused, partly to himself. 'What do we really understand about Flora's secrets, her motivations?'

Jo looked again at the birth chart, ignoring Rowanna's shuffling of paper at the top of the table. 'I'd want to know a bit more about the time Flora spent by herself,' she said. 'When she wasn't in work, she was on her own. We know a bit about her exercise, but Flora is a reflective sort of person. She's not a "doer". Where did she do her thinking?'

Beside her, Jess started to play with her long dark hair, bringing strands towards her mouth and letting them go repetitively. 'Who was following Flora when she was on her own?' Jo persisted.

'That's easy.' Alan started to tick the occasions off on his fingers. 'In six weeks, she went twice to Boscombe library, once a week to knitting and Sainsbury's, plus other little local shops, twelve to fifteen times to the gym . . .'

Macy scanned the list of activities that Alan had provided. 'There were two Sundays she went birdwatching on her own, including last Sunday. What happened then?'

Jess stirred, clearing her throat. 'They were my weekends. Flora took the train to the Quiet Pools near Weymouth in Dorset. It's a nature reserve and sculpture park. She was there walking and looking at birds all day, coming back into Bournemouth station at about five o' clock. Same thing. Two identical Sundays.'

Macy looked at Jess and the small room became claustrophobic with awkwardness. Eyes dropped and fingers fidgeted with phones or papers. 'What did she do when she was there?'

Jess remained very still. 'Just watched birds.' She levelled her gaze back at him. 'She took her binoculars and she bought sandwiches from Greggs at the station for lunch.'

'What else?' Macy pursued.

'I don't know what happened every moment.' She paused. 'All right, look, I wasn't there the second time. There was no point.'

The people in the room took a collective breath.

Jess continued to address Macy. 'I'm sorry, but I went the first time and I can tell you it was a long walk from the station to these deserted lakes. I felt pretty exposed following her as it was early on a Sunday morning. She didn't travel with anyone or meet anyone and then when she got there, she just got on a boat to a sort of island in the middle of this huge lake. Only four people can get on the boat so I just stood there feeling like a loser. After that, I caught the train home and waited for her at Bournemouth station.'

'You could have hired another boat or at least waited on the bank, used binoculars—' Alan protested but Macy cut across him.

'And the second time?'

'I told you, there was no point.' Jess got to her feet, colour creeping up her neck and under her pale make-up. 'I know I've let you down but I stuck out like a sore thumb at that nature reserve and I couldn't do anything. Her voice deepened and she pushed past Jo to get to the door. 'It's OK, I'll leave, I'll go and get my stuff.'

'No, don't do that.' Macy stood up but Jess hurried out of the room, followed by Rowanna.

'That's a whole data set we're missing,' Alan said. 'I'll go down to these ponds tomorrow, ask some questions—'

Macy put out a hand towards Alan. 'No, you've done a great job here.' He waved at the piles of paper on the table. 'Finish it off. Stick with the shredded material and see what turns up.'

Raised voices could be heard from the office and Jo judged it a good moment to leave. She gathered her belongings.

Macy thanked her. 'I'll see you out.'

'No it's all right. I think you're needed in there.' Jo nodded towards the office. Jess was standing by her desk with her arms folded while Rowanna stood beside her talking calmly.

He slid open the glass door. 'I know. I'll see what I can do. Jess was not the right person for that job but she doesn't need to leave. My fault, not hers . . .'

As his sentence tailed off, Jo gave him a hard look. Although he had seemed his usual calm, unshockable self in the meeting, she could tell he was still worried. 'What is it?'

'Nothing.' He shook his head. 'I've got a bad feeling about what I'm going to find at these godforsaken ponds, that's all.'

'I'll come with you if you go on Sunday,' she said. 'The bookshop is closed.'

He hesitated a moment, then nodded. 'I'll pick you up at ten.' Before she had reached her car, he had disappeared to deal with the drama unfolding inside.

CHAPTER TEN

A giant white male torso leaned out at Jo from a yew hedge as they passed through the entrance to the Quiet Pools on Sunday morning. A matching female version loomed at Macy on the driver's side.

He scowled at it. 'What is this? An adult-only nature reserve?'

'Seems the sculpture park is more in your face than the birdy bit,' Jo observed. They passed a woman in wellies chalking bird sightings onto a blackboard.

'Hard to say which of those places I would least prefer to spend my Sunday,' Macy said.

Jo had not had enough coffee to be fully awake and Macy had remained pensive so they'd had a quiet journey. Once out of the car, she stomped ahead of him, determined to ignore his moodiness and hoping to get her hands on some caffeine.

'We're playing way out of our league,' Macy muttered behind her.

'What do you mean?' There were a number of things that were different about this case. One of them was that she had never known Macy to be so rattled and it was starting to get to her. Annoyingly, he didn't reply but just shook his head and hunched into his coat.

'Well, you'll be out of it tomorrow anyway,' she began and stopped mid-sentence. At the same moment, they saw a police car parked half-hidden beside the visitor centre hut.

'Might be nothing,' Macy said. But the dread that he was wrong hung in the air.

Inside the visitor centre, the woman in wellies was now setting out leaflets.

'Is it possible to get a coffee?' Jo asked.

'It's very early.' The woman continued to straighten the piles of leaflets. 'I'm not sure the water's hot enough yet.'

'That's OK, we'll hang on.' Jo smiled. 'Seems busy, seeing as you've only just opened. Quite a few cars in the car park.'

The woman retreated behind the counter. 'They are the serious birders,' she said. Jo felt her red coat and orange bobble hat marked her out as distinctly not in this category. Macy in his wool coat and heeled boots seemed also to have abandoned any attempt to be undercover. 'We've got a coachload coming from Hampshire and another from Wales. Visitors don't usually come in here till later,' the woman continued.

'We're first then.' Jo handed over the exact change for two coffees. 'Milk and sugar, please.'

'Over there.' The woman pointed crossly and stomped into the kitchen. But when she emerged with two mugs of hot coffee, she seemed less edgy. 'Most people didn't want to work today,' she said. 'We're all volunteers and there's been a horrible atmosphere here all week.'

Jo lingered at the counter. 'I suppose someone has to come in if you've got coaches arriving later. Why has it been so horrible?'

The woman took off her glasses and regarded Jo more closely. 'Oh. You don't know? I thought—' she stopped and started again — 'I could see you and your friend don't look like the wildlife types, so I thought you might be journalists or, well, even worse.'

Jo shook her head, deciding it was best to say little but prepared herself for bad news. 'What happened?'

The woman fidgeted with the till. 'It's terrible. One of the volunteers has been murdered. A local woman who lives on the army base found his body on Monday morning. The site's been closed all week. People are saying he drowned but . . .' A mix of fear, apprehension and ghoulish interest criss-crossed the woman's face. 'I can tell you. He was stabbed first. So you can see why none of the other volunteers wanted to turn up.'

'I can,' Jo said with feeling. 'Did you know him? What happened?'

'Of course. Shane Beaman's been here ages. I know all the wardens including the part-timers. He was just a volunteer like me. We both worked Fridays and weekends. Quiet man, lovely, but a bit shy. Used to come to work on his motorbike. He must have been in some sort of trouble though.' She shook her head. 'The most frightening thing is that whoever was after him managed to track him to this lovely quiet place. We like to think we're away from it all down here, away from the London crime and all that.'

'Shane Beaman,' Jo repeated, her voice steady, although her stomach flipped.

'Yes, poor man. They're not letting this out for obvious reasons but I can tell you, there's no way he drowned. Someone had gashed his stomach open. That's how he died.'

'Oh my God.' Jo didn't have to school her reaction. She was grateful that the woman kept talking, adding that it was probably drugs-related, as that's what people were saying. Jo nodded dumbly, thanked her and took the coffees over to Macy. He had become very still, no doubt listening intently.

'That's Flora's friend. It's got to be. Shane Beaman,' she whispered.

'Glad we came,' he said in a normal voice, blowing on his coffee. 'A walk will do us good.'

Before they left the visitor centre, Jo consulted a wall chart showing all the wardens and volunteers at the site. Shane Beaman's picture was still among them. The blurred photograph showed a man maybe in his twenties with an open, square face and wild, untidy hair.

She didn't speak until she and Macy were walking side by side on the footpath leading to the Quiet Pools. 'That's who Flora was going to meet when she was knocked off her bike. The timing fits, doesn't it? He had been missing a few days when I met Flora on Wednesday night. He was the man she was trying desperately to reach by phone. And he was here, dead.'

Macy was shaking his head. 'I've been dense,' he said. 'I should have made the connection when Jess told us they'd met here. This stabbing has been in the local news since Monday, but they hadn't revealed the location. All the same, I should have guessed: local beauty spot, a lake, a missing man.' He sighed, head down, walking quickly. 'We need to somehow find out the time of death as exactly as we can and we need to trace those numbers.' Macy got out his phone. 'Of course, we don't want to get ahead of ourselves. We still don't know for sure. They might not even know each other.'

'But I am sure Flora said his name was Shane,' Jo said. 'And I thought you didn't believe in coincidences.'

'We should at least know exactly where Flora was.' Macy groaned. 'Oh Lord, we could probably have provided her alibi, except Jess was on duty. Or off, more to the point.'

Jo nodded but her thoughts were taking her down another track. 'Why?' she wondered aloud. 'What did Flora and Shane Beaman get up to that was worth a murder and attempted murder? What the hell had they done?'

'We don't absolutely know there's a connection,' Macy said. They took a path downhill, avoiding the sculpture of a stork by a signpost to the Quiet Pools. 'Both very different MOs,' he went on. 'And Flora looks like she will survive, thank God, so that can hardly be called a professional job — and that is assuming the hit-and-run was intentional.'

'But you thought it was,' Jo reminded him.

Their path to the lake was blocked by some temporary bollards and handmade signs pointed to a diversion route back through the woods. The closest they could get to the lakeside was a bird hide on a long spit of land that had a view back towards the visitor centre. Through the slits in the hide, directly in their line of vision, a sign floated on the steely, rippled water: *REFLECT*.

Jo glanced at Macy meaningfully but they didn't speak because an older couple were occupying the bench on the opposite side, sharing a flask of tea and peering through binoculars in silence. Macy asked if he could borrow the binoculars and the chap handed them over readily. While he and his wife enthused about the kingfishers visible on the island in front of them, Macy looked out across the lake.

'That's the army base,' the older man said, moving to stand at Macy's elbow. 'You won't see much beyond the fences from here. That's near where the warden's body was found Monday morning, apparently.'

'He seemed a harmless chap,' his wife added. 'Used to run the boat tours to the island and always said good morning.'

When they left the hide, Macy admitted to Jo that he hadn't learned anything new from his cursory scan of the lakeside. 'I saw a uniform on duty,' he said. 'But I don't recommend we talk to him. We don't know enough yet — we're only working on wild assumptions. There's nothing more we can do here, I can achieve more back at the office.' They tramped along the frozen path, dodging low branches.

'So their meetings may not have been innocent trysts,' Jo mused. 'I mean, suppose Carswell is right and Flora was involved in some sort of insider dealing, then maybe Shane Beaman was part of it somehow. Maybe he had some connection to the company that benefitted.'

'Learning-Into-Work,' Macy supplied. 'That's what they're called, the company that won the contract. A London-based firm that specializes in vocational training. I could ask Rowanna to check out any connection with Beaman.'

Jo followed her own train of thought. 'He was a courier, wasn't he? That's how he and Flora knew each other. Maybe he also worked for this other company and — oh I don't know, maybe someone found out, and, especially if money changed hands, then they were suddenly both in deeper trouble than they'd expected.'

'And this was their meeting place and we didn't know about it.' Macy shook his head. 'This is not looking good for us. We didn't even know they were meeting up when we were supposed to be tailing Flora outside work. I still can't believe Carswell was right about her.' He stared ahead along the path. 'What about Flora and the dead man? Do you think they were in a relationship?'

Jo shook her head, breathing faster as they unconsciously picked up their pace. 'Not according to Flora's brother. She wasn't seeing anyone.' She was silent until they reached the car and she expressed the doubt that had been forming in her mind. 'I know we've been talking about them both as if they were victims, but if Flora was here with him on Sunday, then it looks like she left but he didn't.' She glanced up at him as she buckled herself into the passenger seat. 'And it's hard not to think that the sign, "reflect", wasn't meant as some sort of message.'

'It's certainly working that way on me,' Macy said.

CHAPTER ELEVEN

'One thing's for certain,' said Macy as he drove off, 'I have to let Carswell know this latest development. Maybe he can even throw some light on it.' He took the narrow lanes at a pace and the hedges slapped at the car. 'In fact we might drop in on our way back. He says he lives in the office. Let's see if he's around. Is that OK with you?'

'Not really, I've got astrology work to do,' Jo said. 'Anyway, I thought you were talking to him tomorrow?'

'This can't wait, it's too important. Come on, we'll just pop in. It will surprise him if we both turn up. Carswell likes to throw me curveballs and it would be nice to do the same to him occasionally.'

'So, I'm a curveball now, am I?' Her response was dry but she wasn't deceived by Macy's flippant tone. This was important to him. The Achilles heel of many a Virgo is the need to feel needed. Jo knew this about herself, mulling it over as she listened to Macy setting up the meeting. Yes, Carswell confirmed, he was in the office, despite the fact it was two o'clock. on a Sunday afternoon. Characteristically, Macy gave away little information, ending the call quickly, avoiding questions. He then called Alan, who was at the hospital, and they listened to his report on Flora through the car speakers.

'As far as I can gather, there is no change. My new pal, one of the ICU nurses, tells me they are now able to schedule her operation so I suppose that means she is stable. Theo has just gone back to the flat and Aunt Miriam has taken over the afternoon shift.'

'No sign of their father, I suppose.' Macy tutted disapprovingly.

Jo broke the news about Beaman's death and Alan gave a little murmur of surprise, which was as near to shock as she'd ever known him show. 'Christ, and you're sure this was the man she was trying to reach? And that she met him last Sunday — the day he was killed?'

'Well, we've no evidence they met,' Macy sighed. 'Thanks to Jess.'

'I told you that you should have put me on that job,' Alan said. But Macy informed him that they were immediately stopping all surveillance work so he should leave and go home. Jo felt this was something she herself would like to do. But first she had to face a meeting with the man who paid the piper.

Carswell's office turned out to be as discreet as Macy's own. It was in a warren of streets not far from the bustling commercial area known as the Triangle. Macy left the car on a meter and they walked past silent office buildings and closed sandwich shops until they came to a single frosted-glass door with a small plaque signposting *Planet Events*.

While they were waiting, Jo reflected that Macy would have trawled through whatever data had been published about Carswell's company and probably even some that wasn't. He may have known nothing much about Carswell but it didn't mean he knew nothing about the company. She would have pressed him for more there and then but the man himself was bouncing down the stairs towards them. His silhouette wavered through the frosted glass, then he hit some buttons and pulled the door wide.

'David, this is a lovely surprise.' His eyes fell on Jo and momentarily betrayed that her presence was not quite so welcome. But that was exactly as they had intended. The curveball smiled blithely back at Carswell, whose recovery was so slight as to be almost invisible.

'Come in, come up. I can put coffee on for you.' He led the way past a deserted reception area and upstairs to the office space.

Carswell's physical empire took the form of a narrow first floor, a clutter of cabinets and desks in semi-darkness at one end of the room and his own office area at the back, comfortably fitted out and well lit, including an iconic anglepoise lamp and a substantial chair. He pulled up some seats for them and went to make coffee. The whole floor was open plan so he could carry on chatting to them about Sundays in Bournemouth and other small talk while he washed up some mugs.

'We should get a base in London, really,' he said. 'We would be a lot more central then and closer to Whitehall. But staff are easier to recruit here and it serves as a good base. Plus, Carolyn likes us to be within finger-clicking distance, so at least she's happy.' He chuckled. 'And that's important now we are running her operation so she can spread her wings.'

Macy replied benignly while Jo remained silent, letting her eyes range around the space. There was little to learn from the office. The desks, including Carswell's, were tidy and impersonal. The only conclusion she came to was that it did indeed look as if he had been working there all day, judging by the sandwich wrappers in the wastepaper bin and the neat piles of paper on the desk. And he wasn't acting like someone who was bothered about a dead body having been discovered not far away.

Eventually Carswell brought two mugs over and settled himself behind his desk. He was dressed down compared to when Jo had last seen him at the Metropole. But even his jeans and navy jumper had a military smartness about them and were tailored to his substantial frame.

'So your team are working on the report on Flora Howell? I should get it tomorrow?' He indicated his desk with a rueful grin. 'If you can get it to me as early as you can, I would appreciate it, because we have a huge week ahead. We've got a climate change conference at the Bournemouth International Centre starting tomorrow and a big event on policing, which starts midweek. Same venue, tight turnaround.'

'Both sound controversial, they must need quite a bit of security,' Jo commented.

Carswell shrugged. He held out his left palm at shoulder height. 'Climate change,' he said, and extended his other hand as if weighing the two issues. 'Policing. It's all just business.'

'The report will cover everything we've discussed—' Macy began, but Carswell interrupted.

'Ah, but something tells me that's not so. Otherwise you wouldn't be here. You're going to tell me something that can't go in the report, aren't you?'

'Not at all, we just popped in to be sociable as we were close by at the Quiet Pools. Do you know it? A local beauty spot, apparently.'

Jo sipped her coffee, which was an unusual intense flavour. Not bad considering it came from a capsule. She felt rather supernumerary and wished Macy would just get to the point and tell him about Shane Beaman so they could get on the road.

Carswell shook his head, frowning. 'I don't have time for sightseeing, David. Especially not locally. Now if you'd asked me about Hawaii or Santorini . . .'

'We think Flora has been spending some time there,' Macy went on.

Carswell's eyes flickered with interest but his tone remained urbane. 'No doubt this will all be explained in the report,' he said. 'I am sure you haven't come to bother me with trivia when I can read it tomorrow. I think I know why you came by, actually.'

'That's good,' Jo said. She refused to be passive any longer. If she was going to be part of this meeting, she was going to play an active role. 'Because I haven't the faintest.'

'Ah, David likes his mind games, don't you? You're rethinking your decision to end our contract, am I right?'

'I might be,' Macy said, which earned him a hard look from Jo.

'I perfectly understand that when we last spoke, you'd only just heard about Flora's accident. Let's face it, we're all still getting over the shock. But I thought that once that had subsided, you might reassess matters. Let me see, what can I do to persuade you to stay on a little longer?'

'No more surveillance,' Macy said. 'We can't continue with it while Flora is in hospital, and there's hardly any need. She's as safe as houses there and there are CCTV cameras everywhere, so any unwelcome visitors would know that.'

'But that's the contract, isn't it?' Jo said.

Carswell looked entertained. 'Do carry on, I love the way you two do business. It's novel.'

'I'll complete the research for you at the same rates,' Macy said, not missing a beat. 'So you'll still get the report tomorrow, but we'll complete any unfinished business arising from it. I reckon there may be another week's work, maybe slightly more. We can agree that once you've seen the report.'

'I want you to find out anything you can on Bonnie and Clyde as well, remember,' Carswell said. He smirked at Jo. 'That's Carolyn and Justin to you. And they know nothing about this arrangement.' He stressed the words with small shakes of his head.

Jo remained silent and tried to turn herself into a good poker player. She had no idea what Macy was up to but she was going to have to wait until they had left the office before she gave him her opinion. Which would be within a few minutes, she hoped. Certainly, Carswell seemed to have agreed to Macy's new terms and was looking at his laptop screen. His next words caught her unawares.

'But I want to show how much I appreciate what you've done so far and there is a little something I can do for you. The Rivermill is where you work, isn't it, Jo? Café and book-shop. I'm looking at the website, very shabby chic and charming. How would Ms Hanni Light fancy a stall at the Christmas Festival in Bournemouth, three weeks before Christmas?

Perfect position, corner stand. I will provide the stand and the hardware. It's no problem for me, that's what we do. All she'll provide is the stock.' He grinned. 'And the cash till.'

'No, Hanni would hate it,' Jo said. 'An exhibition is not her sort of thing at all.'

'Take a little coffee stall with you, hand drinks out for free in some nice new mugs. I can find you a comfy sofa, recreate the vibe you have at the Rivermill,' Carswell went on as if she hadn't spoken.

'No. Absolutely no way,' Jo said. She said this many times. She said it to Macy, along with a lot of other, less polite, things on the way home.

'He got that, I think,' Macy said. 'But actually, the negotiation wasn't about you.'

'What was it about? I thought you wanted to give up this contract? It seems to me that all along you knew you were going to extend it, you just wanted better terms.'

'I don't know about "all along",' Macy said. 'But broadly speaking, yes, that's about it. I don't want the surveillance work. I was never happy with it. But we've nearly completed most of the research work, so we may as well get paid for that. It's as simple as that.'

'If it's so fucking simple then why couldn't you tell me?' Jo demanded. The unworthy thought had occurred to her that Rowanna had persuaded him to stick with the contract. 'Instead of spinning me a fairy story that we were going to surprise him and tell him all about Shane Beaman's death, which you spectacularly failed to do.'

Macy made a little moue at the dark windscreen. 'I decided he didn't deserve to know.'

'It's not exactly a secret. Carswell will probably have seen it in the local press,' Jo said.

'When he reads our report, he will make the link with Flora and the Quiet Pools. Meanwhile, we have the advantage of that information.'

The advantage of knowing someone was dead. Sometimes Jo didn't understand Macy at all. He looked more cheerful than she had seen him since the start of the case and it made her want to do something uncharacteristically violent.

Fortunately, as he was driving, he remained unharmed. But when he dropped her at her flat, she was still fuming. He did not improve her mood by adding a word of advice before driving off.

'About the Christmas exhibition offer. Carswell will keep it on the table for a couple of days. I would talk to Hanni before you turn it down again.'

CHAPTER TWELVE

Jo was too angry to wave as Macy drove off. It was seven o'clock on a Sunday evening and she was cold and hungry and, worse still, felt like she had wasted the day traipsing around after Macy like an idiot.

In the two minutes it took to reach her front door via the outdoor steps, past the sturdy back gate and across the short concrete bridge, she planned what she was going to eat. At least she could do something about that. A quick toasted crumpet now and hopefully there was something substantial in the freezer for supper. Halifax, the cat, she shared with the bank below her flat, was waiting for her in the kitchen, delighted to see that she was prioritizing food for once. Jo concentrated on feeding him and herself, trying to put the wasted day out of her mind and work out how she was going to catch up with her astrology work.

Although at that moment she wanted to wash her hands of anything to do with Macy's case, she had promised an astrology consultation with Carolyn Ash at the Upwards office on Wednesday. As she carried her buttered crumpet and a coffee to the sofa, switched on all the lights and settled in front of the gas fire, she considered cancelling the appointment. Jo was still musing on this decision when her phone rang. She glanced at Macy's name on the screen and continued eating defiantly.

'I have my own business to run,' she said out loud to the hiss of the fire. Halifax had already made himself scarce, no doubt sensing the atmosphere. Within a minute her home phone was ringing and she still didn't move. But the ringing persisted long enough for her to remember that Macy didn't have her home number. Unless he had traced it, which would be just like him. She snatched up the receiver. 'Yes?'

'Josephine, is that you?' The voice on the other end of the line was tremulous and unrecognizable. But there was only one person in the world, apart from her mother, who sometimes called her Josephine.

'Hanni? What's wrong?'

'Oh, thank goodness you're at home. I knew you were out all day so I didn't want to call you on the mobile as I knew you'd be busy, but I thought I would just try you at home, because if you're home then — well, you need to know.' Hanni's sentences were running into one another breathlessly. In the background, Jo could hear a man's voice giving orders.

'What's going on? Where are you?'

'I'm at the Rivermill. We've been broken into. They've taken the cash from the tills and a load of stock. The police came to fetch me. Oh, Josephine, it's such an intrusion into our healing space. I haven't dared to look upstairs yet. Some of those crystals are really valuable and they can't be insured like the books—'

'Wait, hold on.' It was out of character for Hanni to talk fast and Jo was having trouble understanding her, especially over the banging in the background. 'When was this? What happened?'

'They broke in as soon as it got dark, smashed the corner window and even trampled over the Christmas tree. The police called me at home at about five o'clock, and when they knew I had no transport, they sent a car for me. They've been brilliant. The burglar alarm at the estate alerted them, which was fortunate.' Hanni's voice was sounding more normal. 'Or the other businesses could have been burgled too.'

'So it's just us? It's just the Rivermill Café and Bookshop?' A prickle of anxiety ran over her skin.

'The police think it's because we're on the corner with those big windows. But the best thing is that the alarms worked so they didn't get away with much stock. Isn't that lucky?'

'I'm coming over,' Jo said. 'Have you eaten?'

'No, April had just put tea on the table when the police rang.' Hanni lived on the family farm, though it was no longer in operation as her mother had been ill with cancer for some time. Hanni had never spoken about her father. Her sister April had recently moved back in as she was suffering from 'anxiety and inner pain', as Hanni had described it.

'I'll bring some chips,' Jo said.

'Oh. Chips?' Hanni's voice held a mixture of delight and uncertainty.

'Don't worry, I'll go to the place where they use vegan oil.'

'Josephine, I don't even care.'

The glazier's van was still in the car park but there were no police cars when Jo pulled up. It was just as well she'd brought extra chips, she thought as she surveyed the damage from the outside and came face to face with the glazier, who was measuring the space from indoors. As Hanni had said, the corner window had been smashed and had provided an easy route in.

Hanni was inside, wielding a dustpan and brush. 'The police said we can clear up and make it secure, so Neil is here, another guardian angel. They took lots of photographs and I have to go into the station tomorrow. Let me introduce you. Neil, this is Josephine, who also works here.'

'How do.' Neil was bending over a large piece of chipboard on a table, which, last time Jo had seen it, had been piled with books.

'Have they taken all that stock?' Jo said after she'd given her friend a hug.

'Yes, a lot of our Christmas stock is gone but the odd thing is they haven't taken anything from the shelves. I suppose they must have realized they had set the alarm off.' Hanni looked around her domain with a puzzled expression and Jo's skin prickled again. She shivered involuntarily and turned to handing out the bags of chips. Hanni had already made tea and coffee and they sat around one of the café tables. Neil hovered nearby with his plate and mug in his hand. 'Thanks for this. I'll keep working, if you don't mind,' he said. 'Then I might get the chance to see the little one before he goes to bed. If you don't mind me chipping in, I don't think the buggers scarpered quick because of the alarm. They would have known they'd triggered the alarms the moment they threw the brick.'

'The police took away the brick in a bag,' Hanni explained.

Jo agreed with Neil. She'd thought the same thing herself. 'What exactly did they take?'

Hanni pointed to a list on the table in green ink. 'Thank goodness I did a stocktake last week, so it's pretty accurate. This is what I need to take to the police station tomorrow.'

Jo picked up the list. There were only about fifty books listed, some paperbacks, some hardbacks. 'This isn't even your most valuable stock.'

'It's all a bit fishy to me,' Neil said. 'It's more like a theft to order. You know, like when they break into your house to steal the fancy car from the drive but leave the cash in your wallet. That's what this looks like to me.'

'Well, I can promise you there are no early first editions here,' Hanni laughed. There was more colour in her cheeks and her plate was nearly empty.

'I'll help you clean up and then we'll take a look upstairs,' Jo said.

Hanni shook her head. 'It's OK, I went up there with one of the police officers while you were on your way over. No damage done. It was still locked as I had left it, so all the crystals and my cards are safe.'

'This gets weirder,' Jo said. 'So someone, or more than one person, broke in here at—'

'About four o'clock, just as soon as it was dark,' Hanni supplied. 'And the police think it was just one man, plus someone else driving a car. They'll be on CCTV if they were in the car park, won't they?'

'OK, so our intrepid burglar throws a brick through the window and takes a bagload of books and then leaves the same way, I suppose.' She peered through the gap where the glass had been.

'In a getaway car,' Hanni put in.

'Mind out of the way, love.' Neil carried the first piece of chipboard to the window and started to fit it in place. 'It makes no bloody sense to me at all. But I can bet you, it will all fall into place when you work out what exactly has been stolen. Believe me, I've seen a few of these. Not bookshops though. That's a new one.'

'We'd better check the list thoroughly then.' Hanni picked up her pen with renewed energy.

Jo joined in the comprehensive search, including the consultation rooms upstairs. But Hanni was right. Nothing up there had been touched and it looked like they had not even bothered to try the lock. She came downstairs thoughtfully and completed her search of the café area. Hanni was tying up the last of the black bags of rubbish. The window was boarded up and even the Christmas tree was back in place, although it looked slightly the worse for wear. Neil shook their hands and went on his way at about eight thirty.

'I hope he gets to see his little boy,' Hanni said. She looked around the shop. 'I think we might be able to open up tomorrow after all.'

'Of course we will,' Jo said. 'I'll cover while you are at the police station.' She gave Hanni a lift home and was relieved to see her friend let herself into the farmhouse. But Jo still couldn't quite relax.

She had realized that there was one thing missing from Hanni's inventory of stolen goods, but she had stayed quiet about it. The stained, smelly and unrevealing report about Upwards Training Company was no longer on the counter by the till in the café where she had left it. She had taken it with her to read on Saturday morning and had emailed her comments on it to Rowanna during her shift. Tonight she had searched the café area comprehensively and she knew it was missing. She had even asked Hanni if she had seen it in case she had thrown the disreputable-looking document away. This would have been understandable, but Hanni assured her she would not have thrown anything of Jo's away because she knew Jo brought her work with her. That was part of their arrangement. It brought her back to the possibility that Neil had raised in her mind. What if retrieving this report had been the sole purpose of the break-in?

Jo told herself she was being fanciful. The report itself was bland and innocuous. Her theory was ridiculous and didn't make sense. But neither did the burglary itself.

That night, she double-checked the front door after she had locked it. On her way up the stairs, she recalled something Macy had said that morning: 'We are playing way out of our league.'

CHAPTER THIRTEEN

However fanciful and unlikely, the question would not go away. It returned to taunt her at 3.40 a.m. She found herself going over, in detail, her movements on Saturday morning, when she had been working on the quality assurance report at the Rivermill. What had possessed her to leave it at the café? Truth was, reading the tedious document had been a chore, which she had completed between serving customers. She had been relieved to send the email to Rowanna at lunchtime and tick that task off her list. The job was done, in her mind. The report was bland and insignificant and she had put it out of her head. She needed to do the same now, she said to herself, because she had to be up at seven in order to be at the Rivermill by eight.

At 4.45 a.m., she was awake again. She'd dreamt she was drowning with ice-cold water choking her and, as she scrabbled for the riverbank, it gave way into a large white sign with letters that made no sense. She retrieved the duvet from the floor and sat up, her heart still hammering as if she was struggling for her life. She laid a warm palm on her chest to calm it down.

An unbidden image of Shane Beaman swam into her mind, blurry like his photo. Had he struggled in the icy cold lake? Had he drowned, bleeding from his stab wounds? Or had he already been dead? She thought again about Flora, sheltering from the rain and staring back at her, uncertain. Was Shane Beaman the friend she'd been trying to reach? If so, he had already been dead three days. Jo was struck by the fact that Flora had not known this. If indeed Shane was her friend, why had no one told her?

She pulled on a jumper that was lying on the floor and slid out of bed. The flat was chilly. On the street below, car windscreens were blinded with frost and tyre tracks showed black on the glistening tarmac. Jo moved the blind aside with her hand and thought, *If Hanni were to die, I would know straight away, because I see her most days. But what if it was, say, Maurisha?* Her old friend from Coventry had a busy job and they didn't see each other as often since Jo's move to the Cotswolds. Even so, surely a mutual friend would tell her any bad news? Or even Maurisha's mum or one of her brothers might get in touch, Jo reasoned as she watched the careful progress of the van from the local dairy farm delivering milk to businesses on King Street.

What if Macy died? Sometimes he disappeared so thoroughly from her life, it was as if he was dead. But if it did really happen, Alan would tell her. Or someone else from the agency, maybe Rowanna.

She shook her head vigorously as if to chase off such morbid thoughts. Rather than continue this gloomy hypothesis for all her friends, she went downstairs and made some peppermint tea. She sat in front of the fire with it, trying to shake off the bad dream. But there remained a cold little worry tugging at her memory. Shane Beaman and Flora Howell couldn't have been close friends or Flora would have known he was dead.

Jo returned doggedly to her hypothesis as she sipped her tea. In three days, surely someone would have contacted her. Unless nobody knew they were friends. An affair? Secret lovers? Thinking back to what Theo had said about his sister being determinedly single, Jo didn't think so somehow. Or maybe Flora had known he was dead or in trouble and that's why she had been so distressed.

'He's always around,' Flora had said desperately as the rain had spattered around them. 'He's just always around. I can't understand it.'

A rattle at the hall window foretold the arrival of Halifax. This was followed by a short, perfunctory mew before he joined her on the sofa. Jo picked up her phone and browsed local news sources in Dorset, peering between the cat's ears. It didn't take long to unearth the reports of Shane Beaman's death. The location wasn't given, although someone who knew the area might have been able to work it out as there were a couple of pictures of the beauty spot in normal times and ones of the white tent erected by the police on the edge of the lake. Shane's blurry photo from the visitor centre had also been much reproduced.

Local man in suspected drugs-related stabbing, ran one headline. There was no mention of family members or friends, nor of his job as a courier. Beaman was described as a local 'conservationist' who lived alone in a 'multi-occupancy dwelling' in Bournemouth. The police were investigating in the area, as a number of car parks at local beauty spots had apparently been associated with drug dealing. She could understand why Macy had missed this. Nothing could have been further from Flora's world, which had appeared to be very genteel and well-meaning.

Jo leaned her head back on the sofa sleepily and the cat stretched his front paws and yawned. Beneath her hand, her phone buzzed once. It was the reminder of a voicemail. She recalled Macy's call from the previous night. She brought the phone to her ear and instantly she was back in the car with Macy. Clearly he was still driving home when he had left her the message.

'I know you're not talking to me at the moment, but I wanted to say thanks for coming today. And I thought you'd like to know that we've traced those two numbers you gave me. And yes, Flora was phoning Shane Beaman on both his mobile and his landline on Wednesday night. Now we know why she wasn't getting any answers. Give me a call tomorrow.'

* * *

Due to her poor night's sleep, Jo could have done with another quiet day at the bookshop, especially as she was on her own for most of the morning. Of course it was exactly the opposite. Most of the customers were other traders on the Rivermill site who had heard about the break-in and wanted the news first-hand. Most of them bought coffees and some even bought books, so it was good for takings. Jo soon got tired of retelling the story, however, and was very glad to see Hanni return just before midday. Her friend's white face with shadowed eyes mirrored her own, but at least she had another pair of hands in the café and at the tills.

They didn't get chance to speak much until after 3 p.m., when the place emptied out. As Hanni served their last customer with some children's books, she sent a meaningful glance across the shop and Jo prepared a couple of coffees. As soon as the door was closed, Hanni flopped onto a sofa. Jo brought the coffees over.

'You should go home, Josephine,' she said. 'You've done more than your fair share today.'

Jo, spreadeagled on the opposite sofa, raised her wristwatch to her eyes. 'I will soon,' she agreed. 'I didn't sleep a wink last night.'

Hanni rubbed her face. 'I'm sorry you were dragged over here and had to get involved in this whole mess.'

'No, it's not that.' Jo sat upright and drank some coffee in the hope it would revive her. 'I'm involved already.'

'Well of course you are,' Hanni said. 'I couldn't do without you at the moment. When Chloe comes back, after she's had the baby, everything will be—'

'No, Hanni, listen. There's something I should tell you. And a — an offer I've got to ask you about. But, first, what kept me awake was worrying that I had caused the break-in.'

104

Hanni gave a short, slightly hysterical giggle. 'Don't be silly. I know you take on all the problems of the world but I'm not going to let you take responsibility for a burglary.' She saw her friend's expression and reached for an extra packet of sugar for her coffee. 'I can see from your face there's another side to this.'

'Last night I kept going over what the glazier said. About it being a theft to order. The books they stole didn't make any sense. They didn't take the most valuable, just the ones closest to hand.'

'That's because they were interrupted.' Hanni stirred her coffee slowly. 'The police said that again today. The alarms worked and the police car was here in a matter of minutes.'

'OK, maybe. Or maybe they only needed a few minutes to grab what they came for, plus some books and cash to make it seem like an ordinary burglary. And, if I'm right, there won't be anything on the CCTV either.'

'The police haven't found anything yet. I asked them but the one nearest our shop isn't working. It was frozen up or something so it just stuck at one angle.' Hanni rested her elbows on her knees, thumbs on her chin. 'So what did they come for then?'

Jo was pleased her friend didn't continue to doubt her theory although she was none too sure about it herself. She told Hanni about the quality assurance report and how it had come to be in her possession. Hanni's eyes widened but she kept listening.

'I couldn't find anything important in the report,' Jo sighed. 'It was just a review of the company's training and they came out of it quite well. Carolyn Ash, the MD of Upwards, was mentioned a few times, but there was nothing about Flora. I've realized since that I left the report in full view of customers, but it wasn't confidential so it just didn't occur to me. I emailed my comments and, when I went home, I left it there.' She pointed to the counter.

'Well, if it was lying around all afternoon and someone wanted it that badly, why didn't they just take it?'

Jo got up and stood behind the counter. She waved at the space beside the till where she had been working on the report. 'It's not that easy for a punter to get their hands on stuff behind the counter with other customers about. Plus, you were here.'

Hanni leaned across the table towards her friend. 'I think you should go home and get some sleep. You know you have a tendency to take too much on yourself. Let me give you a herbal tea. That's good for rest.'

Jo hadn't really expected Hanni to believe her but she felt better for sharing her theory. She took her friend's advice eventually. But first, she explained about the Christmas Festival offer from Louis Carswell. Then she went to the bookshop counter and flicked through the notebook lying there, until she found her own note of a vehicle registration number.

She walked back up the hill, which today seemed steeper than ever, and, once in her flat made herself the herbal brew that Hanni had provided. Although sleep was tempting, there was a natal chart to complete and the long-postponed call to Macy. She managed to procrastinate for another hour or so until it was after five and she judged that the office was empty so Macy would be more likely to be on his own.

* * *

In this she turned out to be right. Macy had reached the end of a busy day that had seemed to consist mainly of phone calls. Most of the staff had left for the evening and he was also thinking of heading homewards when Jo rang on his mobile. He was aware of Rowanna still at her desk in the main room, so he reached over and gently closed his office door.

'Hello, Jo. Found any dead bodies today?' he asked in what, for him, counted as a cheery greeting.

'Ha ha,' came the response. 'I've been too busy clearing up after a burglary. We had a break-in yesterday evening at the Rivermill.'

Macy asked what had been taken, checked that the police had been informed and whether the stock was insured and Jo answered his questions diligently. And yet he was left with a sense that she was holding something back.

'How's Hanni? Is she OK? And you?' Each of his questions received brief answers and he found himself shaking his head, trying to understand his friend, colleague and ex-lover. Not for the first time either. 'So, what's up?' he asked. 'Are you really OK?'

'Yes, yes,' Jo said. 'It wasn't that I was ringing about, actually.' She paused. 'Although there is something . . .'

'Go on.'

'You remember that report I took away to analyse, which Alan found in Flora's recycling?'

Macy frowned and automatically picked up a pen. 'Yes, it was about Upwards. Some sort of training audit. Rowanna got your response and the final report went to Carswell today. What about it?'

'Was that the only copy?'

'I'm pretty sure it was. Why?'

'Well can you check with Alan? Because he took the rest of Flora's rubbish away with him, didn't he?'

'Alan's got his hands full and is still down in Bournemouth. I've got him looking into Beaman's death, as we're still very much focused on Flora here. Turns out Beaman was living in a house owned by the Council for ex-offenders.'

'But the woman at the visitor centre said he'd been working there ages,' Jo said.

'Well, he was released from prison eighteen months ago.' Macy anticipated her next question. 'We don't know what he was sentenced for, or for how long. We're good, Jo but we haven't got access to the PNC database yet. Not directly anyway. But it does make it more likely that it was a gang-related killing. Could have been debts, drugs, anything.'

'It doesn't explain how he and Flora became friends — or co-conspirators, or whatever they are,' Jo said. 'She's from a very different world.'

'Maybe they really did just have birdwatching in common and that type of thing,' Macy speculated, recognizing that he felt more informed about debts and drugs. 'Anyway, Alan's on it, and we should have something more tomorrow.' He paused and turned his attention to something more immediate. 'Now tell me, why the sudden interest in this tedious Upwards report that Alan pulled out the bin? Was it stolen in the break-in?'

There was a hesitation. 'Yes. How did you know that?'

'A wild guess based on years of doing this job. Well, don't worry, I won't be reporting that to Louis Carswell. There was nothing remotely interesting in it, was there?'

'I didn't think so but—'

'Forget about it,' Macy advised, and he might have brought the call to an end but he sensed Jo had more to say. 'Or do you have another little bombshell for me?'

There was an even longer pause on the line and then Jo began a convoluted explanation about how the break-in had meant stock stolen just before Christmas. The upshot of it was that she wanted to accept Carswell's offer of a stand at the Bournemouth Christmas Festival. 'Hanni wants to do it. Provided I'm there. But do you think Carswell will rescind the offer? I'm not looking forward to asking him after turning it down so thoroughly.'

'You were very definite on that subject.' Macy allowed himself a smile. 'But look, there won't be a problem. I'm talking to him in the morning. Tell Hanni she can start to plan.'

There was another short silence.

'Thank you.'

But Macy brushed off her thanks. There was a way to go in this case and he was glad enough to have Jo on his side, although he wouldn't have admitted this to her or anyone else. There was nothing that could be done for Shane Beaman now but Flora was still alive and fighting, according to the latest accounts. Until he knew how she was involved in the murder of Beaman, he was not inclined to tell Louis Carswell anything new. He wasn't even sure how much he wanted to tell Jo.

CHAPTER FOURTEEN

Macy had seemed preoccupied on the phone call, so Jo had decided not to ask if he was travelling down to Bournemouth on Wednesday but to make her own way, as before. In any case, she had her own preoccupations. Despite the fact that both he and Hanni doubted her theory about the quality assurance report theft, she had been unable to dislodge the idea from her mind.

'It's not your fault, Josephine,' Hanni said between phone calls to the insurers and the wholesalers.

'That doesn't stop me feeling guilty,' she replied. 'Put it down to a Catholic upbringing or Saturn opposing my Sun. Either way, I can't stop beating myself up for leaving the report here, and in full view of whoever walked in.'

It made her feel marginally better when Macy rang to confirm that Carswell had booked them a stand at the Christmas Festival. This meant a lot more work for Hanni, as they only had a few days to prepare, but her friend saw it as a way to recoup her losses.

Meanwhile Jo had been racking her memory for anything that could have made the report worth stealing. What had she missed? This was the question that dogged her on her drive south across the Cotswolds early on Wednesday morning. As soon as it turned nine, she even called the number for Cheryl Frost, the author of the report, and left a message but was not hopeful that anyone would get back to her. She harboured a vague hope that she might find a way to ask about the report while she was at the Upwards office later. *Surely Flora couldn't have taken home the only copy*, she thought. And if, somehow, Jo could get another read of it, she might find the valuable nugget she had missed. Getting Carolyn Ash or anyone else at Upwards to discuss it might prove a stretch even for her ingenuity, she suspected, especially as Carolyn still didn't know anything about the surveillance on Flora. At least, that's what Louis Carswell had assured Macy. But Jo remained sceptical. She had seen how close Carolyn and Carswell appeared to be and, given what a sharp brain Carolyn had, it seemed likely that the MD of Upwards knew exactly what was going on.

Jo was curious to know more about the place. All the staff she'd met seemed to love working there and such devotion was unusual, in Jo's experience. Even Vinny, apart from moaning about being overworked, had seemed positive about the company. And Flora, Bex and Liang had all seemed to idolize their boss. She found her suspicious Virgo mind wondering if all was as rosy in the garden as it appeared.

As for the astrological consultation itself, even that was potentially a little risky. Carolyn's birth chart had revealed a complex and driven character and it was going to be tricky to know how best to handle the session. However, Jo was more comfortable with this sort of problem, which happily occupied her until she turned the corner into Belvedere Avenue, where the lime green Upwards logo was flying on pennants tied to the grey stone wall. The company occupied a rambling Edwardian house on the corner of the main road between Bournemouth and Boscombe. Banners also fluttered on the railings announcing it as an *Award Winner for Employability Skills*.

A tall, wide-shouldered man in sportswear was poised under the Gothic stone arch as Jo approached the entrance.

He was wearing bright white trainers and a vest under his maroon tracksuit, but Jo recognized him from his handsome eyes with the sculpted hair and eyebrows. 'Hello again, Andre. Thought you worked for Justin Fielding,' she commented. 'Yet you always seem to be hanging around at Upwards.'

He looked blank for a moment and then, to her surprise, sketched her a smile. Admittedly it was close to a sneer, but he seemed genial enough. 'No, I still do. Wouldn't work for anyone else,' he said as if stating the blatantly obvious. He jingled the car keys in his hand. 'Got a new beast.' He nodded to a gleaming four-by-four taking up a large space by the wall.

'Very nice. Parking's no better though.' Jo grinned to show she meant no harm. 'Justin must be doing well.'

Andre nodded and put his fists together. 'He's on top at the minute for sure.'

'On top? What do you mean?'

Andre's expression filled with scorn. 'Of Carswell. Can't stand him.'

'Oh well, glad your man is top dog anyway.' She pulled her coat closer to her. Looking at Andre in sportswear was making her feel cold. 'I'm meeting Carolyn, so I've got to go.'

'If you need a lift anywhere—' He jerked his head at the car, leaving the sentence unfinished. Jo thanked him and went indoors. In the reception area, there were noticeboards full of numbers to call for advice, links to charities for young people and a list of apparently free courses run by Upwards on IT, marketing and communications skills. *Just ask at the desk*, the sign said. In her head, Jo could hear Macy's voice. *It's all very worthy, but how do they make any money?*

She recognized Liang behind the desk, who quickly ended a call and pushed her mobile under a diary. Pretending not to notice, Jo smiled and asked for Carolyn. 'Yes, you're here to cast Carolyn's horoscope for her.' She smiled. 'I understand you may be doing one for the company too. It's our tenth birthday next week, you see.'

'I hope so,' Jo said and Liang led the way through to the office, where there were four desks in an open space with some part-glazed rooms along one side. Jo recognized Vinny at one of the desks, who was, naturally, on the phone. He waved vaguely at her. On a desk near a window an oversized greetings card lay open.

'That's for Flora,' Liang explained, a troubled expression crossing her face. 'You met her last week at the event. She was in an accident on Thursday and she's in hospital. That's why I was on the desk. We're all having to cover for one another.'

Jo feigned ignorance. 'Oh no, is Flora's accident serious?'

'I'm afraid it might be. Carolyn has been to see her but she's not allowed visitors yet.'

'Flora told me she was worried about a friend so I hope she wasn't dashing off there when she had her accident,' Jo said.

Liang looked up sharply. 'She told me that too. I think she was worried about Shane, one of our couriers. I don't know why. He didn't really talk to anyone else but Flora. Look, why don't you sign the card?'

Jo shook her head. 'Thanks, but she won't know who I am.' She noticed a sympathetic message from Louis Carswell, signed with a flourish. Hypocrite. But didn't that also apply to Carolyn? Flora's boss was, after all, continuing to employ her and take her flowers, but she must have voiced her suspicions to Carswell, or why would he be having her investigated?

As Carolyn was still on the phone, Jo took a seat on one of the sofas while Liang went back to the desk. On the wall above her was a framed photograph of the Upwards team outdoors holding up a certificate like a sports trophy. Most of them were in sportswear apart from Carolyn and Flora, who were dressed in business clothes and stood slightly to one side. The bright green of Flora's jacket was eye-catching, partly because the harsh colour didn't suit her. She wore a familiar, slightly wistful expression as if she wanted to be somewhere else. The rest of the team grinned like Cheshire cats. Under Flora's arm was a bundle of papers and Jo couldn't help wondering if one of them was the elusive report. Judging by the turning colour of the trees, the timing was about right for the date it was issued.

Vinny appeared at her side. 'I'm sorry you're having to wait. But Carolyn really is on a pretty important call.'

'That's OK,' Jo said. Following his eyeline, she realized Carolyn was just about visible in one of the offices, talking animatedly into the receiver.

'It's a government minister,' Vinny added in a confidential tone. 'He's interested in some of the innovative work we're doing here and our success rate in getting unemployed people into work.'

'That's fantastic.' Jo tried to match his enthusiasm. She pointed to the picture. 'I've just been looking at this. Is this another award?'

Vinny peered at the photograph as if he'd never seen it before. 'Oh yeah, that's me there.' He pointed unnecessarily to himself in lycra. 'That was the day — sometime in September — we got our latest Ofsted report. Carolyn and Flora went to collect it and we'd maintained our standard, so we celebrated it.'

'I suppose you have quality audits that go towards the rating, do you?' Jo said, clutching at a faint hope. Just as Vinny was about to answer, however, he was interrupted by a younger, female voice.

'Hello, Jo. Are you looking at our sports day?' Bex appeared from one of the offices clutching a laptop to her chest.

'Yes, it looks like good fun.'

'We played rounders in the park. It was absolutely brilliant. You can see how hot it was. We were all in shorts but Flora had to work. Look at her in her one and only corporate jacket. She only started to wear that because she got promoted, and then she never took it off—' Bex put a hand to her mouth. 'Oh God. I'm sorry. I didn't mean anything bad.' She looked ruefully from Jo to Vinny. 'I forgot about her accident. I really hope she's OK.'

'I'm sure she is,' Vinny said, although he didn't sound it.

The door behind them flew open and Carolyn stepped out looking even more flushed than usual. 'Well, that was interesting,' she said to the room in general. 'We may be getting a visit from a government minister.'

'What does that mean?' Bex asked.

'Great PR,' Vinny grinned. 'National, not just the local media. The MPs will be in touch. Perfect timing for your campaign, Carolyn.'

'Our campaign,' she corrected, and then her eyes fell on Jo. 'Oh, it's my astrology consultation. Today just goes from strength to strength.' She beamed. 'Welcome, Jo, sorry you had to wait. Are you all set?'

'Ready when you are.' Jo picked up her laptop and moved towards the office Carolyn had just vacated.

'Oh, we're not staying here. No, no, no. This is a personal appointment and I don't want to be interrupted by work. Come on, Jo, I've arranged something nice for us. I'll drive.' She led the way out, walking with enviable posture in her high heels.

'Have fun,' Bex said with a trace of envy in her voice. Liang waved them off but her other hand was resting on the phone under the diary, Jo noticed.

Carolyn drove out to a spa in the wooded hills just outside the town. On the journey, she asked about Jo's business and how she had got into astrology and Jo, hoping to find out more about Flora or the missing report, struggled to get the conversation back to the training company. Eventually, as they entered a looping drive between evergreens, she went for the direct approach. 'How is Flora? Did you get to see her on Thursday?'

'She's still in intensive care, poor girl. No visitors except family. I've sent her some messages but she is clearly not able to use her phone.' Carolyn shot her a worried look. 'We are really in the dark. Her brother is not very communicative and she doesn't have much family apart from him. But, as soon as I can, I will take her the card and chocolates. I've got Bex on Flora-watch, phoning the hospital every day, but you get precious little out of them.'

'That's good of you. Not all bosses would go in person.' Jo caught a glimpse of a Victorian manor house with the dome of a swimming pool set among the woods beside it and realized she had limited time to pursue this subject. The place looked very splendid but the trip to reach it had already eaten into her time for a full astrology consultation. As she followed Carolyn up the steps through the grand portico, she gave it one more try. 'I suppose you must be missing Flora at work too. She used to deal with your accreditation and things like that, didn't she?'

'I've got other people for that.' Carolyn frowned at Jo as if she was missing the point. 'Flora looked after me and she's part of the Upwards family and that's why I can't wait to see her. Come on, we have a table waiting.'

Once in the beamed entrance hall, they were greeted by the sweet smell of an enormous fir tree, mingling with the smoke of a log fire crackling somewhere just out of view. 'Wow, nice place,' Jo said. She followed Carolyn up an oak staircase, with two comfortable-looking, worn red sofas on the landing. Carolyn smiled over her shoulder with a proprietorial air, clearly delighted with Jo's enthusiasm.

The table turned out to be a small one between two armchairs in a private room, which looked down from a glass balcony onto a swimming pool, where people were lounging and floating. It would have been easy to be distracted by the sudden, welcome warmth. Jo certainly enjoyed shedding her winter layers and sipping a fruit smoothie, but she hastily set up her laptop. Meanwhile, Carolyn seemed happy enough to talk about the call from the government minister and how Louis's contacts were bringing Upwards the profile she wanted.

'But won't this campaign take your attention away from the business of actually training people?' Jo asked while the chart loaded up on her screen.

'It will help the training business in general. Not just Upwards. That's one of the things I've learned, Jo. After years of hardship when I was striving to make money just for myself, now I believe in abundance. And in fact, you have to be generous to have the biggest impact on the people who matter, who are our young people.'

Jo reflected that this was the sort of approach Hanni would probably favour but she was keen to start the consultation, so she directed Carolyn's attention to the screen. The natal chart showed that Carolyn was a typical warm, charismatic, bossy, self-involved Leo in many ways and her moon in Aries made her even more of a goal-oriented high achiever. She was also headstrong and decisive. This much was music to her ears and she lay her head back on her armchair, accepting her flaws with an easy smile. As she always did at this point, Jo paused and asked if there was anything Carolyn wanted specifically to ask about.

The other woman sat forward. 'Actually, there is. If we have time, can I ask you about — well, affairs of the heart?'

'Absolutely. Do you have a particular question?'

Carolyn hesitated a moment, as if she was making some sort of assessment, and Jo waited patiently. This was about as serious as she had ever seen Carolyn. Eventually, the woman's face cleared and she looked up across her folded hands. 'I feel somehow I can trust you, but this has got to be completely confidential.'

'Of course,' Jo said.

'It's about Justin.' Jo nodded and Carolyn went on. 'He's a Leo too, but we're so different. It's enough to make you doubt the whole astrology thing. He has done well for himself too, you know, but I sometimes think he has run out of ambition.' She pouted slightly, eyes still on her hands. 'In all honesty, I almost think he resents my success. It's as if he doesn't want me to outdo him. But surely he can't be so small-minded?'

'You've been together a long while, haven't you?' Jo remembered from her brief conversation with Justin on this subject that Carolyn's doubts matched Justin's own reservations. He certainly had not seemed keen on her furthering her career in politics. Although somehow Jo doubted that the man was less ambitious.

'For ever,' Carolyn sighed. 'But now I feel—' She looked up at Jo guiltily. 'This sounds a terrible thing to say. But I feel like he is holding me back.'

'That doesn't sound terrible,' Jo reassured her. 'You have plans for a political career, don't you? Looking at your progressed chart, I can tell you that now is a good time to act. The transits in your chart are perfect for realizing that ambition right now, going into early next year. Act quickly though, because after that, the conditions are more difficult.'

'I can make such a difference, Jo. I know I can. I have a lot to offer and I can't do it on a local stage. And Justin is such a small-town thinker. But what's that old thing they say — can't live with him, can't live without him? Are we truly compatible, do you think?'

'Do you have his birth time, date and location? If so, we can look at his chart.'

'Justin doesn't have any contact with his parents. He's not sure if they're still alive. But I know his birthday.'

'That will tell us something.' Without the crucial details, Jo had to stick to general themes, but it was clear that theirs was a relationship where competition for power was important.

'You both want to be in charge,' Jo said, choosing her words carefully. 'Success matters to both of you and neither of you are good at compromise. But there is clearly a strong and passionate bond.'

'He would do anything for me,' Carolyn said in a low tone. 'Sometimes too much. But it's right what you say, once we take a position, neither of us will budge.'

'Astrology can only give you information. It can't tell you what to do, obviously. And in Justin's case, the information is a bit limited.'

Jo tried to return to the wider aspects of the chart, such as Carolyn's business prowess, which was supported by a well-aspected Jupiter and the challenging mix of planets in the Fourth House. 'Family have played a difficult role in your life.'

The other woman laughed. 'Don't think so. Father unknown, mother a heroin addict. You've got a planet in the wrong place or something.' She gave a quick look at her phone and Jo realized that they were at the end of the hour she had allowed for the consultation. Sure enough, Carolyn very politely but noticeably began to draw the meeting to a close.

Although Carolyn was gracious about the consultation, saying how insightful she had found it, Jo felt a sense of frustration as they retraced their steps out of the elegant spa, knowing she had let her preoccupation with Macy's case mar her own professional judgement. As swiftly as they had arrived, Carolyn led them back out, giving generous tips and smiles for the staff. Jo guessed that, as her business manager, Flora had probably enjoyed a few perks and the relationship might not have been as difficult as the younger woman had made it sound when she had turned up in Jo's hotel room.

'I was being a little harsh just then.' Carolyn broke into her thoughts as they walked to her car. 'You were right that family is important. But to me, family is just one person: my nan, who brought me up.'

'Is she still around?' Jo asked.

'Very much so.' Carolyn chuckled. 'She's a strong and wonderful woman. I've seen her physically bar the door to my mother to stop her taking me away to some smelly squat full of strangers. Nan gave me a proper home and made sure there was breakfast every day, gave me the money for school trips and bought me a new school uniform so I wouldn't be the kid with scorch marks on my skirt.'

They stood on the gravel with the soft murmuring of the trees around them and for once the air was mild. Some of the energy returned to Carolyn's voice. 'She's the one I get my drive from. The ambition you were talking about. Well, you can say it's the planets, but I know she's the one who made me write goals for myself and checked on how I was doing. Still does.' She glanced across at Jo with a familiar, impish smile. 'She has big dreams for herself too. She wants to meet the Queen. And I've promised her I'll take her to a garden party at the Palace.'

'I didn't know you could do that,' Jo said.

'You can't. Well, you can't buy it. You have to earn it,' Carolyn said. 'That's why that phone call this morning was so important. It's about influence, Jo. That's how to change things. One company on its own can only train so many kids in juvenile custody centres or those from chaotic homes like me. And Upwards mainly trains local kids. But if the government could provide a separate fund, like they do for apprenticeships, then all training companies would do it. Nationally.'

'That's your campaign,' Jo said. 'I understand how much it means to you.' Jo decided to leave it there and was relieved she had found an amicable way to end the consultation.

Before they arrived back at the Upwards office, Carolyn repeated her request for Jo to attend the company's birthday party for a repeat session on future skills, this time in front of an audience and on video. 'We're going to be over at Justin's studios as we're incorporating some of the celebrations into our next video. And you will do a birth chart for Upwards, won't you?'

Jo agreed, not without some reservations, especially about being on video. However, she had drawn up horoscopes for companies before and it was the kind of corporate business she wanted. As she got out of the car and exchanged a surprisingly warm hug with Carolyn, she felt she could chalk the day up as a success.

CHAPTER FIFTEEN

Jo had not long started out when Alan called. As ever, he didn't waste time with small talk, his voice echoing slightly over the Bluetooth speakers.

'Where are you?'

She looked around her at the anonymous dual carriageway. 'I don't know. I'm on the A-something heading for home. Oh, in Bournemouth,' she added, for context.

'Good. So am I. Macy said you were here. Have you got a few minutes? The thing is, I've managed to get into Shane Beaman's flat and I've no idea what I'm looking for.'

Jo slowed down so she could concentrate. 'Hold on. You've broken into a dead man's flat?'

'Not exactly, no, but let's not quibble about that. I've got limited time. I didn't expect to be this lucky but here I am and the poor bugger's got precious little stuff. So tell me, what am I looking for?'

Jo said the first thing that came to her mind. 'The missing quality assurance report. Or any connection with Flora. Some reason they were meeting up on Sundays. I mean, were they just friends, or what?'

'I don't think he was the type to keep a diary.' She could hear Alan moving furniture. 'Look, I could do with another pair of eyes on this. If I give you the postcode, could you come over? Bring gloves. I'll meet you in the pub car park.'

According to her satnav, Alan was only five minutes away but it could have been twenty miles from the detached residential properties on Belvedere Avenue. The satnav took her to a series of shabby streets of high brick terraces, which seemed to have no fronts, only backs facing outwards, revealing rusting fire escapes and multiple rubbish bins. She saw a young guy in a doorway keeling over to one side, and her conscience tugged at her. Should she stop? What could she realistically do? Perhaps Carolyn or her Upwards troops would have known.

The screen was flagging her to stop at a pub, which appeared to be boarded up. She passed an abandoned car with a 'Police Aware' sticker and heavily graffitied. Alan stepped out from behind it wearing a parka and woollen gloves, looking cold and harassed.

'Thank fuck you're here. I haven't the faintest clue what I'm looking for and I'm pretty sure the police have already taken anything decent. But I do know we've got to be out of there in forty-five minutes because that's when the decorator gets back from his break.' As he spoke, he led the way to a tall gate at the back of a more modern block of flats than the ones Jo had driven past.

'The decorator?'

'They're doing up the block where Beaman lived.'

They walked through a paved yard, which someone had tried to pretty up with metal tables and chairs and Alan opened the door into the flats. She followed him up the worn and stained staircase.

'I got a decorator to lend me his keys for an hour,' Alan explained. 'With a bit of persuasion involving cash, which I shall be claiming back on expenses. This place is council-owned so the workers come in and do a job-lot on all the flats.'

'It could do with it,' Jo commented. They reached the top floor and passed a door that looked like it had been jemmied.

Alan turned the Yale lock on number eleven next door. 'My brief from Macy is to find out as much as possible about Shane Beaman. In particular, why he was stabbed, split open and shoved in a lake.'

'Under a sign saying, "Reflect",' Jo reminded him. She stepped into a studio flat of mean dimensions and small windows. The kitchen consisted of a row of cheap white units along one wall with a blackened hob and a microwave. There was a low table in front of the sofa and a single bed crammed into an alcove at the back.

'I'm going to check the bathroom. Always the best place to find the dirt,' Alan said. He flicked on the light of the small, windowless room. A loud fan started up.

Left to herself, she looked around the small space and wondered what she was doing there. She had no idea who Shane Beaman was or why Flora had been so desperate to call him. It was a fact though that he was now dead and Flora was potentially fatally injured. She found she couldn't dismiss this and not care about it.

No one could call Beaman a hoarder, she mused and turned her attention to the sofa. She felt gingerly between the seats but only turned up the top of a beer bottle and a flattened crisp packet. There was no wardrobe. Beaman's clothes were squashed into a chest of drawers with pairs of jeans and trousers hung over a chair. She emptied the drawers and searched pockets carefully but found only a petrol receipt and another for a local One Stop shop. Small amounts, she noted.

'Why isn't this taped off as a crime scene?' Jo called out. She ran her hands over the bed, glad to be wearing gloves.

'Because they've been and gone days ago. That's why there's nothing personal here. He drove a motorbike and the police have that too,' Alan's voice boomed from the echoey bathroom. 'Did I tell you I went to see the woman who found the body? Her name is Meredith Winney and she lives on the army base by the lake. She's a fierce lady. She looked at me like she was going to stuff me in a pot. Like the fairy tale — what is it? Hansel and Gretel.' Jo heard him chuckling to himself while she peered under the bed.

Alan resumed his story. 'Until I made friends with her dog, that is. Lovely thing, dainty little springer spaniel called Cleo. It was the devil's own job getting onto the base as a visitor. Worth it, though.' He appeared in the bathroom doorway with the showerhead, unscrewed in his hand. 'Aren't you going to ask me what I found out from Mrs Winney?'

Jo, impressed with his thoroughness, redoubled her efforts and took down all the items on the shelf over the bed and laid them out on the thin grey duvet cover. She picked up a model of a motorbike, from which she learned precisely nothing, sighed and replaced it on the shelf. 'Go on then.'

'Beaman's body was stabbed first and then dumped in the lake during the hours of darkness on Sunday night. Mrs Winney could verify that because she was out shooting at first light Monday morning.'

'Shooting?' It was a sport Jo could never quite get her head around. 'Birds and deer and things?'

'Yes. You wouldn't want to pick a fight with Mrs Winney, I can tell you. She met her husband while on active service in Afghanistan. The bobbies are always more open with service people, so she found out quite a bit from the police.'

Jo was flicking through each of the books that Shane had on his shelf. There were a couple of well-thumbed bird-spotting guides. The rest were thrillers. Judging from the pencilled prices on the inside pages, they were charity shop buys and most of them seemed to be about violence on lone women. She supposed she couldn't infer much from this as most drama seemed to revolve around this. All the same, she found her nose wrinkling at some of the covers.

'Meredith — that's Mrs Winney to you — reckons it was a drugs-related killing,' Alan continued. 'She thinks kids have been using the car park at the visitor centre for drug exchanges. She'd reported that to the police.'

'Kids? Beaman wasn't a kid though,' Jo said. 'About thirty according to Macy.'

Alan came out into the main living room and gestured around the small space. 'No, but, living here, you could easily find yourself owing something to the wrong person. Sometimes all it takes with these feral drug gangs is to say something out of line.' He regarded the meagre cupboards and shelves. 'At least there's not much to search. Are you about done?'

'Wait.' Jo paused with her finger in one of the books. Something bright had caught her eye. A coloured stamp on the front page illustrated that this book was *From the Library of Flora Howell*. The name was inked in neat calligraphy. Jo turned the book over. It was a nature book with entries on wildlife for each day of the year, hardback and quite new. She held out the stamped page for Alan to see. 'Flora lent him a book. Or gave it to him,' she murmured.

'Or he took it,' Alan said. 'It's something, anyway. And it's better than what I've turned up, which is sweet FA. Stick it in your bag. No one's going to come looking for it now. And then let's go.' He moved briskly towards the door. 'I've got to get these keys back on the guy's truck.'

Jo dropped the book into her satchel and followed Alan down the narrow, grubby staircase. Thinking of the sparse possessions, the books on the shelf and the neat room, she wondered aloud how Shane Beaman had wound up living there.

'He'd been inside,' Alan said. 'So he was lucky to get a council-run place like this. There are a lot worse out there.'

Jo agreed but added it to the list of unanswered questions piling up in her mind about the dead man. She was struck once again that he and Flora came from different worlds.

'It wasn't a complete waste of time, I suppose,' Alan said. He stopped in the gateway at the end of the yard and sucked in air. 'What the fuck?' He trotted towards his car, parked where he'd left it behind the shuttered pub. Except now it had a flat front tyre.

'It's been slashed,' he yelled. 'Both front tyres. Who the—?' He wheeled around, taking in the back of the pub and the deserted, scruffy garden.

Jo was aware of a movement on the far side of the car. A woman dashed out from behind a wall, black jacket flying behind her. With a bare fist, she caught Alan on the face. He staggered back, shouting.

Jo ran forward. The woman rotated her shoulder and rammed a high kick into Alan's ribs. As he sprawled on the gravel, the woman's bright red hair and sharp chin turned in Jo's direction and she felt a glancing blow at the side of her head. Jo brought up her hands automatically and received a kick in the abdomen. She grabbed for the woman, but their attacker was away, twisting and racing around the corner, leaving Jo holding her bomber jacket.

'I'll — kill — the—' Winded, Alan brought his hand to his face, which was bleeding from under his left eye. Jo searched in her bag and handed him some tissues, which he took and then immediately flopped back onto the ground. 'Some — thing's — broken.'

Jo sank back against the car, holding her side. 'Should we call the police?'

'Are you kidding?' Alan gasped. 'We were breaking and entering. Call Macy.' He stopped struggling to sit up and lay back, holding a wad of tissues to his cheek. 'Tell him to get over here, and tell him I resign. Permanently. I'm too old for this shit.'

CHAPTER SIXTEEN

Alan got to his feet, weaving slightly. The next second, he plunged forward over the car. Jo almost dropped the phone as she sprang forward to steady him. She managed to stop him rolling back onto the ground just as two men rounded the corner. She heard their boots on the gravel as she wedged Alan's unconscious weight against the windscreen.

'What the fuck's going on here?' A bulky man with a muscle-bound gait pointed to her phone, which was lying on the car bonnet. 'Who's that you're calling? You can switch if off for a start.' He made a lunge for it, but Jo got there first.

'It's OK, it's off.' She held up the phone so they could see she'd ended the call. From a quick glance at him and his younger, thinner mate in their builders' boots and paint-stained clothes, Jo realized these must be the decorators, returning to the job and needing their keys. But before she could speak, the larger man thrust a scowling face into hers. 'I should have known he'd be trouble.' He jabbed a stubby finger towards Alan, who had slumped forward, bent oddly. 'But who the hell are you?'

Both men were standing too close. 'Back off,' Jo said, but her voice had a waver in it. She reached into the pocket of Alan's parka, located the keys and held them out. 'Here are your keys. My friend's been attacked and I'm calling an ambulance now.' She dialled 999 while they stood in front of her.

'Attacked? By who?' the younger man scoffed.

Jo ignored him and started giving the details to the ambulance service, and his boss jerked his head, indicating it was time to leave.

'All right,' he said. 'We won't hang around. We'll only get in the way. He might have had a heart attack.' The square red face in front of her registered something approaching concern. Or it could have been alarm. *He's probably heart attack material himself*, Jo thought, watching them leave with relief.

Thankfully the ambulance was as quick as they had promised and within ten minutes a paramedic was checking Alan's vital signs while the other questioned Jo. They soon had Alan seated on the ground, at which point he rallied enough to tell them he was fine, although his skin was still grey-white and the cut was bleeding steadily.

'You've been concussed,' the paramedic said as she prepared a wheelchair. 'So we will have to take you to A&E to be assessed.'

'Did you call Macy?' Alan asked and Jo assured him she had.

'I'll call him again and I'll come with you,' she said. 'I'll follow in my car,' she added to the paramedics.

'You will need to report the incident to the police.'

Jo nodded but was rescued by the ringing of her phone. She couldn't identify the number but knew it was significant. 'Sorry, I'll have to take this,' she said.

A well-modulated female voice spoke in her ear. 'Hello, this is Cheryl Frost of the Quality Assurance Agency. Is this Jo Hughes? I'm returning your call.'

It took Jo a moment to remember her call earlier that morning. What on earth had she been planning to say to the author of the missing report? She mumbled something about the training quality audit while Alan was wheeled into the ambulance. She smiled encouragingly and mouthed that she would see him at the hospital. He responded with a weak thumbs up. For once, he looked old. To her, Alan had always looked an indeterminate age. She remembered the message he'd told her to give Macy about wanting to resign for good. She didn't believe it for a second.

'You can't just request an audit,' Cheryl Frost was saying. 'It has to come through the proper channels.'

'Oh no, it's not that,' Jo said. 'Do you keep copies of past reports? I've read the one you wrote for Upwards, the training company I'm working with in Bournemouth but I've — er — lost it.' She continued with the call through the car speakers as she eased out of the alleyway behind the ambulance. She looked up and down the road but there was no sign of the decorators returning. Nor the high-kicking assailant.

'I can't release copies of past reports. They're confidential,' the woman said in the same calm, measured tone. 'But can't you ask for a copy from whoever gave you the report in the first place? Or they can send you relevant extracts. What work are you doing with them?'

Jo grasped at sudden inspiration. 'I'm helping with their birthday celebrations,' she said. 'Carolyn Ash has asked me to draw up the company's horoscope. I'm an astrologer,' she added, instantly feeling on more comfortable territory.

'An astrologer? That sounds highly innovative, I must say. That must be Carolyn's idea, I was always rather impressed with her as a bold entrepreneur.' There was a chuckle and a short pause. 'Actually, maybe I could help, if you could tell me a bit more?'

'Thank you, that would be brilliant. The report really would help me understand the company better.' Jo was starting to warm to this woman, who appeared, like her, to be an inveterate problem-solver. In front, the ambulance was signalling to turn into the hospital, which was not the same one where she had visited Flora.

'I got the report from Flora,' she said absently, her mind occupied by finding a space to park. 'And I'm sure she would help me out but she's — um — not well at the moment. Look, can I call you back? There's a lot going on here. Or maybe I could even come and see you?' Jo suggested. 'Your office is in Gloucester, isn't it? That's not far away, as I'm based in the Cotswolds.'

To her surprise, Cheryl Frost agreed, saying that if Jo could identify particular parts of the report, she might be able to provide extracts provided they were not 'commercially significant'. It was more than Jo had expected and she thanked Cheryl and raced into the hospital to find out where the ambulance had deposited Alan. She found the A&E queue, consisting of rows of chairs, but he wasn't among the people waiting.

Enquiring at the desk, she was told he was in triage so she sat near the back of the room and called Macy.

He was driving and sounded tense. 'I'm on my way. I've been trying to call you. What the hell's happened? There seemed to be some sort of fight going on when you rang off before.'

'Oh that was just the decorators. You missed the main event when Alan and I were attacked by a kick-boxer, who I think you may know.' She reeled off a brief account, keeping her voice low. 'Alan has a cut on his face that might need stitches,' she added. 'I think he might be getting that fixed now.'

'I'll be with you by three thirty. You can tell me all the details then.' His voice was taut. 'Don't let him go anywhere until I get there.' He took a breath and said in a gentler tone, 'And Jo, please can you stay with him till then? I know you need to get home but—'

'No problem,' Jo said as Alan emerged from the triage room with a wad of dressing on his face. 'Look, I'll have to go, see you later.'

'It looks worse than it is.' Alan had returned to his usual brusque cheeriness. 'What's really bad is they won't let me go yet. I need to see a doctor first. You don't have to wait though.'

'Don't be daft. I've already told Macy I'm staying till he gets here. He's on his way.'

Alan raised his eyebrows and instantly regretted it. He put a hand to his left cheek. 'Ow. Well, I am honoured, I must say, but there's no need. There's a lot for Macy to do.' He sat next to Jo, who soon became mesmerized, like most of the others in the queue, by the rolling electronic message board that announced the order of patients to be seen. Alan was logged as sixth in the queue.

'Not too bad,' he commented as if it was an exam result. 'If I'm still being assessed when he gets here, can you tell Macy what he needs to do?'

'Gladly. I'm looking forward to it already.'

Alan acknowledged this with a lopsided grin. 'I haven't told you the beautiful little nugget that Meredith Winney shared with me.' Jo waited and he went on. 'Beaman was covered in tattoos, which no doubt the police are looking at more closely.' His gaze followed the compelling countdown on the rolling display. 'Although that depends. If they can pin his death on the local drug dealers, then they may not bother.'

'What sort of tattoos?'

'Lots of plants and leaves and intricate shapes, apparently. Like sort of Victorian botanical engravings.'

'Sounds a bit Goth-influenced,' Jo suggested. 'Maybe Jess might have some ideas on those. She's a Goth, isn't she?'

'I suppose.' Alan looked unconvinced. 'But they were quite old tats. All except one, which Meredith Winney said looked new and was very prominent. It was inked below his heart.'

'Don't spin it out, Alan. You've got to go in a sec.' Jo pointed to the board, which showed he had moved up to number two. 'Just tell me what I've got to tell Macy.'

'OK, so Beaman's new tattoo was a large flower, a rose, according to Mrs Winney.' He looked at her for a second. 'Flower. Flora,' he said, as if stating the obvious.

'Maybe. But it could mean a lot of other things too.'

'I know that.' Alan was impatient. His name reached first in the queue and he was called into a curtained booth. 'It needs researching, obviously. Tell Macy to look it up — you know, meanings of names and roses, et cetera.'

Alan disappeared into the assessment room and Jo checked her phone for messages. Idly she looked up the meanings of girls' names and discovered that Flora was the goddess of flowers. There was indeed a rose called Flora but she still felt Alan was clutching at straws.

'Developing new theories?'

Macy sat down beside her and she took in his sudden presence: leather jacket, long legs, dark eyes — which always seemed to hold out a challenge. She felt herself smiling. 'All the time.'

'Well, I have some to test on you,' he said. 'But first, how is Alan?'

'He's being seen. He's had stitches in his face and now he has to have some sort of concussion assessment.'

'What the hell happened?'

'This mad woman, your friend, just came out of the blue at us. After we'd — er — visited Shane Beaman's flat.'

'Can I clear this up?' Macy interjected. 'I don't have any friends who are kick-boxers, OK?'

'I think you know this one. Slim, dyed red hair in a top-knot, very sporty and fit. Ankle bracelet and an ankle tattoo. Oh, and I've got her jacket. It's on the back seat of my car. It's got a label I don't recognize. Maybe Eastern European,' Jo said.

Macy still looked blank. 'You'd better tell me what happened exactly. What was this assault?'

'We were leaving Beaman's flat and Alan noticed his car tyres had been slashed. This woman leaped out from behind a wall, doing some fancy high kicks. He was winded and he must have hit his head.'

When Macy said nothing, she added, exasperated, 'I saw you with this woman at the Metropole my first night down here.'

'She's the least of our problems,' Macy said.

'Seriously?' Jo asked, incredulous. 'You know this woman, and she attacked us. I think you owe me and Alan an—'

'Look, I will explain, but right now it's Alan I'm worried about. I didn't ask him to go breaking into Beaman's flat. Thanks for making sure he got here and for staying.'

'Of course,' Jo said. 'And he's OK, honestly. He's stopped saying he's going to resign now anyway.'

This drew a smile. 'I haven't been entirely idle by the way.'

'Oh, is this the new theory you're going to test out on me?'

'Well, new information, which suggests a theory. What if I were to tell you that I know why Shane Beaman was in prison?'

Jo looked across at him and Macy went on. 'Beaman did two years of a three-year sentence for stalking.'

CHAPTER SEVENTEEN

Jo followed Macy's car to a low clifftop with an open space on one side and the coast path back towards Bournemouth, lined with Christmas lights, on the other. As she switched off the engine and watched Macy walk over to her car, she asked herself what she was doing there instead of driving homewards on the motorway. She didn't have a good answer.

The hospital had confirmed that they wanted to keep Alan in overnight. She and Macy had managed a short conversation with him, in which they had tried to keep him off the subject of the case. Macy had promised he would arrange a repair for Alan's car and drive him home tomorrow if needed.

'Jo will show me where your car is, won't you?' Alan had said and Jo had agreed. Instead of driving back to Beaman's flat, however, Macy had led her to the seafront.

'Thought we could do with some air after all that time in the hospital.'

'I'm not keen on those places,' Jo agreed. She stepped out of the car and shivered. 'But it is a pitch-dark winter night.'

'Well, I can't do anything about that, can I?' Macy said. If she had expected anything romantic from this late-night excursion, however, he quashed that notion with his next words. 'Have you got the jacket from the woman who attacked you?'

Jo reached into the back seat and produced it. They peered at it under a street light for a minute or two but, apart from the unusual, foreign label, it revealed nothing. Macy took it from her and dropped it into his car. 'I'll look at it more closely at the hotel. Come on, let's walk.' He indicated the path that led away from the town. 'Tell me everything you can about what happened to you and Alan first — everything you can remember. Then I'll answer all your questions about Beaman, the stalker.'

As they walked side by side, Jo gave as faithful an account of the assault as she could and Macy said very little. After a minute or two, she realized that she recognized this silence. 'You do know who it is, don't you?'

The path narrowed and dropped towards the beach and he went ahead of her. 'I don't know any more than you do.'

Jo watched Macy's broad shoulders and lean shape descending in front of her and didn't believe a word of this.

'I think you were right not to report it to the police in this instance though,' he said when they able to walk two abreast again. The sea rolled in steadily just below them and now their path was scattered with sand. 'Alan was mad to search Beaman's flat.'

'He just took the opportunity,' Jo said. 'You'd have done the same.'

'That I doubt. But I hope there is no real harm done and that he's OK in the morning.' He pointed to the lights of a bar on the rise of a headland. 'See that place? It does great cocktails.'

She looked at him, or as much as she could see of him, in the patchy light from the clifftop. She hoped her expression was suitably discouraging. 'I've got to drive home.'

'What if you didn't?' They both hesitated on the sandy embankment. 'No need, really. I've got an extra room at the hotel that you can have. I booked one for Alan. Can Hanni do without you tomorrow?'

'I'll have to call her.'

'Can you do that over a cocktail?'

'You're a very bad influence.'

The beach bar was not much more than a shack at the front with some patio heaters and wicker sofas, where people sat wrapped up in blankets. This façade was deceptive, however. Inside, it proved to be a long, narrow place, with rooms leading off one another, built into the hillside, it seemed. It was crammed with locals of all ages, some who were using this as a staging post on the way to the clubs, judging from all the glitz and flesh on display. Seeing a crowd squashed around a long table — a mix of different ages but all wearing work clothes — Jo guessed they were an office party. This made her think of the Upwards birthday party, which was less than a week away and for which she felt horribly underprepared. She pushed the thought to the back of her mind and left Macy to choose the cocktails while she went outside to call Hanni.

When she slipped back into the throng, she managed to find a couple of brightly coloured stools on a raised dais which gave her a good vantage point over the noisy crowd. It was not surprising, given the crush of people, that Macy took a while to fetch their cocktails. While she waited, she took out the wildlife book she had found in Shane Beaman's room. Knowing he had been a stalker made her feel differently about it. Maybe it had not been a gift from Flora, despite the elaborate sticker at the front. Maybe he had taken it. But, as she turned it over, she had to admit it seemed an innocent and attractive book. With its pretty hardback cover, it would have made a nice little present, she thought, noting it had an entry for each day of the year identifying what to look out for in nature.

She leafed through the pages, and noticed one was marked. Someone had underlined '14 September' in blotchy blue pen and added '2019'. She looked up, saw Macy threading his way towards her and set the book aside. He had selected something whisky-based with a delicious citrussy aftertaste and he had the same. 'It's the house special,' he explained and Jo nodded her approval after a couple of sips.

'Alan wanted me to pass on some more information about Shane Beaman,' she said. She recounted what she could remember about Alan's visit to Meredith Winney and what the woman had told him about discovering the body, including the new tattoo on Beaman's stomach.

'Is this Meredith Winney entirely trustworthy?' was Macy's first question. 'We've only got her account and her description of this tattoo.'

'She seems reliable. She's ex-army herself and her husband is still in the service. He works at the base. I think you could say she was a good witness.' Jo was enjoying the warmth of the cocktail after the night air. 'As for the tattoo, I'm not sure it tells us a lot. But Alan insisted I tell you. He thinks it stands for Flora.'

Macy looked out over the crowd and pursed his lips. 'If he's right, it would seem they had more than a business relationship. At least on Beaman's side, anyway. But, like you, I'm a bit wary of reading too much into it.'

'You need to tell me things now,' she said. 'What do you know about the offence that landed Beaman in prison? A pretty disgusting crime, too. Who was he stalking? They'd have a good motive to kill him, wouldn't they? Especially if they thought justice had not been done.'

Macy shook his head. 'We're not going to get that,' he said. 'I can find out about the offence but details on victims are impossible to unearth. Rightly so, I suppose. And, yes, two years doesn't seem very long from the victim's point of view. But there will be safeguards in the terms of his release to ensure he doesn't just start up again.'

'What I can't work out is how this loser had anything to do with Flora.' Jo opened the book she had found in his flat and showed Macy Flora's label in the front. She turned to the marked page. 'There are no other handwritten notes in the book. What's so important about that day?'

'The fourteenth of September? That's only a few months ago.'

'I know.' The photograph of the Upwards team standing in the park holding up a certificate came into Jo's mind. There was no obvious connection except for the turning colours of the trees in the background, but the image remained with her. 'He and Flora seem to come from completely different worlds but this shows they had some sort of connection.'

Macy read over her shoulder. 'You can see red squirrels on the Isle of Wight, apparently.'

'What's this? Literacy hour?' A woman's voice with an Eastern European accent rang out over their heads. Jo recognized the strong, jutting chin, the tied-back dyed red hair and wiry build, and she tensed and pushed back her stool, though she couldn't have said if she was going to run or sock the woman in the eye.

Below the table, Macy put her a steadying hand on her thigh. 'Agnieszka. How wonderfully predictable of you,' he said.

'I haven't just come to collect my jacket. I've come to remind you, we had an agreement. You need to get the fuck out of here.' She didn't raise her voice or change her stance but people nearby moved away slightly and one of the bar staff looked across at them.

'I know what you've come for,' Macy shot back. 'You don't want to attract the wrong attention, so why not go to the bar and get us both a cocktail. We're having house specials. My colleague, Jo, may accept that in lieu of an apology.'

'I might,' Jo said.

'As Alan, my other colleague, is in hospital, you'll have to work harder to apologize to him.'

'Don't be ridiculous, I didn't put him in hospital,' the woman hissed. 'And, as for you—' she jabbed her chin in Jo's direction — 'I hardly touched you.'

She turned on her heel and headed for the bar. A small path opened for her and she had no delay in getting served.

'You could have told me,' Jo muttered. 'What's the game plan now?'

'I like your assumption,' was all he said, his eyes on the crowd around the bar.

Agnieszka brought back two cocktails in record time although, judging from her expression, it would have been easy to believe she had spat in both of them. She dumped them on the table.

'You'll never get a job as a waitress,' Jo remarked, mopping the liquid with a spare napkin.

'Which is unfortunate, really, as you may need a job in hospitality soon if you lose your licence as a PI,' Macy said.

'My business will be very good, thank you very much, as soon as you piss off out of my way,' she snapped back.

'We're not staying around any longer than we need to.' Macy kept his voice low. 'But violence to my team will not get you what you want. When I report this, you will be off the register for good.'

'Do it.' She lifted her chin again. 'Only you won't. Because Louis wouldn't like the publicity. Louis Carswell is *my* client and the only reason he came to you is because he wanted someone to do a botch job. He knew I could never balls things up the way you have.'

'How does that make sense in anyone's world?' Macy demanded and, as she began to answer, he cut her off. 'Let's talk about the work you've done for Carswell, then. Raking up the muck on the previous CEO of Planet Events so Carswell could buy it cheap.'

'That man was a racist pig and deserved to lose his job.'

'The timing worked perfectly for Carswell though, didn't it?' Macy said. 'But it's your methods that I think the local papers may be interested in. Up to and including blackmailing the man's wife about her longstanding affair. When that goes public, Carswell will drop you like a hot brick.'

'Nice way you have of stealing someone's business.' The woman remained standing. She was no taller than Jo, but something about her posture spoke of her strength. And her readiness to use it.

'You've got me wrong. After this week, I won't work for Carswell again. He's all yours and my company will be delighted, believe me, to get back to the Midlands, where life is more civilized. So, you know I could report you.'

'If you say so.' Agnieszka seemed to have perfected the sneer as her facial expression of choice, but Jo could see she was wavering.

Macy pressed home his advantage. 'Meet me at the hospital tomorrow morning at nine. I'll have your jacket and you can apologize personally to Alan and tell me all you know about Carswell. After that, I will decide on what I'm going to do with my report about your assault on them.'

'Piss off,' she said and stalked out of the bar.

Macy picked up his drink and Jo was surprised to see his hand shaking slightly. 'She'll be there,' he said. 'She's made it known we were on her patch but I never thought she would go this far. Right now though, she's the one with more to lose.'

Jo nodded, although privately she had doubts. Her cocktail now tasted cold and sour and she pushed it away. Macy seemed to feel the same and tacitly they both got up to leave. On the patio, among those snuggled up in blankets, they both hesitated. Jo couldn't help looking nervously around. Macy said nothing but he took her hand and they stepped onto the path.

On the way back through a deeply wooded chine, they superstitiously avoided talking about Agnieszka as if it might conjure her up. Jo told Macy about the forthcoming Upwards birthday party. 'It seems to get increasingly elaborate,' she said. 'It's at Justin's film studio, so they are going to video the whole thing.'

'No pressure, then. You know, you don't have to go, as far as I'm concerned. I mean it this time. I'm finished with Carswell after this week. I'm going to hand everything we know to the police on Monday — including the surveillance job.'

'That will not make you popular with Carswell,' she said. 'About the birthday party, which is a sort of rerun of the Future Skills event: I'm committed to it now. I've also taken on the commission of the company astrology chart. It's good-quality work and Carolyn pays well.'

'As does Carswell. Planet Events is a thriving business but I'm not so sure that Upwards can afford this extravagant party, especially since they lost that big contract.'

'Carolyn would probably say you have to spend money to make money or something like that,' Jo said.

Macy seemed to know the way to the hotel and when they came to the clifftop and out in the open again, they decided to continue on foot. Clouds had rolled in from the sea, bringing no warmth, just dampness into the air. Jo could still taste the salt in it, and she filled her lungs after the short, steep climb. Something was preying on her mind about the encounter with Agnieszka.

'So, that woman, the local PI. What if what she was saying was true? I mean, not that Carswell wanted you to do a botch job,' she added. 'But, well, why did he employ you? Why not Agnieszka? He'd obviously used her before.'

'Er, because we're good,' Macy said.

They entered the hotel. It was functional rather than fancy but seemed to be well run. Macy dutifully picked up two key cards and handed her one. She pocketed it and they made their way along a low-lit, narrow corridor.

'I really do have to be home tomorrow,' Jo said. 'I've promised to cover for Hanni while she packs for the Christmas Festival, which starts on Friday. And I'm still trying to track down this stupid report, which I think was stolen,' she went on. 'I've got the author, a woman called Cheryl Frost, to say she'll meet me. I want to take her up on that as soon as possible.'

Macy stopped at Room 106. 'This is me.'

Jo waited for her head to clear and instinct to tell her what to do. It didn't happen. 'I suppose you and Rowanna are a thing now,' she said.

He nodded. 'I suppose you and Teddy are.'

'Yes. He's in Spain, running a golf tournament.'

'Of course he is.' Macy gave the flicker of an eye-roll.

Jo didn't know what to say to this, so she kissed him, rather awkwardly, and said goodnight. 'I enjoyed tonight,' she added, and sauntered off in the direction of her room.

CHAPTER EIGHTEEN

The memory that had bothered Jo during the stand-off with Agnieszka resurfaced in the night. She was restless in the smooth, enormous bed and the cold room and woke up with an image of herself with her laptop at the café table at the Rivermill, waiting for Hanni to arrive and the heating to warm up on a dark, early morning. A shadow had crossed the window and she'd looked up to see a small white van outside. That was the same day that Macy had turned up out of the blue. Later, after they'd eaten at the pub, a van had barged in front to get between her and Macy's cars.

Could Agnieszka be behind this? It could easily have been the same van, Jo decided, and it could have been a woman driving. It seemed dubious, especially as the unidentified van had preceded Macy's visit by several hours. But the woman had clearly been following Alan — Jo had witnessed that for herself. She turned the strange thought over in her mind. If her suspicion was right, it meant Agnieszka was keeping tabs on Macy's surveillance operation. Someone was following the followers.

She must tell Macy. But in the morning. Not now. She rolled over and looked at the clock. 3.41 a.m. Definitely not now. She turned over again and pulled the duvet over her head.

In the morning, there was a perfunctory breakfast in a room where large windows looked out onto steady rain. Macy was late and then spent most of the time on the phone trying to arrange recovery for Alan's car. He tried calling the hospital but he couldn't find out any news on Alan himself.

'You're as bad as Vinny,' Jo grumbled, spreading marmalade on her toast. 'The PR guy at Upwards. He's perpetually glued to his mobile.'

'I'm going to the hospital to see if Alan's going to be discharged,' Macy said.

'I know. You said you would meet Agnieszka there at nine,' Jo reminded him. 'About Agnieszka — what car does she drive?'

'A little Renault van.' Macy bolted his tea and got to his feet.

Jo dug into her satchel and pulled out the crumpled sheet of notepaper where she had jotted the registration. She handed it over to him wordlessly.

He regarded her. 'What's this?'

'I think she's been following you too,' Jo said. 'That van was at the Rivermill the day you came to see me there.'

He folded the piece of paper. 'This is going to be an interesting conversation. Look, I have to go. Thanks again.' He leaned over and his smooth cheek brushed hers. She had a rush of a familiar, warm scent of skin.

'Call me later,' he said. 'I'm going to make sure Alan gets home and then I'll be back here until Jess can take over.'

Jo had to stop herself from offering more help. With Alan out of action, she knew that Macy would be missing more than just a single team member. But, she reminded herself, she had her own business to run, plus her commitment to Hanni.

She smiled and waved and decided that on the drive home, she needed to have a word with herself. This PI business and Macy were part of her past. They were not in her plans to build up her astrology business. And then there was Teddy.

She looked at her phone guiltily. As expected, she'd had two messages and a missed call from him. She attended to these over a second slice of toast and marmalade. Fortunately, Teddy couldn't talk for long as he had a big tourney day but he did ask her if she'd booked flights yet. Jo talked about how busy she'd been. Her reflection looked back at her from the rain-drenched windowpane and she shook her head.

Using her phone to locate her car, she fought against gusts of rain as she trudged up the hill towards it. By this time, the flight to Spain was looking very appealing. Heater on full and windscreen wipers frenetic, she soon warmed up and drove north to the Cotswolds. She had arranged with Hanni to be at the Rivermill at 2 p.m., so she had time for a quick diversion to Cheryl Frost's office in Gloucester.

She had spent so long taxing her brain about the missing report that she was genuinely curious to meet its author. She felt sure that if she could manage to have an open conversation with her, the woman would give her some idea why the report was important enough for Flora to have taken it home in the first place and then for it to be the cause of the break-in at the Rivermill. Or she would establish that there was no connection. Either way, she was convinced that Cheryl Frost could answer a few troubling questions.

The weather was not very different in Gloucestershire except that the rain had a tinge of sleet in it. Cheryl Frost's office was on the wharfside at Gloucester Quays, where many former warehouses had been converted into flats or offices. And indeed restaurants, Jo noted, as she hurried past people having lunch, overlooking the water traffic. The Quality Assurance Agency was situated behind a particularly aromatic Italian place, the delicious smells reminding Jo gloomily of her meagre breakfast.

She followed a cobbled towpath alongside one of the former docks and almost walked past the doorway of the office, which was set into the side of one of the tall, narrow buildings. Jo wiped the rain off the list of occupants and pressed the intercom marked for QAA. The Agency shared its premises with four other companies, all of whom were equally mysterious, as they were also listed as acronyms. Even if she could just find out what QAA actually did, it would be a step forward.

Beside her, the intercom buzzed and the door unlocked. She stepped through into a dark concrete hallway with steep wooden open-tread stairs and felt she had cleared the first hurdle.

Through the slats in the staircase, she could see the sensible shoes and long pleated skirt of a woman making her way down. The woman leaned over the balustrade and peered down. Jo had the feeling of being under scrutiny from a pale, owlish face.

'You weren't expected.' The woman's voice was measured, self-confident.

Jo recognized it from the phone calls. 'We spoke yesterday on the phone,' she said brightly. 'I'm trying to trace a report you wrote for Upwards, the training company.'

'Yes, I remember, but you didn't say you were coming today.' There was a pause, during which they appraised each other through the stairwell. The woman sighed. 'You must be keen as it's such a filthy day. All right, it's my lunch hour so I can spare you a few minutes. You can come up.'

Jo bounded up the steep stairs, following the older woman to a door off the second-floor landing. Cheryl Frost's lanyard pass got them through into an orderly office space. She asked for Jo's contact details and noted them down in a book by the door. 'Antiquated, isn't it?' Cheryl gave an embarrassed laugh. 'But our systems aren't fully working because we're moving out.'

Jo looked around. Most desks were empty. A couple of women sat opposite each other at the far end of the room, staring at their computer screens.

Cheryl offered Jo a cup of tea and led the way to a small windowless kitchen, which was nevertheless better equipped than the one Jo had seen in Shane Beaman's flat. Watching her boil the kettle and find mugs, Jo judged that Cheryl was in her late fifties. She had short, styled grey hair and wore no make-up. All her actions were purposeful and her expression serious but not unfriendly. 'You're pretty determined, aren't you?' she commented after they'd exchanged some small talk about the weather. 'I don't know if I'm going to be able to help you very much, I should warn you.' She handed over a mug of tea. 'How is your astrology going? I had a look at your website after we spoke yesterday. I have to admit, it looks really professional — not my sort of thing, though,' she added.

'Thanks, glad you liked the website. Astrology is not for everyone,' Jo said easily. 'But I find most people can get something from it. When's your birthday?'

'The twenty-ninth of April, I'll be sixty next year. I'm Taurus.'

Jo smiled to herself. It always amused her that even people who had no time for astrology generally knew their Sun Sign. She took a seat beside Cheryl, noticing that, although there were two large screens on the desk, they were both displaying only screen savers. Jo guessed that Cheryl was the sort of woman who would keep all her work password protected, whatever it involved.

Jo decided to come straight to the point. 'What do you do here?' She waved a hand at the spacious office. The other two women across the room continued to work, apparently absorbed in their activities, but Jo reckoned they were close enough to overhear the conversation and tried to keep her voice low.

'We review various services to the government to make sure that the taxpayer is getting value for money and good service,' Cheryl said, 'including things like apprenticeships. That's how I came into contact with Upwards. How did you come across them?'

'Carolyn Ash asked me to draw up a birth chart for the company as it is ten years old next week. It's part of an event where they envisage the future — they've got a futurologist and some business and climate strategists there. I think I'm the light relief.'

'Sounds interesting. Carolyn has a good eye for publicity. She does what she can to help small businesses, I will say that for her. Of course, she herself has thrived despite tough odds, did you know that?'

'Yes, she talked about it at the Future Skills event I attended. She has invited local apprentices to Upwards's birthday party, which is a sort of rerun of the same thing, but they'll get a chance to ask us questions, I think. Did you find in your report that Upwards did a good job with training apprentices and the like?'

'I can't comment on the substance of the report. And in any case, you know what's in it. You said you'd read it.' Cheryl Frost had a way of twisting her neck with a quizzical expression as if she doubted everything that was being said.

'I did.' Jo was relieved to be able to answer this honestly. 'And I couldn't find anything remotely controversial in it. It was pretty positive, in fact. But I — er — just wanted a more thorough read of it.'

Cheryl sent her a challenging look and began a steady series of questions, laying them out like a poker player setting out a good hand. 'How long have you been working with Upwards?'

'Oh, a couple of weeks—'

'How did they get to hear about you? It's quite a specialized service you offer. Was it a recommendation?'

'Through a — er — friend. Well, more of a former colleague, who was working for a company associated with Upwards.' Jo could hear herself floundering slightly.

'Associated?'

'They've just taken over the training company—'

'Planet Events. Louis Carswell?' Cheryl raised a querying eyebrow and, when Jo nodded, she went on. 'So your friend and former colleague was working for Louis Carswell and recommended you for this rather unusual gig?' She smoothed her skirt over her lap and waited.

'Yes, that's about it. And I came by your report when I was trying to get some background on the company. Flora had a copy of it.' Jo trod carefully around the boundaries of truth and omission. 'It seemed to be a sort of audit?'

'Yes, in a way. In the case of Upwards, they asked us for a report as part of their due diligence to help with the sale of the business.'

'It also probably helped them retain their Ofsted rating,' Jo said, thinking of the framed photograph in the Upwards office with Flora standing awkwardly in her corporate clothes while her colleagues were in the middle of a game of rounders.

'I can't comment on that,' Cheryl said. 'It would be reasonable to assume it did not do them any harm.' The woman had finished her mug of tea and shifted in her chair. 'Does this tell you all you need to know? I fail to see how any of this pertains to astrology.'

The statement hung in the air while the two women eyed each other. As Jo's dark eyes met the other woman's steadfast blue gaze, she felt she had been rumbled. She licked her lips. 'Yes, well, it hasn't got anything to do with astrology. It's more to do with Flora, really. Do you know Flora Howell? Carolyn's business manager?'

'It was Flora I mainly dealt with. Although, of course, I interviewed all the key people in Upwards. I always found Flora very helpful. If you want another copy of the report, why not ask her?'

'I would have, but she's in hospital. That's why I came to you.' Jo explained briefly about Flora's accident while the other woman's gaze skewered her with the force of her attention. It was very hard to tell if the accident was news to her or not.

'I assume the police are investigating the accident?'

Jo assured her that they were. 'The thing is, before Flora set out, she was really agitated. She was worried about a friend who had gone missing. And since then, the report has . . . disappeared. So I wondered—' Jo was about to wade deeper into her explanation when the woman opposite shook her head slightly but distinctly. This was followed by a swift glance across the room to where the other two women were working.

'I'm sorry, I've already said I can't discuss the content of the report with a third party. I thought I'd made that clear. There is no more I can tell you.' She got to her feet and Jo followed, thanking her politely for the tea and aware that she was now part of some sort of unspoken collusion with the woman. She allowed Cheryl to lead her to the door and buzz them through to the landing.

'I can't talk about this here.' Cheryl handed Jo a phone number jotted on a Post-it. 'Can you call me this evening? And tell me how Flora is.'

'It's not good, I'm afraid.' It was only fair to warn her in advance, Jo thought. 'She has serious spinal injuries and they can't operate yet.'

Cheryl nodded. Her expression didn't alter but her voice was grave. 'You will call me, won't you?'

Jo promised she would. As she made her way down the stairs, she wondered why this conscientious older woman was so concerned about Flora and, more importantly, why she was so keen to keep her interest a secret.

CHAPTER NINETEEN

The detour to Gloucester meant that Jo was a few minutes late arriving at the Rivermill. Just as she was locking her car, Macy rang. She picked up his call as she hurried past the Christmas tree, which was swaying alarmingly in the wind.

'Are you home yet?' he demanded.

'Just got to the bookshop. How is Alan?'

'The hospital discharged him, but he of course wanted to dive straight into work. He was on about analysing the tattoos found on Beaman's body. I told him the police will be following that up, although I'm not sure they will go into it that deeply if they think it's a gang-related death. Anyway, I put him on a train home.'

'Listen, there is something I wanted to ask you,' Jo said and then interrupted herself. 'You put him on a train? I thought you were going to drive him home?'

'I was, but the police called. They want to interview me about Flora's accident. That's where I am now. I'm calling you from Bournemouth Police station. Alan was OK, anyway,' he added a little defensively. 'He can get a cab from the station and his car is being sorted. I was wondering if you could do me a favour.'

'Another one?'

'I know. But this is really about Alan. He doesn't live far from hippy town so I wondered if you could pop in and see him sometime? Just check he's OK? I need to wrap things up with Carswell, but there are a few things I have to do first, which means I have to be here all weekend.'

Jo was outside the bookshop now and could see Hanni talking to a group of people in the café. 'I don't think I can,' she said. 'Have you forgotten? The Christmas Festival starts tomorrow so I'll be on the stall with Hanni. We've rented a van to take the stock down tomorrow morning. In fact, I think she's just arranging the cover.' She peered in through the glass. 'I've got to go.'

'OK, I'll ask Jess to go and see him. They can discuss tattoos. What was it you wanted to ask me?'

Jo had her hand on the shop door. 'Oh, yes. You know Agnieszka wants to get rid of you? Do you think that's the reason she was keeping tabs on you for a while?'

'Of course.' Macy sounded impatient. 'I'd do the same. If I was operating in a small town and needed the business, that is.'

'If it really was her in the van that stopped outside the Rivermill the day you came to see me, how could she have known you were coming?'

'All I do is drive up and down the M5, it's really not that interesting. But I drove by the Rivermill early that morning because it's not that easy to find, is it? I had no time to stop then so dropped in on my way home. I was after some cake, if I recall.'

'Then I am even more certain she followed you here. And out of the pub in the evening.'

'I'm surprised Agnieszka has the resources for that sort of thing. I've been wondering if Carswell was paying her too, although she wasn't admitting that this morning. Anyway, if you thought I was being followed that night, why the hell didn't you tell me?'

'It only occurred to me after Agnieszka told us how paranoid Carswell is. And I didn't know then what nastiness you were dragging me into,' Jo retorted.

'Thanks, I'll keep my wits about me. Look, I'll see you at the Festival and I'll bring my stalker.'

Jo had to hide her smile at this and went in to the café, apologetically interrupting Hanni's briefing to her temporary team. To cover the weekend, Hanni had recruited her mother, who was eating her way through a catering pack of biscuits, her younger sister, April, who was studiously taking notes, and her business partner, Chloe, whose baby was due on Sunday.

'I've asked the baby to hang on for a day or so.' Chloe hugged Jo in greeting. 'Thanks for looking after the café for me.'

They were all grouped around one of the tables for Hanni's unusual but comprehensive instructions. 'I want the shop to be imbued with the spirit of abundance, generosity and light, reflecting the festival of Saturnalia—'

'Oh good, we can have Christmas music on,' Hanni's mum said. 'It's dead in here, it needs a bit of music.'

'No Christmas music,' Hanni said. 'We want to bring in Spirit energy, not Walt Disney.'

'But you've got a tree,' her mum pointed out.

'The tree is also a pagan symbol of light and regeneration,' Hanni responded while April looked from each to the other from under a cloud of Pre-Raphaelite curls and a knitted brow.

'Maybe you could have the radio on in the kitchen,' she consoled her mother. Hanni sighed and looked across at Jo for assistance.

'The most important thing is to sell as many books, cakes and coffees as you can,' Jo advised. 'We will be doing the same in Bournemouth.'

'Thankfully, it's only three days,' Hanni said, 'with an early close on Sunday. We'll be back Monday.'

Chloe stayed to serve in the café while Jo helped Hanni finish packing the van ready for the drive to Bournemouth the following morning. They sat down together over coffee and cake to go through their plans while April took over at the bookshop counter. Jo had to stop Hanni getting up to help when April struggled with taking a debit card payment.

Hanni took a deep, steadying breath. 'I've never done anything like this before, Jo.'

'We'll be fine,' Jo said and she believed it. On her way home, however, driving up the short, steep hill to her flat, she remembered the atmosphere of mistrust that infected the people she had met in Bournemouth and she was not so certain. Louis Carswell's intense paranoia had clearly rubbed off on the vengeful Agnieszka. There was something about Flora that had provoked suspicion. Even an apparently ordinary woman like Cheryl Frost had not wanted anyone else to know she was interested in Flora. *Why all the secrecy?* she wondered. *What were they all so frightened of?*

Cheryl had said to call after 5 p.m. but it was well after six by the time Jo had returned to her flat, fed the cat and rooted out a freezer meal for herself. With a fish pie in the oven and a milky coffee in her hand, she sat down at her desk to make the call. Cheryl's voice, when she picked up, sounded cautious and when Jo reminded her who she was, the caution remained.

'Yes, I thought you would call. You seemed the type who wouldn't give up easily. I couldn't answer those questions in the office, as I'm sure you understand.'

Jo was tempted to admit that she actually didn't understand anything very much but decided to stay silent.

'I can't promise to answer them now,' continued Cheryl. 'But I need full disclosure from you before I say anything and I need you to start by telling me how Flora is and what you know about her.'

'We both need to be open with each other then.' Jo put down her coffee and gazed up at the darkened arched window over her desk. She had to make a judgement about what to tell Cheryl Frost and there was no time to discuss this with Macy. Which was awkward, because they were his secrets she would be sharing.

'I can tell you about my role and my dealings with Flora,' she said eventually. 'I'm an astrologer, like I said, and have been asked to take part in the birthday celebrations for Upwards on Monday. I met Flora at an event about Future Skills, which turned out to be a sort of dress rehearsal. The day after I met her, she was knocked off her bike in Bournemouth town centre. It was a hit-and-run.'

'How is she?'

Jo gave the latest on Flora's condition and explained that the police were investigating the accident. She was conscious that on both subjects, her information was superficial and she didn't think this would go down well with Cheryl, who seemed a very thorough and authoritative sort of person.

'I'll call the hospital tomorrow, although I don't suppose they will tell me much as I'm not family. Now tell me,' Cheryl said, 'why are you concerned about Flora?'

'All right, this is where it gets complicated. I was asked to keep an eye on Flora by a friend who thought she might be in trouble.' Jo had wanted to avoid bringing Macy or Carswell and the whole surveillance operation into it. However, as soon as the words were out of her mouth, she knew they wouldn't be enough.

There was a disbelieving silence on the other end of the phone. 'Does this "friend" work for Planet Events or Upwards by any chance?'

'He's working for Louis Carswell. But I'm not.' Jo felt the need to distance herself from Carswell. 'I'm just helping my friend out.'

'And do you believe Flora had an accident?'

'I'm not sure — but I do think she was in some sort of trouble.' She found herself wanting to be as honest as possible with Cheryl. 'Who would want to do that? And why? I thought you might be able to help. Was there something I missed in the report you wrote on Upwards? Did you uncover something that Carswell would want to keep under wraps?'

There was nothing forthcoming from the other end of the phone for some moments.

'I'm not prepared to talk about that now and certainly not on the phone,' Cheryl said at last. 'I don't even know who you are really, do I? Or what your intentions are. Let me think it over and maybe talk to Flora, if they'll let me, and then we can meet up — at the weekend, maybe. Not at the office though. Don't come to the office again.'

'The thing is, I'm in Bournemouth until Tuesday,' Jo began. She looked at the clock on her plain, painted work-room wall. If Cheryl worked in Gloucester, surely she couldn't live that far away? She had to grab this moment. 'What if I came to see you now? You're not at work now, are you? And face to face, we really will both be able to talk freely. I think then we will both know what to do next.'

To Jo's surprise, there was a chuckle on the other end of the line. 'I am working actually,' Cheryl said. 'I'm working at what I love doing most and yes, you could come over if you wanted. I'll be in my workshop, which is behind my house in Uley.'

'Workshop?' Jo echoed while she hurriedly searched on her laptop for directions.

'Yes, that's why I'm so interested in what you've done,' Cheryl said. 'I want to work for myself like you do, set up a business by myself. I upcycle furniture in my spare time, but obviously that is limited because of my job at the QAA. So I can only take on a couple of pieces at a time. But when I leave — I've just accepted their redundancy offer, you see,' she added. 'I told you we were closing, didn't I? There's only a handful of us left now and we're just winding down our cases. Then I'll be free to do my own creative thing. Like you do.'

Jo smiled. 'I wish I'd taken redundancy to do it. Instead I just walked out of my job about six years ago. I don't think my mother has forgiven me yet. No husband, no mortgage, no grandkids and no proper job either. It's lucky for me that my sister is doing all that stuff.'

'Well, I admire you,' Cheryl said. 'And I expect Carolyn does too or she wouldn't be putting business your way. She likes to do that — especially for entrepreneurial women. She's shown an interest in my little enterprise, came up to see my set-up and has even talked about investing when the time is right.' She sighed. 'My problem is, I'm nearly sixty now and I wish I'd done it years ago. I'm worried I've left it too late.'

'It's never too late,' Jo said. 'Talking of which, I can be with you by seven thirty, is that OK?'

'All right.' Cheryl's voice became cautious again. 'But I need to know you're on Flora's side in all this.'

Jo hesitated. 'I'm not sure as I didn't know she had a "side". But I can promise you, I don't mean her any harm.'

This seemed to suffice as the woman gave her directions and explained how to reach the workshop at the back of her house. Jo switched off the oven, abandoned her pie and the cat, and grabbed a packet of wafer biscuits as she headed for the door.

The short drive took her across the back of the common and out of the narrow lanes onto the high, flat open land, which was turning silver with frost, then quickly back down into the valleys again. With the risk of ice, she paid attention to her driving, especially on the twisty route into the long, stretching village of Uley. Cheryl's house was on the road towards Gloucester and, before she reached it, Jo passed a line of similar houses, driving slowly to read the names and numbers. Number 139 was a plain double-fronted bungalow, standing in its own little plot of land.

Jo parked across the drive. Behind low, double gates, she could see a small car parked in the driveway. There were no lights showing in the house and only a porch light in the brick archway over the front door. Although Cheryl had never said so, Jo had gained the impression that the woman lived alone and, walking past the silent bungalow, she congratulated herself that she had guessed right.

Exactly as Cheryl had described, the workshop was in an old-fashioned detached garage standing a long way back from the house. Only as Jo approached it from the unlit drive did she start to notice her heightened heartbeat. She had closed the gate behind her and the plastered wall of the bungalow loomed to her right, with a dense, thorny hedge on her left. It took only a few seconds for her to feel suddenly vulnerable and alert. She fumbled for the torch on her phone, keeping her eyes fixed on the thin slits of light showing from under the garage doors.

Reaching the workshop in half a dozen fast strides, she rapped on the wooden door and called out Cheryl's name at the same time. She looked up at the stars and the frosty, green-hazed moon while she waited for a response. When she was met with silence, she banged harder on the door until it rattled and shouted Cheryl's name, half-hoping a neighbour would hear. Again, nothing.

When she tried the handle, one of the doors opened easily and light flooded out. Then the smell hit her throat. It was acidic and almost sweet in her nostrils, but it seemed to close off her airways as she inhaled. She gasped and stepped back.

Lying over a workbench, Cheryl was bent double, like an old doll, her grey head flopped almost onto the floor. One hand, which had been holding sandpaper, dangled onto the tiles. The other arm was tucked underneath her body. A cupboard door jutted out from under her at an angle and a metal bottle dripped colourless liquid from the bench onto the floor.

Jo crooked her arm over her nose and clamped her mouth shut and took a step or two inside. Her eyes streamed instantly from the harsh chemical smell. Dizzy, she grabbed at the door handle and it swung unreliably away from her as she reeled backwards, throwing her head back to gulp the night air.

Icy burning compressed her chest, pressing down on her like strong, flat hands and another cold force seemed to push her throat inwards. She found a garden bench with her fingers and gripped it, trying to catch her breath and pull herself onto the seat. A searing pain streaked behind her eyes and still her lungs couldn't get any air.

She located her phone with a fumbling hand and dialled 999.

'There's a woman, Cheryl Frost. Lives in Uley,' she croaked. 'She's collapsed and I can't get to her.'

CHAPTER TWENTY

Jo couldn't understand why she didn't feel cold. She was outdoors and it was night-time. There were stars overhead, oddly close. All she could see was a strangely tilting night sky. She clutched at blades of grass to stop herself falling off the planet.

It should be colder than this. It bothered her. Except in those sick moments when nothing bothered her except clinging onto the ground.

Someone was speaking to her now but she paid them no attention. The woman's voice was just an irritation that distracted her from her main job, which was holding on. The harsh voice called her name and someone started pummelling her, gloved hands reaching into her coat. She couldn't even fight back. She had to allow herself to be wrapped and plastic clips attached to her skin. Still they kept on with her name. Jo found it helpful if she closed her eyes.

All around her the gravel was scrunching and churning and there was a background crackle of electronic hissing and muffled words. She identified two male voices as well as the woman's voice.

'Jo Hughes. Jo, Jo. Can you talk to us?' One of the men was stooping over her. A face covered the sick-making stars.

It was a round, baggy-eyed, wrinkled face and she decided she liked it very much. She wanted to make an effort for it.

'Yes,' she croaked. After that, all she did for the next four hours was answer questions. At first the questions were simple and mainly concerned with how she felt and what she could physically do. Sitting upright and swigs of water from a plastic bottle helped at this stage. Gradually the questions became more complicated until she was being asked if she understood that she was being taken for questioning to Gloucester Police station and did she want to call anyone? By then, Jo was in yet another hospital, sitting on yet another hard plastic chair. The kindly-looking PC was the person to explain to her that the questioning was just a formality because she was a key witness to a death, which they had to treat as suspicious.

'If you give me the keys to your car, we'll have someone pick it up and bring it to the station,' he said, 'so you'll be able to drive home later. He glanced up at the nurse. 'She's all right to drive, is she?'

'Yes, breathing and blood pressure is fine now.' The nurse smiled at Jo. 'You're good to go.'

Jo still felt heady when she stood up to follow the uniformed PC. She could recall everything up to making the 999 call. However, her brain still didn't feel fully functional and so she decided it was best to remain quiet and follow orders. Her first instinct was to call Macy but she decided to wait until she felt more coherent. She took heart from the mention of driving home later. She would make her calls then.

At the police station, they gave her a plastic cup of coffee and a jug of water and left her to herself in an interview room for about half an hour. Jo was glad of the time to try to come to terms with what she had seen. How could Cheryl be dead? Cheryl, who had been lively and full of optimism at seven o'clock when they'd talked on the phone. Less than an hour later, the woman was dead.

Jo sipped the revolting coffee, which oddly seemed to quell the insistent banging in her head, and went over in meticulous detail what had happened leading up to making that emergency call.

The image of Cheryl's body, clad in overalls and flopped over the workbench kept interfering with her careful mental reconstruction, every detail bright under the workshop spotlights. She shook her head and cupped her face in her hands. As soon as she closed her eyes, she saw the scene from the garage doorway and Cheryl's body. Her first thought had been: heart attack. But instantly the choking, acidic smell had reached her. The fumes must have caused Cheryl to lose consciousness. She remembered a metal canister lying on the bench, upended with clear liquid running out of it. What had Cheryl been using that could have been so toxic? On the face of it, she had knocked over a whole bottle of it and then been overcome.

If Jo had hoped for more light to be thrown on what had actually happened when the police finally arrived to question her, she was to be disappointed.

DCI Conway introduced himself as the senior investigating officer, a black man, soberly suited, tall and grave with a trace of a London accent. The DS with him, DS Brookes, was the harsh-voiced woman who had tried to rouse her when she'd been lying on the ground. Face to face across the table, she actually seemed quite friendly, unlike her boss. She was older than the DCI, probably in her fifties with reddened cheeks and sandy hair. 'Feeling better?' she asked.

'Yes, thanks.' Her voice still sounded hoarse. Her instinct was to say as little as possible until she could figure it all out but, at the same time, she knew that if she had phoned Macy, he would have encouraged her to be open with the police. This would mean telling them about Louis Carswell and the surveillance on Flora. Jo sighed inwardly. She could be here hours if she told the whole story, she thought, and reverted to her instinct.

'How did you come to be at Cheryl Frost's house this evening?' DCI Conway opened the questioning.

'I had met her earlier in the day. I went to her office to find out about a report she had written on a training company I'm working with. She didn't want to talk about it in the office but she gave me her phone number and said I could call her. So I did and we ended by agreeing to meet up.'

'On an icy night? At her house?' DCI Conway had wonderfully expressive eyebrows. Jo agreed it sounded odd but, yes, she had wanted to see Cheryl as soon as possible so she'd offered to drive over. DS Brookes scribbled avidly in her notebook.

'Tell me about this report,' the DCI went on. 'What was in it and why were you interested in it?'

Jo took a breath. She stuck to the version of events she had given Cheryl, which meant omitting Carswell and the surveillance operation, although she knew this might be unwise. She started with Flora's accident, adding that it was being investigated by Bournemouth Police.

'We'll talk to them, of course,' DCI Conway said. 'It seems a whole lot of trouble for you to go to just to get hold of a report.'

'I felt bad I'd lost it and Cheryl didn't want to talk about it in the office. When I phoned her, we both agreed to be open with each other. That's why I went over there.'

'Remarkably conscientious of you.'

Although the officers said little, their scepticism about her account was palpable. As the minutes of intensive questioning dragged on, Jo began to see the sense of Macy's policy of not holding anything back from the police. Although he didn't always stick to this himself.

DCI Conway had taken down Macy's details and said he would be calling him so this policy would be tested again soon, she noted. She was relieved when they changed tack and questioned her about her arrival at the workshop, the timings and what she had seen and done.

After about half an hour on this, they called a break and Jo told them she was expecting to drive to Bournemouth with a van full of books in the morning. This didn't go down well with DCI Conway, who said they would want to go over her statement and would rather she remained local.

Jo used the time to call Hanni and briefly explain. Hanni took the news in her stride and simply asked if she could do anything to help. Jo nearly gave way to tears at that point but said there was nothing her friend could do and she would be in Bournemouth as soon as she could.

Thankfully, the interview didn't continue much longer after the break. Maybe her commitment to return at 9 a.m. was sufficient, Jo mused, as DS Brookes signed her out unsmilingly. The uniformed PC was around to hand over her car keys and suddenly she was standing on the steps outside, shivering with relief and shock.

It was 11.05 p.m. when she drove away. The first thing she did was to call Macy to warn him.

'I didn't tell the police everything,' she said when she had summed up her evening. 'But I told them about Flora, so they might find out about the surveillance. I said you were a friend who had got me an invitation to the Future Skills event.'

'I'll expect their call,' Macy said.

'I can't believe it, Macy. This must be some massive cover-up if it's worth killing both Beaman and Cheryl. She knew something though. Cheryl knew something about Flora. She was very concerned about her.'

'Look, stop thinking about it now,' he advised. 'Go home, get some sleep. I'll go and see Carswell in the morning so he is forewarned too. And if you need any advice tomorrow, I'll send you the number of a good solicitor.'

'Thanks,' Jo said drily. 'That makes me feel a lot better.'

The next morning proved just as gruelling but not so bad that Jo needed to call on Macy's solicitor. DCI Conway and DS Brookes patiently went through their questions again and particularly pressed her on her reason for meeting up with Cheryl Frost and the missing QAA report, about which they seemed equally sceptical.

'When the Rivermill Bookshop and Café was burgled, did you list this report among the missing items?' DS Brookes asked with the air of one who already knows the answer to her question.

Jo admitted she hadn't and that she hadn't realized it was lost until after the police had left.

'Did you mention it to the proprietor, Ms Hanni Light?' the sergeant continued.

'No, I didn't want to worry her,' Jo said, unnerved that she was starting to doubt her own story. The interview had been going for an hour and a half, her head and chest were still sore and her own words had begun to sound meaningless. Maybe DCI Conway sensed this, as he looked at his chunky wristwatch and called a break. Today she had found out his name was Chris and he had even unbent enough to tell her that ingesting the paint remover fumes was the most likely cause of Cheryl's death. He fetched her a coffee in a proper mug, for which she felt unreasonably grateful and she drank it while she waited for the officers to return.

It was 11 a.m. and she was due to be in Bournemouth by now, unpacking books and, later, attending a rehearsal for the Futures event with Carolyn her team. She had called Carolyn that morning and made up an excuse about 'urgent family business'. Carolyn's response had been polite but distant. 'That's a shame. I thought you were here to attend the Christmas Festival too?'

'Yes, I'm missing that at the moment too,' Jo had said. 'Look, I will be there sometime today and I'll let you know.' This had to suffice for Carolyn because she had no intention of telling her about Cheryl Frost's death. She supposed it would become public knowledge soon enough and wondered how Macy's meeting with Carswell was going. She didn't envy him.

When Conway and Brookes reappeared, equipped for another session with notebooks and coffees, Jo wondered if she was going to need Macy's solicitor after all. Her stomach clenched at the thought and she took some deep breaths as the questioning began again. After another hour or so, it became obvious that the two police officers had nothing new to ask and Jo had nothing new to tell them and so, after another short break, they presented her with a comprehensive statement.

'If you get in touch with the Dorset police, they can tell you all about Flora's accident and Shane Beaman's death,' Jo said after she had signed it. 'They will know far more than I do.' By then, she had her coat on and was standing by the door ready to leave, which had increased her confidence.

'Thank you.' DCI Conway graced her with one of his lifted-eyebrow stares. 'You can rest assured that we have already contacted them and we will be talking to David Macy too.'

This time, Jo didn't even bother to take a moment on the police station steps to savour her sense of release. She got straight in her car and set out for Bournemouth. She had packed her bag the night before, which was just as well, because had she returned to her flat, she might have felt tempted to fall into bed and not emerge for a few days. It wasn't just her chest and throat that felt battered and bruised. Her headache remained, despite consuming regular doses of aspirin and seemed to echo the confusion in her brain. She was still grappling with the fact that Cheryl had died within minutes of their last conversation. This meant the murderer must have known her movements and habits. Maybe they even knew about Jo's involvement?

Jo glanced in her rear-view mirror. Everyone in this case seemed to mistrust one another. Maybe Louis Carswell's need to have everyone under surveillance, especially his employees, was getting to her. There was nothing to be seen in her mirror except lines of other cars heading south but she couldn't shake the unsafe feeling. *Paranoia is infectious*, she thought.

When she arrived at the exhibition centre, the Christmas Festival was in full swing. Jo picked up her exhibitor's pass and found the Rivermill Bookshop stand at a good site at the top of an aisle and complete with mini sofa, coffee and cake, exactly as she and Hanni had planned. She stood back for a moment or two, realizing with some satisfaction that customers were browsing the shelves and Hanni was busy at the till. She noticed in surprise that Liang from Upwards was restocking the shelves. Liang saw her at the same moment and gave her a quick wave.

'Carolyn knew you were delayed so she asked me and Bex to come over to help. Bex has been here all morning, but I've only just arrived. She's refilling the coffee pot — there are some kitchens over there.' Liang indicated vaguely.

'That's brilliant, thank you,' Jo said, momentarily overwhelmed. 'I must find Carolyn and say thanks in person.'

Hanni, unusually flushed, was still busy serving and looked at Jo wide-eyed. 'It's full on. Thank goodness you're here. Could you open up the other till?' After that, they hardly had time to exchange a word until there was a brief lull later in the afternoon.

'I can't believe it,' Hanni said. 'You've brought us true abundance, Josephine.'

'It's mainly down to Macy, really.' She was reluctant to give Carswell any credit as she didn't want to have to feel grateful to him.

'Oh, he's been here too.'

Jo looked up sharply as Hanni went on. 'Your friend Macy brought Bex over and helped unpack the van. He asked me to call him David, by the way, but you don't, do you?'

'He's always been Macy to me,' Jo said with a shrug.

'Well, he's been amazing, and it was very good of Carolyn to send the extra help. I'm not sure we would have been ready on time without Macy and the others. But how are you, Josephine? You've had an ordeal, haven't you? It's shaken your usual equilibrium.'

'I'll tell all later, but I'm sorry I wasn't here to help. The police in Gloucester were hard work, I can tell you. Look, I need to apologize properly to Carolyn too. I missed her rehearsal for the birthday party. Can you manage without me for a while? I might just catch her at the office if I go now.'

'Yes, you must. They say this is the quiet time when people are travelling back from work. Apparently, it gets busy again between seven and eight o' clock.'

Jo assured her she would be back by then. She knew the Upwards office was only a few blocks away but there was a soaking, drizzly mist in the air so she took her car. It was past five thirty but she was pretty sure she would find Carolyn still at work. Her punt turned out to be a lucky one as Carolyn was clearly visible working at her desk, the blinds raised and the light blazing out across the dark car park. The rest of the office was deserted with no one at reception. The large greetings card for Flora remained open on her desk in the corner. Clearly no one had yet been to the hospital deliver it.

Jo glanced up at the framed photograph on her way through to Carolyn's office. Although only taken in the autumn, it struck Jo that it represented Carolyn and Flora and the team in happier times. *What went wrong?* she wondered. She felt a tingle of anticipation mixed with apprehension at the sudden sense that if she could answer this question, she would uncover what was hidden and understand all the secrecy.

Rehearsing her little speech of thanks, Jo knocked softly on Carolyn's office door and turned the handle. It was immediately obvious that Carolyn had been crying. Her eyes were puffy and the tip of her nose red, although she put on a bright and welcoming expression. 'Jo, you made it. How's the family? Everything sorted?'

Jo quickly reassured her that they were and thanked her for sending Liang and Bex to help with the Rivermill stall. 'You really didn't need to do that and I know Hanni was very grateful too. They have worked hard.'

'We women must stick together in business,' Carolyn said and her eyes teared up again. 'There are enough bad bastards out there and we must win out against them.'

'I'm really sorry I missed the rehearsal,' Jo began and paused. The woman opposite her looked uncharacteristically weary and dejected. 'Look, are you all right? Is there something wrong?'

Carolyn's hazel eyes filled with tears. She began to shake her head in denial but then reached for the tissues in her desk drawer. 'Vinny just told me he's leaving us. Louis is furious, and that's just adding fuel to the fire. I know it's silly, but it feels personal. Like a betrayal almost. Vinny has been with us for five years and he will be such a loss, especially as we get a higher profile and win back our government contract. I need his expertise.' She blew her nose. 'Sorry, I realize this must look like a terrible overreaction but, coming straight after Flora's accident, it's a tough one to take. I relied on them such a lot.'

'Yes, I know, it must be hard. Why is Vinny going?'

'That's what makes it worse. He's got a Head of PR job with Learning-Into-Work — that's the company who stole the contract from us. That's why it feels like a betrayal, and what's worse is that I really feel if Louis hadn't lost it with Vinny, I could have persuaded him to stay. Louis wouldn't let me offer him any incentives to stay and rang him up and bawled him out. Well, that was never going to work, was it?' Carolyn concluded with a return to her more composed, businesslike expression.

'No, I can imagine.' She had heard few people criticise Louis Carswell and, coming from Carolyn, who was usually so loyal, she was keen to get her to say more. Admittedly this was partly because it chimed with her own opinion of the man. She felt her way into the conversation. 'It must be difficult to take orders from Louis when you are used to running the business yourself. He doesn't seem to be the easiest man to work for,' she tried.

'It's the first time we've clashed,' Carolyn said. 'Mostly, he lets me run things. I remain the MD, that was the deal. And I had to do it for the long term. The business will reap the rewards in time because of Louis's powerful network, to say nothing of his knowledge and energy.'

And saying nothing of the personal rewards to Carolyn herself, Jo thought. Outwardly she kept quiet, reminding herself that she had effectively left these unresolved questions in the hands of the police. All she had to do now was to fulfil her own business commitment to Upwards and she could return home and enjoy some of the Rivermill's success. Maybe she could even take Teddy up on his offer and fly to Spain? With this vague plan in mind, she asked Carolyn how the rehearsal had gone.

'It's going to be a brilliant party but, more importantly, we are going to create an amazing little movie. I'm thinking now of a series of videos all focused on the skills of the future.' Her brow creased for a moment and Jo guessed that the impact of Vinny's departure was already making itself felt, but she shrugged this off and gave a reassuring smile. 'We went through your presentation that you sent over and it was fine. You've got nothing to worry about.'

Carolyn got to her feet and began to gather her belongings together. She glanced at the darkened window. 'It's looking so gloomy out there and I'm clearly not doing any good sitting and moping here. It's time for me to go home.'

The two women left the building together, with Carolyn talking some more about her plans for the business while she switched off lights and set alarms. 'I want to help Flora get back to work as soon as she can,' she said. 'I appreciate it might be months but I'm sure we can work something out.' Once in the car park, Carolyn took out her phone to call a cab, explaining that her car was at home and she was going to Justin's apartment.

Jo offered her a lift. 'It's the least I can do.'

Carolyn beamed. 'That would be marvellous, thanks. Justin sometimes sends Andre to collect me if I'm going to the studio—'

'Andre with the notched eyebrow and sulky good looks?' Jo smiled. 'He sort of works for both of you, doesn't he?'

'No, no, he works at the film studio with Justin, but I can see why you thought that, he's often at our offices. You know what it's like between our three businesses: Justin, Louis and me. We're a bit incestuous.' Carolyn gave a little laugh as she climbed into Jo's car. 'That's the way to thrive in business, you've got to help one another out. We're not competitors, after all.'

'Belief in abundance,' Jo murmured, thinking that Hanni would approve.

'Abundance,' Carolyn agreed. 'That's exactly it. And speaking of which, Jo, you should see Justin's apartment. He's got a penthouse suite in one of the new architect-designed blocks in Boscombe with the most fantastic views over to Studland Bay.' She threw a look across at Jo. 'I bet you're surprised we don't live together, aren't you?'

Jo shook her head. 'I hadn't thought about it.' Though now, reflecting back on her conversation with Justin in the Snug Bar, she found she wasn't surprised at all, but said nothing.

'I like to keep my total independence,' Carolyn went on. 'Although it's crazy, given the amount of time I spend over at his place. You must come in and have a cocktail with us tonight and have a peep at it. Honestly, it's like something you see in the magazines.'

'I'll have a coffee with you, thanks, but then I will have to get back to Hanni. The exhibition is open till eight o'clock.' Jo glanced at the clock on the dashboard and knew she should just have politely declined. Yet curiosity had driven her to accept, and it was nothing to do with Justin's home décor. It was more to do with the fact that two people had died and she was as clueless about it as she had ever felt. If these three powerful people and their businesses were as intertwined as Carolyn had said, maybe they were all in some way connected to the deaths?

Beside her, Carolyn was continuing to enthuse about Justin's apartment and an original artwork that covered virtually all of one wall and was meant to represent struggle. The woman's earlier, tearful mood had apparently subsided and, as Jo was only required to listen and drive, her thoughts drifted to Vinny's move. There was an obvious conclusion to draw from his departure, which she couldn't believe Carolyn hadn't considered.

As they drew up to the gated apartment block, Carolyn blithely announced over the intercom that she was 'bringing Jo to see the flat.' Jo could only guess Justin's reaction as he buzzed them in. Somehow, she didn't think he would be pleased to see her, and she wanted to tell Carolyn her insight about Vinny before they arrived. She seized her moment as they stepped into a spacious lift.

'Now you know where Vinny is going, it gives you a good indication of where your leak came from,' Jo said. She saw herself reflected four times over in the different mirrored tints of the lift walls. In all of them she looked tired, her wavy hair dishevelled and any make-up she'd applied worn off. Carolyn, on the other hand, looked as striking as ever in a mulberry business suit with a satiny black frill at her neckline.

A short silence stretched out while Carolyn checked her reflection and tidied her hair. 'You were sure someone was leaking information to Learning-Into-Work to help them win the contract,' Jo went on.

Carolyn's gaze snapped to Jo's in the mirror. 'I get it. There's no need to put in simple language for me. It's just, I really don't know what you mean by it.'

Jo had a strong sense she was digging a hole for herself but, having embarked on it, didn't seem to be able to stop. 'It's just that, you were wondering who had given out your prices and contract details to your competitor. Now Vinny has shown his hand, it seems likely it was him. He's probably been planning this move for a while. People don't just make a big jump like that overnight, do they?'

Carolyn had gone back to applying lip balm, her eyes on the task in hand. 'I don't believe Vinny would do that to us. It's so . . . so . . .' She searched for the word. 'Calculating.'

'But you thought Flora did?'

'I never suspected Flora,' Carolyn retorted. The lift had come to a halt but she didn't move. 'Louis blamed her. Not me. I knew she was too loyal to do anything to harm us.' Carolyn clearly considered this was the last word on the subject. She made one final adjustment to her hair and stepped out in front of Jo.

As Jo sought to make sense of the woman's many contradictions, she realized the wide apartment door was open in front of them and Justin was standing there, arms folded, listening with interest.

'What's this about Carswell? Who is he blaming this time?' His narrow blue gaze alighted on Jo. 'You can tell us better than anyone, as you're working for him.'

'You're not, are you, Jo?' Doubt crept into Carolyn's voice. 'Is that how you know about our little contract issue? It's not something we advertise.'

'Of course she is. I told you that the first time I met her.' Although Justin's tone was far from welcoming, he left the door open for them to follow him into the large, open apartment space. A shining, ceramic floor, glistened with low-level lighting and a vast open-plan kitchen gleamed in front of them. There were soft, pale blinds over the windows but in daylight, Jo imagined that the wide room would be flooded with light from the sea and sky.

'You were wrong then and you're wrong now,' Jo said, but she found herself hesitating on the threshold with a sudden sense of being outnumbered.

Carolyn brushed past her, unbuttoning her jacket and flinging it onto one of the leather sofas. 'Don't be silly, Justin,' she said as she took off her high heels. 'Anyway, what does it matter if Jo is working for Louis? He's my business partner, after all, and he has certainly let me know it today. Jo is only having coffee by the way, but I'm definitely up for a cocktail.'

Justin crossed the apartment in a few strides to the kitchen. 'No problem.' He emptied some coffee beans into a grinder, took a cocktail shaker out of the fridge and located two identical glasses.

'Where were you today?' He shot his question at Jo. 'I would have thought an astrologer would be able to foresee "urgent family business". If these things can still take you by surprise, what's the point of astrology?'

'Astrology is not just about future events but about many things. Such as character, for example. That's much more my sort of thing.' Jo's voice sounded a lot calmer than she felt.

'Character?' He passed her closely, carrying a cocktail for Carolyn, who was virtually lying on an armchair.

'Didn't I tell you this place was amazing, Jo?' she murmured, her eyes half-closed. She reached up and took the cocktail without looking at Justin.

'It's a fabulous apartment,' Jo said, as admiration seemed to be required.

'And let's not have any more nonsense about Jo working for Louis.' Carolyn sat up suddenly, rubbing the frown line between her eyes and glaring at Justin. 'Her first loyalty is to me, isn't it, Jo? And we're going to have a world-beating, innovative event on Monday.'

Justin looked at Jo across the kitchen counter. He poured out her coffee from a chrome coffee machine and added hot milk from another shiny appliance. 'I hear differently.'

He padded around the warm, aromatic apartment, his voice and actions as smooth and easy as his black cashmere jumper and yet, as he performed these little domestic duties, Jo felt a tangible sense of menace.

'I hear that Jo has more than one boss, isn't that right?'

'Doesn't everybody?' She accepted the coffee at arm's length and sipped it warily.

He laughed. 'Don't worry, you're quite safe here.' He slid his eyes towards Carolyn. 'Believe what you want, darling, but even if she's not working for Carswell, her boyfriend is, and that amounts to the same thing.'

'My boyfriend is running a golf tournament in Spain,' Jo said, finally feeling on firm ground with this statement.

'Oh, that boyfriend.' Justin laughed again. 'And the sooner you join him there the better, if you want my advice. And, while I'm at it, I'll give you a couple of other pearls of wisdom. Firstly, there is nothing much goes on around this town that I don't know about. If you think differently, then you'd be underestimating me, which some people have regretted doing.'

'Well, whatever you decide, you're not to go anywhere before Monday,' Carolyn interjected, draining her cocktail glass. 'We need you at our Futures event, don't we, Justin?'

'Yes, no more urgent family business on Monday, please,' Justin added.

Jo could have acquiesced and taken that as the right moment to leave. She was very aware that Hanni would be wondering where she was. But she had come here with a purpose, which had nothing to do with admiring the swanky flat. Maybe she hadn't even known it herself until that moment, but suddenly she was speaking up and her words felt right and steady.

'It wasn't family stuff at all,' she said. 'Actually, I was being questioned by the police about a possible murder. Cheryl Frost. Heard of her?'

She had the satisfaction of seeing Justin's shocked expression before it dissolved into his usual handsome mask. Carolyn was still in shadow on the armchair, but as she sat up and moved under a light, Jo saw her face was pale and troubled. 'I do know that name,' she said. 'It can't be the same one — the Cheryl Frost I knew worked for a government agency. Quiet, pleasant, unassuming woman. You're not saying she's dead?'

'The police are investigating her possible murder,' Jo continued, although her thoughts were barely a step ahead of her words. 'In fact I could have been killed too. Suffocated by the fumes in her workshop.'

'Workshop? Government agent? Who is this woman?' Justin tried to brush off the facts with abrupt irritation.

Carolyn came to stand at his side, speaking slowly. 'I don't know about the workshop but I remember Cheryl Frost. She did some work for us for a while. Flora had the most dealings with her.'

So far, so consistent, Jo thought and wondered how far she dare go with her plan to flush something out.

'But, Jo,' Carolyn went on, her tone becoming more normal, more like her work persona. 'How on earth did you know her? And you were questioned by the police? That must have been disturbing. You should have just been straight with us. We might have been able to help, mightn't we, darling?'

Justin's face showed no inclination to help. He moved closer to her and reached out a hand.

She couldn't stop herself stepping back automatically. He laughed and took her empty coffee mug. 'I don't want to burst your bubble, but I don't really give a shit about you, your little adventures or this unfortunate accident. What I do care about is that this event goes well on Monday because Carolyn and I have invested a lot of time and resources into it. So I want you there. Carolyn has had just about enough of people letting her down, so make sure your stars are aligned so that you show up this time.'

Carolyn had turned away to pour herself another cocktail. Any support she had shown to Jo had evaporated along with her tears about Vinny. Jo decided on balance that it was time to leave. She mentioned Hanni and the exhibition as a reason to get on her way.

Carolyn reverted briefly to a few chatty comments but it was obvious that neither of them were going to detain her and she was back in her car in ten minutes, thinking, *What was all that about?* She had made herself late for Hanni and had learned precisely nothing.

As the gates opened for her, she imagined Justin hovering over the button, enjoying her discomfort. Maybe her little ruse to flush something out hadn't quite paid off, she conceded as she drove to the exhibition centre. She felt relieved to be going back to something practical and useful, where she couldn't do anything rash.

She had taken to parking the Seat on a sunken piece of ground behind the centre, which had possibly been the foundations of a former hotel but now formed a rough car park. She was jogging up the steep steps to reach street level when she became aware of a bulky figure at the top. She slowed and tried to damp down her fevered imagination, which was feeding off her new-found paranoia. It was just a man standing there. He was not necessarily waiting for her. But she slowed her pace so she wouldn't be breathing fast and transferred her keys to her hand as a weapon.

The man turned. It was Louis Carswell. The street light caught the breadth of his shoulders in his well-fitting suit and glinted on his teeth. 'I thought it was you,' he said. 'I was just paying a visit to the exhibition and thought we could walk down together. I expect you want to know how Hanni is doing? I popped down to see her this morning and she was coping splendidly and making some good sales.'

'Yes, I'm a bit late.' Jo matched his friendly tone.

'You are indeed. I wonder where you've been all this time? Seeing Carolyn, I suppose. She has been very generous providing some extra hands for your friend.' Jo agreed and Carswell went on, 'It looks like the Rivermill Bookshop and Café will have a successful Christmas. I don't know about you—' he sighed expansively and addressed the night air — 'but, in business, I've always found it worth knowing when to cut your losses. Hanni is going to need you back home in the bookshop before Christmas or these gains could be for nothing. That's her bread and butter after all. It's just my view, but I think you will be more valuable there than at the Upwards birthday party on Monday.'

They rounded the corner of the exhibition centre. 'I've said I'll be there. It's a professional commitment.'

'Maybe so. But you weren't at the rehearsal today, were you?' he pointed out. 'And they coped. Upwards have got plenty of proper scientists at this event and the national press are attending. It's only a word to the wise, but some of these journos can destroy your business if they take against you.'

They had reached the conference doors, where a woman with a clipboard, recognizing Carswell immediately, headed determinedly in his direction. Jo felt grateful to her. Carswell paused, caught Jo's elbow and turned her towards him.

He leaned down as if for a farewell peck on the cheek. 'From one businessperson to another,' he murmured, 'I suggest you go home with the books and crystals tomorrow and leave Carolyn to me. Or you might find the police take an even closer interest. After all, you have no real alibi for Cheryl Frost's murder, have you?'

CHAPTER TWENTY-ONE

As soon as she could, Jo found a moment, half-hidden by the bookshelves, to call Macy. He was the one person in the world who would have a hope of understanding her dilemma.

'In the space of half an hour, Carswell warned me not to attend on Monday and Justin Fielding was full of vague threats if I didn't go.'

'You don't have to do anything right now,' was Macy's response. 'I'm meeting Agnieszka tomorrow morning at the Quiet Pools. Alan and I are making some progress on Beaman's death and she thinks she can help. If we can understand who killed him, I am convinced it will unravel this whole sleazy mess. Why don't you come with me and hear it first-hand?'

'Yes, if it's early. The exhibition doesn't open until ten a.m.'

'Eight o'clock OK for you? Wrap up warm.'

'Did you tell Carswell about Cheryl's death?' Jo asked. 'Because he knows.'

There was a short pause. 'I told him yesterday evening as it's relevant to the case. Why?'

'I thought you were quitting this contract? You were going to have no more to do with Carswell.'

'There is more to be gained from having him believe I'm on his side.'

'Well, I don't get it. But look, I'll see you tomorrow.'

Sometimes she didn't understand Macy at all but she had no energy left to explain this to him and rang off. She dwelt momentarily on Macy's twisted loyalties and wondered how a meeting with the violent and untrustworthy PI was going to help them. But, seeing no easy answers to these questions, she was glad to return to the simple task of selling as many books as possible to a dwindling evening crowd. When the doors closed, she counted the takings while Hanni restocked the shelves and tidied the café area. As she returned to their stall with a tray of clean crockery, Jo gave her the good news about the day's profits.

Hanni shrieked and threw her rubber gloves in the air. 'Josephine, we've done it! We've rescued Christmas!'

'And there's still tomorrow.' Jo grinned, glad to have something positive to think about. But later, over what was meant to be a celebratory drink in the hotel bar, she couldn't help her mind turning to the threats she'd received from the two very different men.

She found Justin Fielding easier to understand. His air of fake friendliness and domesticity was an easy sham to see through. He was used to allowing people to see the menace below the surface. At least his motives seemed obvious. On the face of it, he was trying to ensure that Carolyn's event was successful. He just had a heavy-handed way of going about it.

Carswell was a lot more opaque, she thought, as she sipped her warm Prosecco and tried to listen to Hanni enthusing about the day's events. It was due to him that she and Macy were here in Bournemouth. She had to admit that her own business was benefitting from the relationship she had struck up with Carolyn and it was only due to Carswell's largesse that the Christmas Festival was proving a saviour for Hanni's business. This evening, however, he'd made it clear that she couldn't leave town soon enough.

'You're very reflective tonight,' Hanni said. 'It's not surprising. Your encounter with death has left a wound that hasn't even started to heal yet.'

'The encounters with DCI Conway didn't help either,' Jo said. 'For someone who doesn't say a lot, he is certainly a force to be reckoned with and I expect it won't be long before they are wanting to talk to me again.'

'Maybe it's too soon to celebrate. Let's just see if we can manifest another good day tomorrow.' Hanni finished her drink and set down her empty glass. Jo was glad of an excuse to abandon her Prosecco.

Setting her alarm for an early start the next day, she realized she had forty-eight hours to decide which of the two obnoxious men she was going to disappoint. Considering her day had started with a police interview and ended with a double threat, Jo slept surprisingly soundly.

The next morning, she drove while eating a piece of toast, which she had grabbed from the buffet, in order to avoid being late for her strange rendezvous with Macy and Agnieszka. His car was the only other vehicle at the nature reserve when she drew up alongside it. She stepped out to the hollow sound of birds rising from the water and watched them fly over. The sharp tilt of her neck reminded that her throat was still sore. She hunched her shoulders and paced towards the visitor centre, still mulling over her dilemma.

The wooden cabin was closed and Macy was sitting outside at a picnic bench, muffled into his red scarf and winter woollen coat. He pushed a Starbucks coffee towards her. 'Twenty-four-hour drive-through,' he said.

'You're an angel,' she said and saw his eyes warm up. She realized she didn't often tell Macy how much she appreciated him. Maybe never in fact. 'So, what's the plan?' she asked, rather than pursuing this thought. Life was complicated enough.

'Agnieszka has offered a lead but she wanted to meet here at this ungodly hour. You were right by the way, she was following my surveillance team and being paid by Carswell.'

'Very trusting of him,' Jo commented.

Macy was surveying the little clearing where the wooden tables stood. The dawn light was strengthening every second but they sat in the shadow of the cabin and the soft, indeterminate shapes of trees in a small copse creaked and rustled on their other side.

Jo followed his gaze. 'Am I your bodyguard?' she asked with a sudden grin.

'Witness at least,' Macy admitted. 'And I wanted to tell you what we've got on Shane Beaman. They have to be connected — Flora's accident and Beaman's death.'

'And Cheryl Frost,' Jo added.

'If we crack one, the others will become clear. All we've got on Flora comes from the police investigation. They're planning to interview her again on Monday. Or at least to try to. I gather that the first time wasn't very successful.'

'That's an understatement,' Jo said. 'It put her recovery back several days, so Bex told me.'

Macy nodded. 'I heard that too and it will have delayed their investigation no doubt. Alan found out that they've traced the white van that hit her. It's a rental on a corporate contract and the firm is one of the nightclubs that Justin Fielding used to own. The club's records are so poor, they can't tell who was driving it. Conveniently.'

A nearby rumble of car tyres made him pause but it soon passed by on the lane and he turned back to Jo. 'So there is a link between Flora's accident and Fielding, but it's tenuous. Your turn. How is the inquiry into Cheryl Frost's death going? Have your Gloucestershire lot been able to make a connection to whatever is going on here?'

'Getting anything out of DCI Conway is like getting blood out of a stone, but they did confirm Cheryl was overcome by toxic fumes. The paint stripper she was using was industrial strength. She was a furniture restorer in her spare time, so you'd think she would know what she was doing but it seems she used the wrong stuff. I told them about what had happened to Flora and Beaman but I'm not sure what they are doing about that or what they made of it all.'

'You can hardly blame them. We're a lot closer to it and we can't make anything stack up.' He sighed. 'Not yet anyway.' He looked at his watch and at the car park entrance, his expression doubtful.

Jo sipped her coffee. 'At least Conway's team have stopped quizzing me about the whole thing. I was worried I was a suspect for a while. I don't think my mother would ever have forgiven me. On top of my other failings.'

Macy was about to pose a question when they both heard the unmistakable scrunch of tyres on stony ground.

'We're out of the picture of those two inquiries,' Macy said, speaking rapidly, 'so Beaman is our best bet, and Agnieszka reckons she is close to that investigation. I have to trust her — at least for now.' They shared a look that clearly expressed both their misgivings and a tacit agreement to go with this plan.

Low, conversational voices reached them in the cold misty air, accompanied by the tramp of two sets of boots. Agnieszka was bringing company. Jo tensed and avoided looking at Macy so he wouldn't see how scared she suddenly felt. It was obvious, however, as soon as the two figures appeared on the path, shoulder to shoulder, that their gait and manner were confident and relaxed. Agnieszka raised a ski-gloved hand and pulled the snood away from her mouth to greet them.

'Early start today.' She turned towards the man at her side. 'This is DC Craven from Poole station. He hasn't got long, so make the most of him.'

DC Craven was tall and narrow with a neat beard. His cord trousers looked new, and his shoes were too shiny for the terrain. He stood awkwardly while they introduced themselves.

'Sit down,' Agnieszka demanded. She took her place beside Macy, which meant that DC Craven perched beside Jo. 'Nat and I have worked together many times,' the PI went on. 'We need each other, don't we?' Her steely grey eyes regarded them all as if daring them to disagree.

The DC rubbed his nose with a gloved hand and nodded. 'Mutually beneficial,' he acknowledged in a surprisingly low-pitched voice.

Agnieszka smacked the table. 'OK, let's get started before we freeze our bollocks off. Nat, Macy does the same job as me. Only not here,' she added with emphasis.

'I'm located in the Midlands and Jo works with me,' Macy said and, for once, Jo didn't argue.

'So, treat Macy as you would me. I can vouch for him.' When the DC remained silent, she added, 'I owe him one. That's what this is about.'

DC Craven cleared his throat. 'And you owe me after this little rendezvous, Aggie.' He didn't wait for a reply but turned to Macy directly. 'I'm working on the Shane Beaman inquiry. I'm here to pay another visit to Meredith Winney. That's the woman who reported finding his body. It's probably best if you ask me questions. I can't promise I'll answer them, but you can try me.'

'Shane Beaman's record,' Macy began. 'I understand he had a conviction for stalking and harassment. What was that about?'

'Beaman used to work on the doors of various nightclubs in Poole and Bournemouth and his speciality was to harass women he met through his work. I don't know how serious this got as most of his offences never reached us, I suspect, but one woman took it all the way. She was stalked and could prove it so we were able to get him and he was sentenced for three years and served two, released about eighteen months ago.'

'Can you tell us who the woman was?' Jo asked.

Craven shook his head. 'I cannot, but she was no gormless holidaymaker, I can assure you. Beaman chose the wrong victim that time. The woman used to manage Le Mystère — it was a nightclub near the Triangle back in the day. Anyway, the point is she knew her way around the Bournemouth scene. She was savvy and she had balls.'

'It shouldn't take that to bring a sex criminal to justice,' Jo said and received a look of respect from Agnieszka.

'I can tell you that the woman is no longer living locally,' the policeman said, pursing his lips. His nose was pink with the cold. 'I don't know if that helps.'

'The owner of Le Mystère,' Macy said. 'That was Justin Fielding, wasn't it?'

Craven nodded. 'Yes, we are talking about four years ago when Fielding owned two clubs in Bournemouth and one in Boscombe. He's not in the nightclub business anymore. He sold them all and has only got his film studio now, which was his father's business.'

'Is it all above board?' Macy asked.

DC Craven pulled a sceptical face. 'I doubt it. Let's just say we don't take anything for granted with Fielding. He was charged with supplying Class A drugs when he was running the clubs but we didn't have enough to get him, and since then he has stayed just about the right side of the line. He has all the local contacts to follow through on a nasty threat, that I don't doubt. But in the case of Beaman, there is no motive and no evidence.' Craven ended on a superior note as if hoping this would bring the conversation to a close.

'So if you don't have anything more on Shane Beaman,' Jo said, 'why are you seeing Meredith Winney again? Surely there's nothing new to ask her?'

'There is one new piece of evidence, which involves Fielding actually,' the DC said with a telling glance at Agnieszka as if reminding her of the magnitude of this favour. 'We know that Beaman visited Justin Fielding at his studio on Friday the twenty-third of November. We have it on CCTV. Now—' he held up a cautious hand — 'we don't know the significance of that visit.'

'It was two days before his death,' Macy said. 'That seems pretty significant to me.'

'Yes, but maybe he visited him regularly. We can only speculate about the reason for the visit. We are going through more CCTV and seeing witnesses again.'

'Since Beaman has been out of prison, has he been in any trouble?' Macy asked. 'What's his probation record like? Any signs of renewed stalking behaviour?'

When Craven said blandly that he wasn't aware of anything, Jo followed up with a question of her own. 'Was he stalking Flora Howell? We know he was meeting her after work on his motorbike because the staff at Upwards told me.'

'Nothing reported,' Craven said.

'That's not illegal,' Agnieszka pointed out. 'Maybe the woman was OK with him waiting on his bike outside work.'

'What about his phone?' Jo asked. 'Have you found that and was there anything on it?'

Craven shrugged. 'Absolutely bugger all. He did call and text Flora Howell, but his texts are completely banal and innocent.' He dragged out a pause while the little group around the picnic table waited for more. 'There were a few odd messages. He occasionally texted her with a date: the fourteenth of September 2019. Just that, nothing else. This was every few weeks. We're assuming that's the date they met.'

Jo's mind immediately went to the nature book she had taken from Shane Beaman's bookshelf and the same date scribbled on the page. She said nothing. Meanwhile, Macy tried to ask about the investigation into Flora's accident but there seemed to be nothing Craven could tell them about that.

'What about Louis Carswell?' Jo said suddenly. 'Are you investigating Carswell for anything?'

Agnieszka shot her a sharp look. 'Don't forget he is my client. And I am very choosy about who I work for.'

'Louis Carswell has just won Director of the Year or some such award from the Chamber of Commerce,' DC Craven said. 'I wouldn't trouble yourself with him. Your other man, Fielding, is a much more likely suspect, providing you can get something on him. And if you do, you can contact me via Aggie.' The police officer got to his feet, smoothing out the wrinkles in his cord trousers as he did so. 'Now, I really must love you and leave you.'

Agnieszka laughed. 'He's not serious. He doesn't really love you.'

Macy quelled this jollity with a look and got up to shake DC Craven's hand.

'I've got another question,' Jo interrupted. 'Have you found anything interesting about Beaman's tattoos? I'd heard he had a new one of a rose.'

The officer huffed impatiently. 'He had a load of tattoos, which we're looking at, but they seem pretty standard, including a couple of prison tats. Most were very old so he must have got them as a kid. That's about it, I'm afraid.' He directed a look at Agnieszka. 'I'll be in touch.' He walked away in his shiny shoes without a backward glance.

'I'm sure he will,' Agnieszka said. She looked at Macy as if to say, 'Are you satisfied now?' They exchanged a few words in parting but Jo wasn't listening. She was searching for something on her phone, which was slow to respond because of their remote location.

As they watched the other PI stride back to her car, Jo shivered. She was chilled by sitting still in the damp air. 'Let's go for a walk,' she said.

Deep in thought, Macy fell into step with her and they walked in silence for a while. The growing daylight was amplified by the large expanse of water rippling beside the bare trees and they took the path towards it. There was still a faint mist over the lake, which drifted into the layered soft browns of the winter woods.

'Craven wasn't exactly a mine of information, was he?' Jo said.

'No, but there were a couple of gems. We now know that Beaman knew Fielding. Used to work for him, in fact,' Macy said. 'That seems significant, although I don't know why. Yet.'

'I'm sure this date of the fourteenth of September is important. He underlined the day and month in Flora's book and wrote in the year. Or someone did, and I don't think it was Flora. She is neat and precise and this was just a scribble. Anyway, I looked it up again. That date was the day Louis Carswell's company took ownership of Upwards.' Jo tapped her phone and held it out to show Macy the photographs from the training company's website. 'They had a celebration party at the Metropole.'

'Where else?' Macy murmured.

'They're all there.' Jo flicked through the pictures. 'Carswell, and there's Fraser, one of their apprentices. The other Planet Events people, I don't know.'

They paused on the path to study the photos. In one, Carswell was pouring champagne, smiling widely, with the Upwards staff grouped around him. Carolyn, in her usual stand-out colours looked as delighted as anyone with her glass held high. Wearing emerald green this time, Jo noted.

'Not surprising she looks so smug, she made a quarter of a million from the deal,' Macy commented. 'I can see Flora, Liang and Vinny from the Upwards team. All our usual suspects, except Fielding.'

'Fielding doesn't work for Upwards so he wouldn't have been invited,' Jo pointed out. 'He's just Carolyn's other half. He provides the space for their video filming, that's all.' Something resurfaced in her mind about their very first meeting. Justin had made some jibe about Carolyn being 'too busy partying' to approve the apprentices' final video. She wondered if this was the event he was talking about. She voiced her thoughts to Macy. 'Carolyn said she was double-booked. Now I come to think of it, that seems like a fairly major diary cock-up.'

'That was Flora's job. Looking after Carolyn's diary was a big part of what she did.' Macy said. 'Or didn't do in this case.' They picked up their pace again. It was too cold to stand still for long. 'Beaman wasn't at the Metropole either of course,' he went on. 'Although maybe he was loitering in the background. That seems to have been his style.'

'Waiting for Flora perhaps,' Jo said. She watched her breath condense in the air and thought about Theo's comments on his sister's love life. He'd said she wasn't uninterested, just shy. It still gave her a private, inner smile, thinking of the very modest but sensitive way he had expressed it. 'I wonder if Flora knew Shane had been a stalker. Even if she did, maybe she was fond of him. She gave him the nature book after all. And they used to come walking here on Sundays.'

Macy looked at his watch. 'Well, we can't do any more of this hiking business. You have to be at the exhibition in twenty minutes and I'm going into the office, so I've got a drive ahead of me.'

'Oh. You're going back?' Jo realized that she had not given any more thought to her decision over whether to attend the Upwards birthday party on Monday. But she already knew what she was going to do. She couldn't renege on a business commitment. Nor could she let Carolyn down. In addition, she now wanted to confirm her suspicions about the day of the party and the making of the video, and Bex was probably her best source.

'I've got to,' Macy was saying. It sounded like he was going to say more and Jo would normally have prompted him but she was still following her own train of thought.

She queued almost the whole way to the BIC in the morning rush hour but eventually she swung down the ramp into her usual car park at the back of the exhibition centre. Before getting out of the car, she checked for any messages on her phone and idly scrolled through the photos again. She paused at the one showing Carswell and Carolyn drinking champagne and called Macy.

'It's the same jacket,' she said. 'The emerald silk jacket that Carolyn was wearing at the Metropole is the same as the one that Flora was wearing two weeks later when they collected their Ofsted certificate. I've seen a picture of her standing in the park. She was wearing it again when I met her that first evening at the Metropole. Why would Flora wear Carolyn's jacket?'

'Maybe Carolyn gave it to her. You know what she's like,' Macy said. 'Lady Bountiful.'

'Flora wore it all the time once she'd been promoted. Bex told me it was her "one and only" corporate garment. Maybe it was a hand-me-down from the boss. Seems a bit odd though.'

'The police will go over everything that happened on that date in September. Hold on a minute, I'm just picking up a coffee for the journey,' he said. She heard him make his order and then he picked up the thread. 'I get the impression that if the local police can find something on Justin Fielding, it will give them a lot of pleasure. Agnieszka thought so too.'

Jo gave a scathing snort. 'She also maintains Carswell is as pure as the freshly driven snow, which is such bullshit. We know for a fact he was looking for some dirt on Flora so Carolyn would have to sack her.'

'Carolyn could have sacked her if she'd really wanted to get her out of the company. There must be more to it than that for Louis to run expensive surveillance on her. He believes he's still employing me now in the hope I will turn up something to discredit her, and the poor woman has been in hospital for two weeks.'

'Don't forget he was probably also paying someone to check up on us at the same time,' Jo said. 'Paranoia run rampant.' She could hear Macy walking back to his car and glanced at her watch. If she ran up the steps and in through the exhibitors' entrance, she would hardly be late at all. 'You do see that now, don't you? That Carswell was keeping tabs on your operation?'

'Yes I do.'

Jo's hand paused on the door handle as she heard the new certainty in his voice. 'What is it? What do you know?'

'I'm going back to the office to sack Jess,' he said. 'Alan found out. He got her talking about why she didn't follow Flora to the Pools and she confessed. Jess has been working for Carswell, giving him information about what we're doing. They met when he was first working for me. Apparently they kept in touch.' His voice, although weary, injected layers of meaning into these last four words.

Jo listened in silence. Knowing how betrayed he would feel, she struggled to find a response. 'I'm sorry,' she ended up saying, which sounded inadequate to her own ears.

'It's my own fault. I knew all along Carswell was a ruthless bastard who uses everybody and trusts nobody, but I still took the job. I met him yesterday morning, to finally tell him what I think of him. It wasn't as satisfying as it should have been.'

He sighed. 'I should never have gone anywhere near this.'

CHAPTER TWENTY-TWO

'A ruthless bastard who uses everybody and trusts nobody' played like a refrain in Jo's mind for the rest of the weekend. When the team arrived to take away the sofas and coffee machine at the end of the exhibition, she was reminded uncomfortably that Carswell was the man who had supplied them. She said nothing to Hanni, as she didn't want to burst her friend's bubble of euphoria over the Rivermill's success, but it only added to her unease. They had been friends a long time and she felt she was lying by omission.

The refrain was still on her mind, although for a different reason, when she arrived at Justin Fielding's film production studio on Monday morning. The studios surprised her by being tucked away in a respectable and discreet pair of Georgian mews houses behind a parade of shops in the neat little suburb of Westbourne. To reach them, Jo had driven past people shopping at delis, an artisan bakery and an old-fashioned chemist's shop. A sharp turn took her to the quiet cul-de-sac, behind the shops, which was home to an engraving workshop, some rented properties and, right at the end, the two houses that made up Westbourne Studios. She couldn't help looking out for Carswell's black Mercedes as she walked alongside the other parked cars, although she knew he was not expected at the Upwards birthday event. *No doubt his spies will soon tell him I'm here*, she thought. *And then what?'*

The entrance to the studios looked more like two back doors, side by side, with a small brass nameplate beside one of them that would have been easy to miss. Justin Fielding was standing in the narrow doorway, arms folded, watching her walk up the mews.

'Wise decision.' He nodded towards a staircase through the open door behind him. 'They're all up there, getting ready.' Music blared briefly from the windows above their heads as if to prove his point.

'I bet your neighbours love you.' Jo looked around at the other Georgian buildings' white stucco walls, closely packed together in the quiet mews.

He shrugged, flicking ash from his cigarette in the same movement. 'Thing is, I *am* the neighbours.' He gestured at the buildings opposite. 'The stone engraver rents from me and, as the other residents gradually moved on, I bought each property one by one. My tenants never complain.' He grinned.

'Odd that.' A part of Jo wanted to move past him quickly and get on with the ordeal that lay ahead, but she also realized she had never seen him so relaxed. She decided to make the most of this. 'Carolyn told me you inherited the film studios from your father?' she said, leaning against the wall as if she had plenty of time to chat.

'That's right, it's a family business.' He inhaled deeply from his cigarette and peered at the blue sky showing between the tops of the buildings. 'We actually made movies here back in the fifties and sixties. And some dodgy stuff in the seventies and eighties, I admit, but now we only do TV work and music videos. Most of the money is made in the editing suite, to be honest. I employ great technicians.' He indicated the closed door next to him. 'This is where we do the TV work. I'll show you around if you want?'

Jo accepted. Although it made good sense to have no more to do with this man, she couldn't resist her innate need to find out more, to resolve some of the unanswered questions. It felt as natural as if she had been an investigator all her adult life. She followed him into the neighbouring building.

He led her down a narrow corridor with bare, polished floorboards to some double doors. They opened onto a cavernous space resembling a large, dark warehouse except for the gantries for lighting and screens overhead. All the screens were blank and the sound desk and windows into the production rooms at the back of the auditorium were in darkness.

'It's like a blank canvas,' Jo said, surprised that such a space was hidden behind the genteel Georgian exterior.

'That's exactly it.' Justin reeled off a list of music videos and parts of TV shows that had been made there, most of which she recognized. She made appreciative noises and was reminded that, as with his swanky apartment, this was what he seemed to expect and crave. Of course, he was a Leo, she reminded herself, which led to another thought.

'Thanks for showing me round.' She turned back towards the exit. 'I'd best go and let Carolyn know I'm here. You and she are both Leos, aren't you?'

'Yes, big cats, both of us. Big on everything,' he said. 'But we fight like cats in a sack.'

She laughed, recalling her consultation with Carolyn, when she had said similar. 'What do you fight about?'

'Oh, stupid things mainly. We like to manage things quite differently. She's a control freak, whereas I'm quite relaxed with my staff, to a point, anyway. Sometimes she thinks she owns my business too, like when she starts trying to tell my people what to do. But we need each other and that's a fact.' He pointed to the long windows into offices at the back of the room. 'That's the editing suite, where the actual work is done.'

'You share staff too sometimes, don't you?' Jo followed him down the cavernous room. She had to look down to avoid tripping on a cable or metal stanchion, whereas Justin strolled ahead of her, sure-footed. But she had gleaned the merest hint of an opportunity and she was not going to pass it up. 'Like Andre? And Shane Beaman. Carolyn used Beaman as a courier, but he also worked for you in the past, didn't he? As a bouncer.'

'Shane Beaman?' Justin threw the words over his shoulder, dismissing the name and the man. 'He did not work for Carolyn. She might have used the courier company he worked for but that's a totally different thing, and as for him being one of my doormen, well you're going way back in time. I haven't had anything to do with Le Mystère for five years or more.'

Jo noted that, despite his flippant tone, he had been ready with all the relevant facts, which suggested he'd been prepared for questions about Beaman. Looking down the long, darkened studio, she was struck by the emptiness of the space. It occurred to her that it was also likely to be very well soundproofed. She began, unhurriedly, to return to the exit door and Justin followed close behind.

'He came to see you here, didn't he? Two days before he died.' She turned her head so she could see something of Justin's face in the shadows. But she also kept moving forward. 'What did he want?'

There was a heavy sigh from behind her. 'Money, of course. What else?' Justin's tone altered slightly, becoming more businesslike as he went on. 'He wanted a job, but I had to tell him that I just don't employ that kind of person these days. I need highly skilled people.' As they re-entered the dim corridor leading back to the front door, he took her arm. 'What's your interest in all this? You're a long way off your natural hippy-dippy territory, aren't you? Is all this going in a report to Carswell?'

She shook her arm free. 'No,' she assured him, with feeling, but she could feel him close behind her as she put one steady foot in front of the other along the hallway. He was not a large man but he was near enough that she had a physical sense of his strength. Her heartbeat seemed loud in the narrow space and she traced her hand along the wooden panelling to stop herself from hurrying. She could smell his scent: cigarettes and musky perfume masking his own hormonal, chemical smell, which made her feel claustrophobic, and his breath, which was too close on her neck.

'You're an odd one anyway, aren't you?' I can't work you out.' His gravelly voice rumbled in her ear. 'What star sign are you, dare I ask?'

'Virgo,' she replied. Her own voice sounded strangely high and echoey. She turned a corner and saw the front door was now closed. Slanting, dusty fingers of cold sun from the fanlight showed the shape of the architrave around another closed door to her right. She had a sudden frightening memory of a visit to the dentist as a child and, in response, she quickened her pace.

'The Virgin, eh?' He grabbed her arm. 'Wait. Slow down. You'll hurt yourself.'

Jo could feel the pads of each of the fingers of his right hand pressing into the fleshy part of her arm. His other hand brushed her neck.

She jerked back instinctively, crashing against the panelling. Her eyes were fixed on the front door, her every muscle leaning towards it when it flew open. Daylight flooded the hallway. Fielding dropped his hands instantly as a man's shape appeared.

'Boss, are you in here? Carolyn's having a serious hissy fit. She wants me to—' The man stopped when he saw Jo, but she had already recognized him — first from his accent, which was a mix of Hispanic and London, and then from his unusual profile, with its quiff and sharp chin.

'Andre,' she said, remembering that she had last seen him at the Upwards office. Relief made her giddy and her laugh was light-headed. 'We always seem to meet in doorways.'

Andre seemed floored by this and said nothing, his eyes going to his boss. Fielding stepped between them. 'What did I say about fighting like a cat?' he remarked to Jo. He placed his hand on her back as if to shepherd her outdoors.

She stepped smartly aside as soon as she could. If her questions had aggravated Justin, it was Andre who now bore the brunt of his temper. Justin barrelled his chest out and bawled at the younger man, who stood head and shoulders taller than him, looking confused.

'What the fuck does she want now? Have you still not learned, you don't have to jump every time she breathes! Remember who your boss actually is.'

Justin pushed past him through the doorway and into the building next door. His footsteps clattered up the stairs to the conference room.

Jo raised her eyebrows at the show of temper. 'And who is your boss, then?'

He puffed out his lips, placing his fingers deliberately on the waistband of his tracksuit. It was the closest to any emotion she had seen in him.

'Right now, I don't actually know.' After this statement, he took refuge in injured silence.

Andre remained outside while Jo turned into the next-door building and followed Justin up the stairs. Lagging behind, she used these moments climbing the steep stair-case to compose herself. She had been strongly tempted to simply run to her car once she was in the fresh air and free of Fielding's advances, or whatever they were. She had made a conscious decision to return indoors, although it felt instinc-tively wrong. She took some quiet breaths, kept her distance from Fielding and reminded herself that in two hours, she would be out of this horrible studio, out of Bournemouth, and out of the lives of Carolyn Ash, Justin Fielding and Louis Carswell.

Justin preceded her into the large conference room that extended across the top floor of both houses, so she had a moment at the threshold to simply observe the Upwards team in preparation for their big event. Carolyn, at the centre of the room with her team scattered around her, spoke wel-coming words, but her colour was high and an air of nervous tension pervaded the room. In the corner, Bex wobbled off a chair while trying to tie some balloons to a pelmet. She landed gracelessly but unhurt.

'I've told you not to climb on things,' Carolyn snapped. 'Leave the decorations now. Our guests will be arriving any minute and we need to be in our places.'

The large airy room looked festive with banners in primary colours, flowers on each of the tables, which were set out in cabaret style, and a birthday cake on a sideboard.

'Justin, can I have five minutes of your time?' Carolyn added icily.

'Certainly. By the way, one guest is already here.' Justin stood aside to reveal Jo, who was still deliberately hanging back. 'She's very keen,' he added. 'No urgent family business this time. Someone must have encouraged her to come.'

'Well, it certainly wasn't your group director,' Jo shot back. 'He actively tried to persuade me not to attend.'

A frown crossed Carolyn's face but was swiftly banished. 'Nonsense,' she laughed. 'He was probably joking. He's got a very dry sense of humour, you know. Louis always wants the best for us and you *are* the best, Jo.' She beamed. 'No need to be nervous. Find your place. Each guest speaker has their own table.'

Whatever the reason for her anger with Justin, it had clearly been shelved, and with the arrival of more guests, Carolyn quickly transformed into her usual hospitable, light-hearted self. But Jo knew she hadn't imagined the tense atmosphere.

A minibus arrived in the mews below, bringing apprentices and other young workers from across the town and various industries. Bex, at a vantage point by the window, was the first to spot them.

'Now these really are our special guests,' Carolyn said. She swept across the room to greet them by the door. Of the fifty or so apprentices who arrived in the next half an hour, she appeared to know most of their names and remembered what they were studying while the rest of the Upwards team handed out badges and table numbers in their well-drilled fashion. Soon a convivial babble filled the room as people helped themselves to coffee or juices.

Jo noticed that Justin took advantage of the crowd to make himself scarce. When the other guest speakers turned up, she forgot about him and began to be nervous all over again about her presentation. Klaassen, the climatologist from Bournemouth University, treated her with the same remote, barely polite manner as before, whereas Bal was just as charming and friendly as she remembered. Jo tried to settle her nerves with a cup of coffee and a chat to the apprentices at her table. They were from very different jobs, but they all seemed to have a high opinion of the training from Upwards and they cheered Carolyn to the rafters when she got to her feet to welcome them and open the event.

Carolyn had selected a black-and-white dress with a striking necklace, which somehow made her look more severe. She beamed radiantly across the room as the cameras started recording. Behind her, a monochrome film showed scenes of Bournemouth in the eighties and nineties as she talked about her upbringing and how much the company meant to her.

Despite her unease about Justin Fielding, Jo had to admit that the studios seemed to be a professional outfit. An expert speaker gave their presentation of the future from each table, which meant plenty of work for the camera and sound operators. During the time for questions after each session, Carolyn and her team tended to stay quiet to ensure that most of the questions came from the apprentices, but Bex was as vocal as ever. Jo noticed that Liang looked subdued and kept glancing in her direction. She decided to seek her out as soon as she could to find out what, if anything, was wrong.

First, however, she had the ordeal of her own session on what the planets said about the future. She focused on the benefits of a more spiritual age, a better understanding of the earth's needs and the required skills and qualities of science, empathy and collaboration. She had been worried about scepticism, particularly from the scientists in the room, but there were so many questions from the young apprentices that they took up all her attention. Even so, she was mightily relieved when the time came for Baljit's session and the cameras turned to him.

In the break afterwards, while people queued for coffee, juice and birthday cake, Jo sought out Liang. She was handing out a quiz that she was going to run after lunch. Jo had a feeling that, given the chance, Liang would tell her what was on her mind and, sure enough, after some chat about Jo's session, she confessed in a low tone that she'd been offered a job with an insurance company.

So that explains the hidden phone and calls, Jo thought. From Liang's quick description, it sounded like the new job had far better prospects. She waited to hear what was bothering her.

They drifted towards a quiet corner, where Liang poured out her concerns. 'I can't tell Carolyn. I can't do it to her, she'll be so disappointed. Especially after Vinny and Flora.'

Jo had noticed that Vinny was conspicuous by his absence. 'He's been kept back at the office to look after the phones,' Liang explained. 'With no Flora around, one of us had to do it and Carolyn said she wanted me here. So, you see, that's another reason why I can't bring myself to tell her. And, to make things worse, the new company want to know my answer today.'

'Carolyn is a grown-up,' Jo said. 'Just tell her the facts. It won't be the first time someone has left for a better job, and it won't be the last either.'

Liang still looked troubled and may have said more but they were interrupted by Bex.

'What are you two whispering about?'

'An Upwards birthday surprise for Carolyn,' Jo replied. 'Justin told me he's planning something special for her,' she added with a sudden mischievous impulse.

Liang looked askance at her while Bex plied her with questions. While Jo fended off the young woman's interrogation, already regretting her rash flight of fancy, she wondered if Bex was also on Louis Carswell's payroll. She checked herself and remembered what Agnieszka had said. 'Paranoia is infectious.' She didn't want to become as bad as Carswell.

'Carolyn deserves it anyway, whatever it is,' Bex was saying. 'She fills me with optimism just listening to her. If she can be so successful after the start she had in life, then we certainly can.'

Jo agreed and smiled at Liang. 'It just takes courage sometimes, that's all.' She was starting to feel a wave of relief. She had survived the ordeal by video and Justin Fielding's ominous presence. Flora was recovering and at this very moment, if all went to plan, should be opening up to the police, placing the blame firmly at Carswell's door, which would get the persistent DCI Conway off her back. She found Carolyn as soon as she could and made an excuse for an early exit.

'I loved your session. It captured imaginations, and that's the most powerful thing of all,' Carolyn said, standing back and looking Jo in the eyes.

'I was pleased with it too,' Jo admitted, 'especially because of all the questions.'

Carolyn hugged her. 'You must go, you've got a long drive home. But keep in touch. I want to go over that birth chart for the company.'

Jo could have been forgiven for racing down the narrow stairs and out into the mews with a lighter step. But there was one more thing she wanted to establish and this was her last chance to find out.

She approached Bex, who was cutting the cake into smaller slices. 'Do you know how the cloakroom system works?' She held up her ticket. 'Someone took my coat when I arrived and I can't seem to find it.'

Bex masked her irritation well and managed a smile. 'Follow me,' she said, wiping her hands on a napkin.

Jo allowed herself to be led into the small room near the top of the stairs, which was stacked with racks of coats and bags. Bex kept up a flow of chat as she sorted through the racks, but Jo knew her red down coat couldn't easily be found, having dropped it at the back of the room earlier.

She brought the conversation easily enough to the previous Upwards movie. 'You were heavily involved in making that video, weren't you?'

'Yes, that was how I learned all about production and marketing. I'm going to go for Vinny's job,' Bex said. 'I know you might say it's a bit soon, but why not? You've got to take a risk sometimes, haven't you?'

'Absolutely,' Jo agreed. 'And your experience in promoting the first video is bound to help — especially as you were up against a tight deadline. Weren't you waiting here for Carolyn to watch it on the day you finished it?'

Bex frowned. 'Oh yes, that's right. She was at the Metropole at the Planet Events takeover do. Sorry, I shouldn't call it that, should I?' She laughed. 'Justin was pissed off, I can tell you. He told her to get her arse over here. Those were his actual words.'

Taking pity on the young woman, Jo started searching herself, moving closer to the spot where she had dumped her coat earlier. 'Did he tear her off a strip when she arrived? I'd like to have seen that.'

'Me too,' Bex said. 'But he bottled it. She said she'd view it at his place so he downloaded it onto a stick and sent us home. He was in a foul mood.' She shook her head in admiration. 'She did it, though. Carolyn, I mean. She was as good as her word. The video was in Vinny's inbox the next morning, edits marked and ready to be finalized. And you've got to admit, she does manage both Louis Carswell and Justin brilliantly, even though they hate each other.'

Jo made a pretence of finding her coat and held it up triumphantly. 'It must have fallen off a hanger. Thanks for helping, I'll be on my way.'

Bex looked relieved and was clearly eager to return to the action. But, as they left the little cloakroom side by side, Jo decided to chance one more question.

'That day we were just talking about — the day Planet Events bought out Upwards? Can you remember anything special about that day?'

Bex shrugged, her eyes on Carolyn, who was holding court with a bunch of apprentices in the other room. 'Just the making of the video and being here at the studio and working in the editing suite. I mean, that was pretty special.' She paused for a moment. 'Well, goodbye, Jo. It was lovely to meet you. Oh, hang on—' she dug in her pocket and pulled out a little wad of shiny business cards — 'I had these made for my new career in marketing.' She flourished them proudly. 'You can have one. You've got to build your own dreams, haven't you?'

On that optimistic note, Jo finally made good her escape from Justin Fielding's studios and was already thinking fondly of the deep Cotswold valleys. She was jogging by the time she reached her car and reversed so speedily out of the mews that she nearly collided with a white van parked at an odd angle by the studio door. She recognized Andre at the back, busy stacking it with boxes, and they exchanged the briefest of nods.

She drove for about two miles until her heart rate calmed down and she started to think more clearly. She noticed she was close to the clifftop where she and Macy had walked on the night they'd met Agnieszka in the cocktail bar, and she decided to head there to get some air.

It was a damp, mild day, with the branches of the trees nodding gently and the sea flat calm. She took some steadying breaths while she stood on the cliff path looking towards Purbeck. Then she steeled herself and looked at her phone. As expected, there were a few missed calls, including two from Macy. There was also a text from him.

Told Carswell I quit. Went straight to police but they don't believe any of it and are holding me for questioning re Flora's accident. LC is powerful here. Try your Gloucester pals, they might be better listeners.

CHAPTER TWENTY-THREE

It was easy enough to follow Macy's advice because her other calls had been from the Gloucester Police, who'd left a voicemail asking her to call them. She sat on bench on the cliff top, battling with the wind and trying gamely to explain that the murder of Shane Beaman and Cheryl Frost were connected to Flora's accident, but DCI Chris Conway interrupted her. 'I have some questions for you first. How soon can you get to the station?'

'I'm in Bournemouth but I'll set off as soon as I can. I can be with you in a couple of hours but this is urgent.' Jo could hear the tiredness in her own voice. 'My friend — colleague — David Macy is being held by police in Bournemouth and they don't seem to believe that Louis Carswell arranged a break-in to the Rivermill Bookshop and Café, where I work. You need to get hold of Cheryl Frost's report, which he stole from the Rivermill. There must be something valuable in it, which Carswell wants hidden. He may also have tried to get Flora killed. Honestly, Carswell is ruthless and paranoid and he has influence in Bournemouth, that's why they won't listen to Macy.' As Jo went on, her volume had risen and she could feel herself growing more agitated.

'My team is going through Miss Frost's report, and I am in touch with my colleagues in Bournemouth,' DCI Conway said. 'Now, what's the earliest you can get here?'

'You mean you don't believe us either?' Unable to sit still any longer, she began to pace towards her car.

'It's a question of evidence, Miss Hughes,' came his rather monotone voice. 'I've spoken to the accident investigation team dealing with Miss Howell's unfortunate hit-and-run incident. We have recovered the full details of the vehicle involved, which has no connection whatsoever to Mr Carswell. And there is no evidence of any connection with Shane Beaman's death either.'

This silenced Jo for a second. She was getting a sense of what Macy must be up against in Bournemouth and realized all they had was conjecture with no strong evidence. She made another valiant attempt to persuade the DCI, pointing out that Carswell had no direct involvement in any of the crimes. 'He probably has perfect alibis for all of them. But he *is* organizing them.'

DCI Conway remained polite and implacable and she had to agree to meet him at the police station, after which point, she realized she had better get on the road to Gloucester. She tried Macy again but he didn't pick up, so she assumed he was still being interviewed. She expected to be in a similar position herself very soon and wondered how close they were to being charged.

It was a frustrating journey as the traffic was heavy. She had no idea how Macy was getting on and was fairly sure of a frosty welcome at the police station. Once there, she spent a few minutes sitting in her car, tensely touching up her hair and make-up. 'Stay calm,' she muttered to herself. But it wasn't easy to quell her nerves when there was so much at stake. What if they charged Macy with withholding information or, worse, interfering in a police inquiry? A criminal charge could ruin his business. She didn't fancy her own prospects much either and was not looking forward to doing battle with DCI Conway again. He was bound to focus on her untimely appearance at the scene of Cheryl's death. She noticed that her hands left sweaty patches on the swing doors as she pushed her way into the police station and repeated in her mind that she was completely innocent of any crime and therefore could not be a serious suspect.

Whether under suspicion or not, there was no doubting the gravity of DCI Conway and his team. They were more interested in her actions than anything to do with Louis Carswell. Conway sat mainly in silence while a different officer questioned her about Cheryl's report on Upwards.

Jo surprised herself by showing she could be as patient as they were. Macy's advice over the years had always been to be open with the police whenever possible. Based on his last message to her, she decided to keep nothing back. She trusted he was doing the same.

The whole interview took about two hours, by which time she was hungry, shaky with too much caffeine, and her brain felt numb from the extensive questioning. She drove into McDonald's, which was the first food outlet she encountered on her way home, ordered a random selection of items and sat in her car, eating stolidly and watching the muddy sky grow darker.

Afterwards, she felt slightly sick but less shaky. There was still no reply from Macy, for which she felt irrationally grateful as she didn't really want to talk. She drove home with the radio switched to the news, not taking any of it in. Nor did she think about anything very much except to envisage a warm bath and a very early night. After a good night's sleep, she reckoned she would be able to cope with her shift at the Rivermill and further dealings with the police. DCI Conway had promised to be in touch, which she regarded as more of a threat.

She drove past her flat to park around the back, as she always did, Fleece Alley being too narrow. The bank on the ground floor was closed as it was after five o' clock. All her windows were in darkness and the little cobbled street was quiet and empty as usual. On the corner by the bank, a woman stood with her hands in the pockets of her trench coat, which she was wearing over a long skirt. There was something about her uncertain stance that caught Jo's attention. She dithered between the archway entrance to Fleece Alley and the street lights, shoppers and commuters in King Street. The tall, thin woman looked like a commuter herself in her sober work clothes, loafers and with her laptop bag over one shoulder.

Walking up the alley from the opposite direction, Jo saw the silhouette of the woman still hovering on the corner. The gate to Jo's flat was close to King Street. The woman watched her approach, seeming to freeze like a statue. They stared at each other across the unlit cobbles of the alleyway.

'Can I help you?' Jo heard herself say politely and wondered at herself. All she really wanted to do was go to bed.

The woman hesitated, and if she had dithered a moment longer, Jo would have been through the gate and up her outdoor steps in a single swift movement. But just as Jo released the lock, the stranger spoke. 'Are you Jo Hughes?'

Jo merely nodded. After the day she'd had, words were at a premium.

'I'm a friend of Cheryl Frost's. I was in the office on Thursday when you came in to see her around lunchtime. I don't suppose you noticed me.' Now that she had started speaking, the woman didn't seem to be able to stop. 'I got your details from the visitor's book, where you signed in. I'm sorry about that, I should never have done it, but Cheryl wanted me to contact you.' She paused and her voice wavered slightly. 'What I mean is, she would have wanted me to contact you.'

Jo moved forward and the woman stepped back like a startled deer. Under the street light, Jo could see she was in her fifties, and her narrow lips had a harsh colour on them, which gave her a stern expression. But she had heard the wobble in her voice and sensed the courage behind the hesitation. 'You'd better come in.'

Jo didn't usually drink tea but the woman, who introduced herself as Eloise Pindard, requested tea with milk, so she made a pot. Eloise perched on the edge of the sofa and held the mug on her knees, while Jo waited patiently. 'What did Cheryl want you to tell me?' she asked eventually when Eloise had admired the cosy room and thanked her for the drink.

'The police came to the office on Friday morning. That's how I heard the news,' Eloise said, answering a different question. It seemed to Jo as if some of the horror she'd felt then remained imprinted on her face in shock lines and crumples. 'What a way to find out your friend is dead. Of course they have a very professional way of telling you but even so . . .'

She rubbed her finger on the rim of her mug to erase the trace of lipstick she'd left there. 'It was an awful thing to hear in the office with other people around. We've been friends for twenty-two years.' She swallowed. 'I'm so sorry. You're a complete stranger. I shouldn't be going on like this. And drinking your tea. I don't even know you. I should be at home.' She looked at the clock over the fireplace. 'It's late.'

'You may as well finish your tea.'

'Cheryl's death has affected me oddly, I don't recognize myself,' the woman admitted. She took another gulp from her mug.

'What did you want to tell me?' Jo tried again, this time more gently.

'It was the fact that she was in her workshop at the time she died,' Eloise said, again on some track of her own. 'What she really wanted to do was to work on her furniture and make neglected things beautiful again. She couldn't wait for the office to close so she could use her redundancy money to start up her own business.'

'She told me a bit about her plans too.' Jo sat back in her armchair. 'Her dreams, really.'

Eloise nodded. 'The police said it was an accident, but Cheryl was far too careful to do anything stupid like using the wrong paint remover. I told them she would never have bought anything dangerous. She was smart and knew what she was doing. And even if she had, she would have known how to use it. With the right PPE and all that.'

'She wasn't wearing any special equipment except gloves,' Jo said.

Eloise shook her head slowly, her face tense. 'I don't believe it was an accident. I tried to tell the police that sometimes our work puts us at risk, which is why confidentiality is so important. And I know Cheryl had severe doubts about a case and the people she was dealing with. The trouble is, I don't know much of the detail.'

'What sort of case do you mean?' Jo was finding the woman's rambling account hard to follow.

'We deal with whistle-blowers. And when we investigate a claim, we are not always welcome, as you can imagine. I told the police all this and they took notes but I've no idea what, if anything, they're going to do about it.'

Jo wondered if she should mention that she had spent hours with the police or explain that she had been the one to discover Cheryl's body. Somehow it seemed important just to let the woman talk so, for once, she resisted asking questions and instead topped up their mugs of tea and pushed forward a plate of ginger biscuits. The woman opposite her took one absently and continued to speak her worries.

'I live on my own as well, but I'm not entrepreneurial like Cheryl. I don't know what I'm going to do when the office closes. She said you ran your own business and that you're an astrologer. But I don't think I have any special skills to be able to do anything like that. And I'm too young to retire.' She looked into her mug. 'And, as for Cheryl, she was far too young to—' Eloise broke off, collected herself and looked Jo squarely in the eyes for the first time. 'So that's why I came to see you. Because I'm not sure the police took me seriously. I don't know the finer details, but Cheryl told me you had found something out about a case of hers: Flora Howell.'

'Flora was a case of hers?' Jo repeated.

'Yes. We don't share the details of cases. Not even among one another in the office. It's all completely confidential. It has to be, but Cheryl was my friend, so I know enough. Can I ask — what did you tell Cheryl that worried her?'

Jo leaned forward and set down her mug. 'I told her that Flora had been involved in a hit-and-run accident and was nearly killed. It happened in Bournemouth on her way to see a friend and Flora's injuries are so severe, she has hardly spoken to anyone since.'

'That makes sense,' Eloise said. 'You see, Flora Howell was a whistle-blower and Cheryl had taken on her case. They met when Cheryl was doing a quality audit on the training company that Flora worked for. It doesn't mean Cheryl believed everything that Flora said but I know she was concerned about her and I know the complaint concerned bullying.' Eloise seemed to find the conversation easier now she was describing work processes. 'Cheryl was at stage one of the investigation, which means she had met with those involved and submitted her initial report.'

'Would she have met the directors of the company? Carolyn Ash and Louis Carswell? Did they know about this complaint?'

'I don't know their names, I'm afraid, or the details of the case, but Cheryl knew Flora was under pressure to drop her claim. She'd said that a director was trying to get her to sign a non-disclosure agreement, which would mean she would have to leave the company and not discuss anything about working there. For a tidy sum, no doubt, and he was very persistent. It happens, unfortunately,' the woman added matter-of-factly.

'And Flora refused,' Jo murmured. Her mind went back to her hotel room at the Metropole, the night she'd met Flora. The woman had been drunk and propped up on the opposite bed, sipping water, claiming people were after her, trying to tell her what to do. She thought about what Agnieszka had told her about Carswell's tactics. 'Would it make any difference to her claim if she was discredited in some way?' she asked. 'Would that count against her?'

Eloise assumed a rather superior expression and her face returned to its harsher lines. 'Cheryl was looking at the whole context in which the claim was made. So if the claimant had other motives for bringing the case then this would come to light. That's the reason for formally interviewing the people concerned.'

'What did Flora hope to get out of all this?' Jo wondered out loud, realizing the question was as much to herself as the woman opposite.

'Not financial gain, I can assure you. This is not like an employment tribunal where costs are allocated. However, any malpractice or unfair treatment is made public and the company has to take appropriate action. If anything illegal comes to light, then we inform the relevant authorities.'

Jo sighed. 'But you don't know what's in Cheryl's report. And it hadn't reached that stage yet anyway?'

'No, it's with our boss in London. Obviously, I told the police all this but I'm not sure they will pursue it. They seemed more interested in Cheryl's hobby and what I knew about her business and where she bought her materials. I couldn't really help them with that.'

'If it's DCI Conway's team, then I can assure you he is very thorough,' Jo said. As the police already had Cheryl's audit on Upwards, surely it wouldn't take them long to get hold of her report on Flora's whistle-blowing claim? Even without that, they should have enough evidence to charge Carswell. In her own mind, this proved conclusively that he was behind the burglary at the Rivermill, although DCI Conway would no doubt require more convincing. Still, it was worth a call to them, she decided, and then Bournemouth Police would have to release Macy.

'You will let me know, won't you? I need to follow this up for Cheryl's sake,' Eloise said when Jo showed her out of the flat. Having unburdened herself, she seemed eager to be on her way home but on the doorstep, she hesitated. 'It's not that Cheryl was emotionally involved with the case. She was far too professional for that. But she was concerned about Flora. I want to make sure I do everything I can, so I will be pushing London to release this report. Don't worry,' she added with a bitter smile. 'It's not as if I care if it's career-limiting.'

'I'll keep you informed,' Jo promised.

As soon as the front door closed, she picked up her phone, eager to tell Macy about this breakthrough. She should have remembered that conversations with Macy never went to plan.

CHAPTER TWENTY-FOUR

The first surprise was that Macy was driving and so clearly no longer incarcerated in Bournemouth Police station.

'I've got a good lawyer,' he said before Jo could even ask the question.

'You could have told me,' she complained.

'And you could pick up your phone occasionally. I've left at least two messages to tell you I'm on my way home. I can't put enough miles between me and Bournemouth, quite honestly. Don't ever suggest a seaside holiday to me. I never want to see the place again.'

'Listen, I've found out something about Flora that makes sense of everything she did. She was a whistle-blower and she reported the directors at Upwards for bullying. Carswell knew and he was trying to get her to sign an agreement to withdraw her claim and pay her off. So this definitely lays the blame for her accident and the Rivermill break-in firmly at Carswell's door.' She explained rapidly what she'd learned from Eloise but was met with a sceptical silence.

'Hmm,' Macy said. 'It gives him a motive for ensuring nobody gets their hands on that whistle-blowing report, but it's not going to be enough to convince Bournemouth Police that he would try to kill her. And it's not Flora's report that was stolen from the Rivermill but some other fairly bland document.'

'But Carswell wanted to cover up Cheryl's involvement with Upwards. I suppose he was worried we would find out about the whistle-blowing, which we have,' Jo said. 'After all, he knew from Jess that I had that report.'

'I suppose it explains why he roped me into all this too,' Macy said. 'He wanted to see what we could find on Flora. Because what we could find, then others could find.'

'And he hoped to get something on her that would make her story look bad. Not that we know what her story is,' she added before he could make this point. 'That's still a big gap. But the police are interviewing Flora again so it will soon be out there. Now maybe they will charge Carswell too.'

Again Macy sounded doubtful. 'To be honest, the police are more interested in Justin Fielding. They've been going through the CCTV footage and they've got enough to bring Fielding in to question him about why Shane Beaman went to see him two days before he died. That's part of the reason they lost interest in me, I think,' he said. 'And even if you're right about Carswell wanting to silence this whistle-blowing report then it still doesn't make sense of the hit-and-run accident. Especially not when he was the person who had put Flora under surveillance.'

'But we now know he was pressurizing her to sign something, offering cash for her silence. She virtually told me that herself,' Jo said, 'though I didn't know enough then to understand what she was saying.'

She heard the car engine turn off and guessed Macy was home. She wondered where that was these days and whether Rowanna was waiting for him.

'Yes, Flora being pressurized to sign an agreement, that I can believe. Agnieszka told me Carswell makes use of NDAs. He gets her to dig the dirt on a rival and then decides how he's going to use that information.'

'Delightful,' Jo said.

'A bit shady maybe, although still nothing they can convict him on. But listen, you've got something and you should tell the Bournemouth lot. I've had it with them for today, so just let me know tomorrow how you get on. Ask for DCI Jill Bellis.'

That was as much as she was going to get out of Macy tonight. She rang off and dutifully called Bournemouth Police.

As she waited to be put through to the right team, the information that had seemed like a breakthrough when Eloise was sitting in her lounge gradually began to diminish and the gaps emerged, partly because Macy had done such a thorough job of pouring cold water on her theories. By the time she explained it to a detective constable on the inquiry team, even she was beginning to have doubts. The detective constable took it seriously, however, and assured her they would take action if needed.

'Does that mean you will call Louis Carswell in for questioning?' Jo asked.

'We will be talking to him in the morning,' came the cautious reply, 'and we are also meeting with Flora Howell later in the day. We have arranged to see her in hospital. No doubt she can corroborate your information.'

Jo had to be content with that but was left feeling oddly excluded. All the work seemed to be in the hands of others and she had to sit back and wait. There was astrology work to do but knowing this didn't make her feel any better. She wandered to the window of her lounge and looked out moodily. A couple were strolling by below, leaning into each other. Jo imagined they were probably on their way to a restaurant, where they had a table booked with candles and, for good measure, she included a festive and cosy atmosphere — possibly with carol singers dropping by — to complete her mental picture of a romantic Christmas meal.

She brought herself up short and reminded herself that it was only this emotionally charged month of December that made her yearn for an idyllic Christmas. She had probably also been provoked by the stray thought she'd had earlier about where Macy was spending his nights. It was time to seriously consider her own romantic offer, she decided, so she picked up the phone and called Teddy. He was about to go to dinner with his golfing group but was clearly delighted when she told him she was going to book her flight to Spain.

'Work here is winding down,' she said, gleefully making it up as she went along. 'And Hanni can do without me now her sister is trained up and she's not so worried about takings at the bookshop. I've decided I need a break and a romantic dinner in a posh restaurant.'

'Well, that can certainly be achieved,' Teddy said and Jo laughed and told him she would send him her flight details.

Her mood lightened after this conversation. There was no doubt that putting all their information into the hands of the police had taken a load off her mind. And why did she care where Macy was spending his time? While she ran the bath, she booked her flights to Malaga and messaged Teddy. After that, all it took was a hot, sudsy bath, a ready meal from the fridge and a glass of red wine and she finally went to bed with a good conscience.

When the alarm woke her at 7 a.m., she rolled over into the pillow, hit the snooze button and was, for once, glad of the dark morning. Hanni had told her she was not needed that morning and that she should have a lie-in for her own well-being.

Scraps of dreams and images returned to her in the half-light. She recalled the moment she'd first seen Flora, although she hadn't known that the woman locking her bike and bundling up her purple waterproof was the so-called 'target'. A few minutes later, she had seen Flora pulling on the green silk jacket, which she'd worn all evening. Carolyn's jacket, Jo now knew. Or, at least, the jacket that Carolyn had been wearing on the fourteenth of September at the Metropole. What had Bex called it? The takeover do. She'd not thought of that moment since but going over it in detail now was a pleasant excuse to put off getting out of bed.

She remembered then why she'd not given more thought to that first encounter with Flora. It was because of her little spat with Andre, the obnoxious but handsome driver of the BMW. She had almost forgotten Flora's modest but effective intervention and how the young woman had then quickly erased herself from the scene by scuttling into the hotel, almost succeeding in erasing herself from Jo's memory too.

Jo threw back the duvet and grabbed a sweatshirt and tracksuit bottoms. She didn't even make coffee or feed the cat. She went straight to her workroom, opened a drawer and pulled out Flora's natal chart. She reread her own notes about the importance of the Jupiter return, which brings a chance to start over or put something right. In Flora's case, it had been the courage to blow the whistle. But surely that couldn't just be about bullying at work?

There had to be more to it than that. Jo put down her notes and stared out of the arched window unseeingly. Whatever Flora had said to Andre had taken him aback and had also been effective. Maybe Flora had surprised herself too when she had decided to take Cheryl into her confidence and tell the truth about Upwards. Whatever it was she had chosen to reveal, it had put her life in danger. And others' lives. Jo pushed back her office chair. She'd have a shower and a coffee and then she had to make some phone calls.

Her first call was to Hanni to ask if her friend could manage without her. 'I have to go back to Bournemouth,' Jo explained.

'Of course I can,' Hanni said. 'But do you really have to go back? Are you going to get David released?'

Jo laughed. 'No, he's rescued himself. It's something I've got to do for Flora. The police told me they're going to interview her again and I think it's going to be a disaster.'

'Last time they went to see her, they blocked her healing,' Hanni said.

'Yes, because they told her about Shane's death and I am sure she blames herself for that. So she still won't tell them anything for fear of putting other people in danger. I have to find a way to make it easy for her,' Jo said. 'Because she is the only person who can unlock this.'

'It's not just her body that is healing, but her spirit,' Hanni said. 'Listen, Josephine, you must protect yourself too.'

Jo assured her she would, gathered her things together and hurried to her car.

* * *

Two and a half hours later, she was pulling up behind a low, uninspiring block of flats in Boscombe, which looked like it had been built in the 1970s. Signs of wear gave a tired look to the fancy tiling and paintwork. She rang an old-fashioned, low-tech doorbell, which buzzed somewhere internally.

The glass door popped open and Jo stepped into a spacious, if shabby lobby with a staircase ahead. Flora's flat was on the ground floor. As she hesitated, the door on her right opened cautiously.

Flora's brother Theo stood in the gap. The young, dark face wore an exhausted, defeated expression, and even his clothes looked creased, as if he had just picked them off the ironing pile.

'Hi, Theo. Thanks for letting me come and see you.'

'I doubt if we'll find anything useful.'

'At least Flora will listen to you,' Jo said, 'and you've got a better chance of persuading her to talk to the police.'

'Nothing I've said so far has worked.' He stepped back to let Jo into the flat. 'I haven't got any milk for tea or coffee or anything like that,' he said.

Jo followed him into a small hall with two doors leading off it. One was ajar, revealing a tidy bedroom and the other led into a lounge, sparsely furnished but comfortable enough. What money had been saved on furniture had clearly been spent on books, Jo thought as she let her eyes roam over the shelves.

'I can do you a coke, though.' Theo had continued through to the kitchen and was now standing in the doorway with two cans of Coca Cola.

'Thanks,' Jo said. 'Now, let me tell you what I think has happened.'

'As long as I can pack while you talk,' Theo said. In the middle of a low coffee table was a half-full holdall. 'Flora has given me a list of books that she wants me to bring to the hospital.'

Jo stood in the middle of the lounge, sipping her coke while Theo gradually built a pile of books. She took a breath and began to explain the sequence of events that she had carefully constructed on the drive down.

'Flora discovered that Upwards was doing something wrong or illegal. I don't know what. It could be something to do with the loss of a contract to another firm or the takeover from Planet Events. I don't know how long Flora had known about it or what prompted her to take it to the authorities. It might have been simply that she had met someone she liked who she felt she could trust. That woman was Cheryl Frost, who works for an agency providing a whistle-blowing service.'

'Hold on.' Theo held up his hand, looking pained. 'Who is this Cheryl Frost? The police asked me about her but Flora's never mentioned her.'

'Flora met Cheryl when she did an audit on Upwards last September. The audit gave them a clean report, which helped them get their Ofsted rating, but I think Flora knew they didn't deserve it and maybe that bothered her.' Jo remembered the picture of Flora standing aside from the team while they proudly waved their certificate.

'DCI Bellis told me that Cheryl Frost had been killed in an accident at home and they're treating it as suspicious. Obviously, I told them this had nothing to do with Flora.' Theo bit his lip. 'Are you saying I was wrong? It did have something to do with her?'

Jo nodded. 'As a whistle-blower, Flora would have been assured of complete confidentiality and she would have had to keep her side of the bargain and stay silent too. Even to you,' she added. 'At least while the investigation was going on. And it had only just started, from what I can gather.'

Theo sat down suddenly, holding a Regency romance novel. 'So, let me see if I've got this straight. My big sister is a whistle-blower. She's actually done something pretty brave, in fact. And she's kept all this to herself to try to protect others. Because, whatever it is she knows has put her life in danger.' Theo chewed on his bottom lip, staring at the worn green carpet.

'I think so,' Jo said. 'Maybe that's one of the reasons why she is still not speaking up. She knows from the police that she has lost her friends and supporters. Shane, Cheryl.'

'Not me.' Theo looked up at Jo, shock driving out the sadness from his face. 'So you think Cheryl Frost was actually killed because of this?'

'Yes — and Flora's friend, Shane Beaman.'

'Christ!' Theo put his hands to his face. 'What is it that Flora knows? Some sort of state secret? And if so, why aren't the police protecting her instead of torturing her with questions?'

Jo sat down on the nearest armchair. It was as though speaking the words out loud had made Flora's courage and vulnerability more real to her. She was taking a risk of her own, too, because she didn't have much hard evidence and there were some troubling gaps in her analysis.

'As soon as the police get hold of Cheryl's whistle-blowing report, which should be today, they will know a lot more than we do,' Jo said. 'Then she should feel safer.' *And so will I*, she mentally added.

'Will they know before they see Flora?' Theo asked. 'They're due to be meeting her at two o' clock.'

'That's why I wanted to see you first. To make sure you're there with her and that you understand.'

'Don't worry, I was always going to be with her.' He didn't move. 'I can't get over it. My sister being so brave when she's always been so — well — so meek and mild.'

'She certainly found her courage.'

'Like the lion in *The Wizard of Oz*.' Theo gave a sudden laugh, which turned into a strangled sob. He pushed his fingers into his eyes as the tears coursed down his face. 'I should have been here for her. I was away, always studying, and she was working to help me pay my fees.'

Jo searched for a box of tissues but had to settle for some kitchen roll from beside the cooker. She silently handed it to Theo.

'Whatever it is she has found out, I'm proud of her. Even if it's some piddling accountancy dodge and not a national secret after all. She has done the right thing,' he said. 'She's always had a strong sense of right and wrong.'

'Scorpio Sun and Moon, along with the Jupiter return means it was the right moment for her to exercise her strength,' Jo murmured while Theo returned quietly to the packing.

'Obviously I don't know what you're talking about and probably wouldn't agree with you if I did,' he said over his shoulder.

'It doesn't matter.' Jo smiled. 'One thing you've made me realize is it's not about the nature of the secret but the people Flora is dealing with. Louis Carswell has been pressurizing her to drop the case by offering her cash, and he has power and influence locally — and even in government circles, apparently.'

'I can see why she has refused to say anything and I'm going to make sure the police don't see Flora before they know the full story. Otherwise it will just be a repeat of the last time they interviewed her, which was a nightmare. Will you come to talk to them with me?'

'Of course, as much as they'll let me.'

Between them, they found the last few items from Flora's list and Jo zipped up the holdall while Theo went to fetch his coat and keys.

'I'm borrowing Flora's room while I'm staying here,' he explained. 'When we shared a flat in London, we had a bigger place, but we needed money for my university fees so she moved down here.' He carried on talking while he locked the doors and they walked to Jo's car. 'I'm going to persuade her to come back to London and we can rent a place together. As soon as she's well enough.'

'She certainly seems to have got in with a toxic little clique here.' Jo shuddered, recalling her encounter with Fielding yesterday and realizing that she, like Macy, would be relieved never to see any of the Upwards team again.

She stopped suddenly and looked at Theo over the bonnet of her car. 'Do you remember you told me that Flora got a speeding ticket?'

'Did I?' He looked at her, his face all light and shade in the low December light.

'Yes, it was when I first met you in the hospital waiting room. You were describing your sister to me and you said she could never do anything wrong. You said she was so law-abiding that she cried when she got a speeding ticket.'

'Vaguely.' Theo had his hand on the passenger door, eager to get to the police station now he had made his decision. 'I was here when she got the ticket through the post and I do remember that she was upset, which was slightly over the top, I thought. After all, we've all—'

'Can you find it?'

'Yes, I suppose I could. Flora always files everything neatly. But let's get to the station first, I want to make sure I see them.'

'No, this is important,' Jo said. 'Can you go and look now. Please.' She followed as he trudged back indoors and stood over him while he wordlessly went through a box file holding all Flora's bills, bank statements and other papers. It didn't take him long because, as he'd said, his sister was very organized.

When he held up the penalty notice with a flourish, Jo took it carefully from his hand. Her lips went dry as she spoke the date out loud.

'OK, we can go now.' She made for the door.

'What's up?' Theo demanded. 'Are you OK? You've gone very pale. What's changed? What's happened?'

'I'm fine,' she reassured him, her voice even. 'Nothing's changed. It's exactly as we thought. Come on, I'll drive you to the police station.'

However, while Theo locked up again, she hurried ahead and made a single phone call.

'Bex, I need you to tell me one thing and you need to be quick and completely honest with me.'

CHAPTER TWENTY-FIVE

When they arrived at the police station, Jo had to tell Theo that she couldn't come in with him. She simply said she needed to be somewhere else for her own peace of mind.

His disappointment was palpable. 'But you can explain it all a lot more convincingly than I can.'

'I doubt it. You're her brother and you understand Flora better than anybody. Just be open with them. And, look, you can still phone me if needed.'

Jo, for once, didn't phone anybody on her journey to the hospital. Once she had watched Theo walk into the police station, she drove in tense quietness. As she retraced her route past the now familiar tree-lined roads of smaller hotels and B&Bs, she remembered her first visit, when she had just learned of Flora's accident and found herself fully engrossed in this case of Macy's. Strangely, she found she didn't regret any of it and the fact that Macy had now apparently washed his hands of the investigation didn't bother her.

She found a parking space easily and within minutes was walking purposefully towards the entrance. A white van stopped at the kerb as she approached and she recognized the handsome Andre at the wheel. Her heart rate sprinted and she realized she hadn't seriously expected to be right.

Carolyn stepped down from the van, holding a large bouquet of flowers. Jo drew back as the vehicle accelerated past her and away, but she was a fraction too slow. Carolyn had spotted her and instantly her face broke into her usual warm smile.

'Jo! How lovely. Have you come to see Flora too?' She held out the bunch of red roses and holly, spotted with mistletoe berries. 'Look, this is all I could get. It's a bit Christmassy, isn't it? But at least it's better than a wreath.' She ended on a little laugh.

Jo suddenly doubted herself. A cold intake of breath seemed to stick in her chest and she couldn't form a sentence.

Carolyn was all concern. 'Jo? Are you all right?'

'Please don't go and see Flora today,' she said, finding her voice. But Carolyn was already moving ahead of her and into the noisy and bustling hospital lobby.

'Of course I will — I said I would,' she said over her shoulder. 'You can come in with me if you want. Although I don't think Flora knows you very well, so it might not be such a good idea. It's the first time they've allowed visitors and I need to tell her how much she is missed. We really do miss her, you know.' She strode down the wide corridors of the hospital with Jo keeping pace at her side.

'You can't see her,' Jo said. 'The police are interviewing her later. They've forbidden all visitors.'

'Nonsense, I'm her boss and I'm not staying long, anyway.'

They had reached Flora's ward, where a list of patients was posted alongside the official signs and instructions. Another visitor walked ahead of them, an elderly man with a slow, shuffling gait. Not pausing to look at the list, Carolyn pushed ahead of him. A ward nurse stepped out of a side room and demanded to know who Carolyn was visiting.

'Flora Howell. It's all right, I did notify you and I am expected,' Carolyn said with breezy authority, keeping up her pace, the bouquet held out like a trophy.

'And you?' the nurse detained Jo with a look.

'The same. I'm visiting Flora too.'

'Only one visitor at a time,' the nurse said. 'You're not Flora's family, are you?'

'No. Theo's coming later with the police.' Jo tried to edge past, her eyes on Carolyn as she turned right into a private ward. 'Look, I know it sounds odd, but please can you let me through. I'm concerned about Flora and I just need to see her.'

From her expression, Jo guessed that the nurse knew nothing about the police interview. She regarded Jo through narrowed eyelids. 'Flora is in the best possible hands. What's your relationship to her?'

'I'm Flora's friend. Jo Hughes. Can I see her?'

A couple of other visitors had arrived to form a small queue behind her and one raised a complaining voice. The nurse turned, distracted, and Jo slipped past her.

In the private room, the deep red flowers and white berries lay on the empty bed as if on a grave. Still connected to a bank of screens and an intravenous drip, Flora was at the window, propped in a chair. Carolyn was standing over her, clutching a pillow.

Flora's pale face, marked with dark freckles, whipped to Jo as she entered the room. She gaped at both of them, gripping the side of her chair. Her eyes flicked from each to the other. 'What do you want?' she whispered.

'Just to see how you are.' Carolyn's voice was soft and she held out the pillow towards Flora's white face. 'Do you want this? You don't look comfortable.'

Jo stepped forward, her body shaking, and was about to speak when Flora straightened her neck and fixed Carolyn with a stare.

'I was frightened of you once and now I know what you've done to my friends, you must believe I'm terrified, but I'm not. It's all going to come out, Carolyn, and not even you and Louis can prevent it.'

'She's right,' Jo broke in. 'Flora's brother is with the police now. They will see Flora's whistle-blowing report.'

Flora looked at Jo, her eyes widened in relief.

'I know too,' Jo went on. 'It's taken me this long to work it out but I'm not going to stay quiet.'

Carolyn took a few steps back and sat on Flora's bed, seemingly relaxed. The pillow dangled from one hand and she let it fall to the floor.

Jo took a breath and faced her. 'You were driving drunk, weren't you? On your way to Justin's apartment to view the video. You were late and you'd come straight from the Metropole, where you'd been celebrating with Carswell. That's right, isn't it?'

'Well, you seem very certain.' Carolyn didn't falter.

'She was angry as well as drunk,' Flora was hoarse but clear. Her round brown eyes switched from Jo to address Carolyn directly. 'You were angry because you'd missed the appointment with Justin and it was all my fault. You were going on about how I'd made too many mistakes. Then you stupidly had to race that guy on the motorbike who was trying to overtake us.' Flora's back straightened and her voice gained strength. 'Only the police saw it all from the opposite carriageway.'

'What happened then?' Jo kept her voice calm and her eyes on both women.

'She pulled over before they could reach us and made me change places with her.' Flora's energy was gathering with every word. 'We were standing on the edge of a heath in the dark and she was just yelling instructions at me. I hadn't driven in — I don't know — years. I was scared.' She turned to Carolyn again. 'But you knew I had a licence and you just kept shouting. "It's an automatic, it's dead simple, just indicate and pull out. Drive."' Flora's head dipped for the first time and she shuddered.

'Go on,' Jo said.

'I am here, you know.' Carolyn's face had whitened to her lips. She directed her words at Flora. 'I was right to do it, because you were as sober as a judge. You just got a ticket, whereas I would have been . . .' Suddenly her confidence wavered and the sentence hung in the air.

'Just in case they'd got a glimpse of you or in case of cameras, you gave Flora your jacket,' Jo said.

Carolyn's mouth hardened and her gaze snapped to Flora. 'You taunted me with that jacket afterwards, not giving it back, wearing it to the office every day. Just to make the point that finally you had a bit of power. The worm had turned.'

Flora shook her head. 'That was Shane's idea, so you couldn't forget it happened. And so I couldn't forget either,' she said. 'Shane knew. He saw it all, because he'd come to meet me on his bike like he always did.' She sighed. 'He reminded me constantly about the date in case I gave up. He was the only one on my side. He said that Louis pressurizing me to sign that NDA was corporate bullying. And he was right. Actually, you and Louis are just plain, nasty, power-mad bullies.'

'But Flora, why not just go to the police?' Jo could see Flora was close to tears but she had to ask.

'Louis said they wouldn't listen. That he is powerful and has influence in this town, and the only option for me was to leave the company. And look what has happened to everyone who helped me.'

'So instead, Shane went to his old boss,' Jo said.

'A lot of good that did him, Justin knew nothing about it,' Carolyn broke in, her voice scornful. 'Louis and I know when and how to keep something quiet.'

'Because it wasn't Justin who arranged to have Shane Beaman stabbed, was it? You paid Andre, didn't you? With your windfall from the sale of Upwards, you paid Andre for the hit-and-run on Flora and the stabbing of Shane Beaman.'

Carolyn looked across at her with something close to respect. Her voice when she spoke was as steady and rational as if she was making a case in the boardroom. 'Beaman was a loser and a liability. No one except Flora was going to miss him. Given time, Louis said he could make the report disappear into the long grass, and that was all I needed.'

'But that meant you had to silence Cheryl too. You pretended to be interested in her business but you took her some lethal, probably doctored, paint stripper and just waited for it to do its job.'

'Her little so-called business was a totally amateur set-up.' Carolyn looked down at the hospital floor, her tone reflective and calm. 'You have to realize, it was down to me in the end to make my future secure. Let's face it, has always been down to me.' For once, a shadow of weariness crossed her face. 'At the end of the day, no one else is going to look after me. I didn't give Andre all the money by any means,' she added. 'I still have my plans.'

'I would put that in the past tense, if I were you.' Flora lifted her head with an unexpected light in her eye.

Jo could see from the clock above Carolyn's head that the police were due to arrive in five minutes. She was also aware that Andre was probably even now speeding in the white van towards Southampton airport. But there were things she needed to get straight, and she turned to the woman. 'Did Andre refuse when it came to Cheryl?'

'Andre would have done it but Justin stopped him.' Carolyn faced Jo, her eyes fiercely defiant. 'Don't think it's because he grew a conscience or got cold feet. No, it's because, to him, Justin was still his boss. Fucking little idiot.'

'So you had to resort to more direct methods,' Jo pressed on. She could hear a commotion in the corridor behind her. 'And the police will find that Cheryl's is the one death you don't have an alibi for.'

'The kid already had more money than he ever expected to earn,' Carolyn said, the bitter words tumbling out. 'That was a mistake, I admit it. I shouldn't have paid him at the Metropole. I should have made him wait.' She shook her head. 'And now Louis will say he had nothing to do with it. He likes to pretend everything he does is legit, but he knew all about it — most of it anyway — so he's just as guilty.'

'He was the one trying to make me sign that agreement,' Flora said. 'You both nearly drove me mad with that, saying how the money would help Theo.' As she covered her eyes with her hand, the drip above her forearm rocked.

Jo turned to her quickly. 'Not all your friends are lost, Flora, and not all your courage was wasted. Your brother's here and your report to Cheryl won't be silenced.'

Theo was in fact the first person to appear in the doorway, closely followed by DCI Jill Bellis and two uniformed officers. Flora looked up and Theo gave her a nod, and a moment of complete understanding passed between them.

Carolyn rose to her feet and straightened her dark blazer. She turned to DCI Bellis with her usual welcoming smile as one of the officers began to read her rights on arrest for murder and conspiracy to murder.

CHAPTER TWENTY-SIX

As the room filled with people, Jo found herself strangely alone. DCI Bellis made it clear that they would be in touch for a statement but, for the moment, she wasn't needed. The medical staff were attending to Flora and the police attention was focused on Carolyn. She wasn't even sure if Flora had remembered her from their brief meetings at the Metropole.

Free to go, Jo retraced her path with leaden steps through the warren of hospital corridors. She felt a sense of sadness due to the losses: Shane Beaman, who had been a loyal friend to Flora in his way and Cheryl Frost, who she'd met only briefly but, somehow, they had seemed to understand each other.

'Cheer up, you've just played a blinder,' a familiar voice said and she nearly collided with Macy in his woollen coat, scarlet scarf loose at his neck.

'I thought you were never coming back to Bournemouth.'

'When I heard the police were going to take Carswell in for questioning, I just had to be there.' He grinned. 'Even if they can't actually charge him with anything, it was still a sweet moment.'

'Who told you?'

'Jill Bellis, of course. She even let me accompany her to his office. That's what I call job satisfaction.'

'She's a busy woman,' Jo said. 'They're arresting Carolyn Ash upstairs.'

'I know. I was at the police station when Theo arrived. He told me all you'd done. That's why I came over here.'

'Andre Souto still needs to be brought in. He was the one doing Carolyn's dirty work, for a price. And if they don't stop him, he'll be using that money to get on a plane. But I've given DCI Bellis the van registration, so hopefully that's enough.'

They walked outdoors together into the fading winter sunlight. 'So you drove down this morning too,' she said. 'I wish I'd known. You could have given me a lift.'

He put an arm around her shoulders. 'How about I buy you a late lunch instead? There's a pub I've got to know on the seafront in Southbourne, which does a very good fish and chips.'

Jo nodded.

'I should warn you. There is one hitch,' Macy added. 'Alan will be joining us. He's just working through something with Agnieszka. It didn't seem fair to keep him out of the fun.'

'You've got a very strange idea of fun,' she said. 'But then so has Alan.'

Macy smiled. 'The old gang.'

'You Cancerians.' Jo sighed. 'You love a bit of nostalgia.'

'You can leave your car at the pub if you want to have a celebratory drink. I've got our usual two rooms at the hotel.'

* * *

The large corner pub was sitting in a deceptive splash of sunshine. The strange amber sky lightened the whole place inside, filling the little booths with winter light and jarring with the tinsel and decorations. The tables were mainly occupied by workers from the local high street with the odd huddle of well wrapped-up tourists. They took a booth along the sea-facing side but neither of them moved to order anything.

Macy studied her for a moment. 'So, Carolyn was pulling the strings all along.'

'She so wanted to control everything.' Jo sighed. 'All her ambitions of meeting a government minister, reviving Upwards and getting to Buckingham Palace so her nan could meet the Queen. All that in jeopardy.'

She glanced up and saw Alan making his way towards them, spruced up with a shirt collar poking out over his jumper and his hair slicked into its side-parting.

'You look a lot better than when I saw you last,' Jo said.

'Still got a shiner though.' Alan pointed proudly to a trace of a bruise on the inside of his eye and along his nose. 'As a result of which, I will never trust the mad Polish PI as much as he seems to.' He jerked his head towards Macy, who had gone to the bar. 'Although I have to admit, she's come good today. I hope you've ordered cheeseburger and chips for me,' he added as Macy returned to the table.

'Of course. What was that about not trusting Agnieszka? Tell us what you've been up to.'

Alan took his time over his first sip of beer before bestowing a self-satisfied smile on Jo and Macy. 'Oh well, yes, that was rather good, if I say so myself. You see, once we found out that Flora had a speeding ticket on the critical date, then we had a place, date and time to work with. Agnieszka can get access to the CCTV through the traffic control centre. Don't ask me how, but she can. So it was easy enough to find the incident.' He took another sip to create a dramatic pause. Macy hurried him on with a chivvying hand.

'Turns out there was a third party involved. A motorcyclist, not Shane Beaman. He was driving erratically and, you could say, he provoked the incident, but Carolyn definitely overreacted. She was already speeding and she cut him up dangerously. That's what the police saw. They were driving in the opposite direction, but they hit the blue light and went after them. It all plays out brilliantly.' Alan beamed at them.

'Justin Fielding should make a little movie,' Macy said.

'No wait, here's the good bit. Agnieszka and I tracked him down — the mad young motorcyclist. He's a bit half-soaked but he remembers it all right because he reckons Carolyn nearly killed him. He even got a glimpse of her at the wheel.'

'So it verifies Flora's story. This is what must be in the report she made to Cheryl,' Jo said. 'She blew the whistle on Carolyn for breaking the law.' She stared out of the window at the sunny promenade and the passers-by in their winter coats. 'And the whole staff of Upwards always seemed so positive. I never could quite believe that.'

'If you let the video run a bit, there's Shane Beaman on his bike behind them,' Alan added. 'But there's no way either he or the other motorbike rider were going to give witness statements to the police. Not the type.'

'Beaman's an odd one,' Macy said. 'Reformed stalker, or not? I wonder if he put his own pressure on Flora.'

'Yes, he was a bit weird, the way he followed Flora around. But I think maybe she liked him,' Jo said. 'And he did try to sort it out for her by going to his old boss and telling Justin what Carolyn had done. He wouldn't let her give into the pressure from Carswell either.'

'Carswell dressed up his involvement in this very effectively, or I'd never have taken on the case,' Macy said. 'All that stuff about psychological profiling and really understanding Flora,' he sighed. 'Such bullshit.'

'That's presumably why he couldn't just employ Agnieszka,' Alan said. 'She would probably have asked too many questions, having seen it all before.'

Macy nodded. 'She knew him too well. And they'd had a falling out. Not difficult with Agnieszka,' he added with a wry smile. 'But I don't believe that Carswell knew anything about Carolyn's violent plans. That was why he was just as shocked as we were over Beaman's death and Flora's accident.'

'He's hardly an innocent bystander,' Jo pointed out. 'Apart from the bullying and pursuing an NDA for an illegal act, he took extreme steps to keep Cheryl's involvement with

Upwards quiet. And he might deny it to the police, but I'm convinced he arranged the break-in at the Rivermill. Not to mention the fact he was assuring Carolyn he could use his influence in government circles to make the report disappear. He's a fixer, isn't he? That's the reason Carolyn told him about the whole drunk-driving incident. Because she needed his help.'

'He and Carolyn were determined that the whistle-blower report would never come to light,' Macy agreed.

'Do you think he was using his contacts in government to keep it quiet?' Jo asked. 'Is that why Cheryl's initial report was delayed once it got sent to her boss?'

'Of course he was,' Alan put in, but Macy was shaking his head doubtfully.

'I don't know,' Macy said. 'I was never convinced his contacts were as good as he said they were.'

'They certainly won't be now,' Alan remarked. 'Ooh look, grub's up.'

Jo sat back as their food was brought to the table and, realizing that it was a day or two since she had sat down to an actual meal, began to look forward keenly to her fish and chips.

'Reckon we've earned this.' Macy raised his glass to them both.

'It would have been a lot simpler for Carswell to just distance himself from Carolyn,' Alan said.

'The timing was all wrong for that. He'd only just bought Carolyn's company when she dropped this bombshell on him,' Macy said. 'I expect he was going to ditch her as soon as he could.'

'He almost got me as paranoid as he is, because I even wondered if he was behind the closure of Cheryl's office,' Jo said. 'She and Eloise and all the other people who worked there had been given notice. I don't know what was happening to their cases, but it would have been bound to cause delays and disruption at the very least.'

Macy looked at her, his scepticism clear from his arched eyebrows.

Jo laughed. 'OK, one theory too far,' she said. 'Maybe. Let's see what comes out of the police investigation.'

Alan frowned at Macy across the table. 'Do you think he'll get away with it then?'

Macy shrugged. 'Some things are beyond me. He's certainly not as implicated as Carolyn Ash and Andre Souto. And if the police can find anything that will stick to Justin Fielding, they'll be delighted, believe me. But Louis Carswell? I don't know.'

Alan had finished his beer and mopped his face with the napkin. He offered to get a round but Jo and Macy were content with their bottle of wine. 'This really is an occasion,' Macy said, watching Alan walk to the bar.

Jo glanced up at him. 'You know you said you had two rooms at the usual hotel? Is that you and Alan sharing?'

'That wouldn't be my preferred configuration.' He met her gaze.

This time, Jo was in a decisive frame of mind. It was helped by the fact that Alan had decided to go home to his bungalow in Cheltenham so, after a few beers, they had packed him onto a train and waved him off. Her impulsive decision to fly to Spain to see Teddy was at the forefront of her mind too and she still intended on using the ticket she'd booked to Malaga. And maybe it helped that she'd made another, bigger decision, which made the choice of spending the dark December evening in bed with Macy easier. In fact, they were still there in the morning when other commitments and empty stomachs forced them to make a move towards breakfast.

Jo lay back on her pillow, contemplating the ceiling. 'I need to tell you something,' she said. Outside a delayed dawn had struggled its way through and pale sunlight filled the room.

Beside her, Macy became very still. 'Go on.'

'I've decided I really love this.'

A heartbeat of a moment slipped by. 'You do?'

'Yes. I actually want to do more of it.' She lifted herself on her elbow to face him. 'I love resolving things for people

and it puts my astrology knowledge to another purpose. So .
. .' She paused and looked into his opaque eyes. 'I'm going to
be a PI. I'm going to set myself up in business in Stroud. I'll
still continue with the astrology business, of course.'

Macy sat up and looked straight ahead. 'You're going to
set up in competition with me?'

'That's a detail.' She brushed this off with a dismissive
wave. Then she turned his serious face to hers and reached
up and kissed him. 'We'll always be friends though and help
each other. I can never see that changing.'

THE END